PRAISE FOR THE WORK OF RICHARD C. WHITE

"Entertaining, old-school sword and sorcery, in the tradition of Fafhrd and the Gray Mouser."

—Jim C. Hines, author of the *Magic ex Libris, Jig the Goblin,* and *The Princesses* series, on *For a Few Gold Pieces More*

"What a fantastic ride! If you like sarcasm and snark reminiscent of Harry Dresden, good doses of magic, treachery, and myth, this is the book for you."

—Goodreads, on *For a Few Gold Pieces More*

"White's *Terra Incognito* is a solid introduction to the subject of world building. It succeeds in helping the apiring writer in creating a skeletal framework on which to hang the moving parts required of a believable fictional setting."

—The Gaming Gang, on *Terra Incognito: A Guide to Building the Worlds of Your Imagination*

"A very good spin on the tried and true 'good-guys-for-hire' formula. All in all, an enjoyable read that I would recommend to anyone."

—*Word of the Nerd*, on *Troubleshooters, Incorporated: Night Stalkings*

"An accurately dialogued epic set in a place and time of fantasy. If you like pirates or elves or fantasy adventure or pure swashbuckling, then pick it up."

—*Comic Genesis*, on *The Chronicles of the Sea Dragon Special*

STARWARP CONCEPTS TITLES BY RICHARD C. WHITE

SCIENCE FICTION AND FANTASY
Harbinger of Darkness
For a Few Gold Pieces More
On Wings of Steel: The Darkside Chronicles, Book 1

DARK URBAN FANTASY
Chasing Danger:
The Case Files of Theron Chase

PULP ADVENTURE
Cry Havoc: The Furies, Book 1

NONFICTION/WRITERS' REFERENCE
Terra Incognito: A Guide to Building the Worlds of Your Imagination

GRAPHIC NOVELS AND COMIC BOOKS
The Chronicles of the Sea Dragon Special
Troubleshooters, Incorporated: Night Stalkings

ALSO BY RICHARD C. WHITE

NOVELS
Gauntlet: Dark Legacy: Paths of Evil

NOVELLAS
Battletech: No Rest for the Wicked
Strikeforce Falcon: Flashpoint
Strikeforce Falcon: Operation Komodo
Star Trek: S.C.E.: Echoes of Coventry

ANTHOLOGY CONTRIBUTIONS
Doctor Who: Short Trips: The Quality of Leadership
Star Trek: The Next Generation: The Sky's the Limit
Star Trek: Corps of Engineers: What's Past
One for All: Tales of the Musketeers
The Ultimate Hulk

CRY HAVOC

THE FURIES, BOOK 1

RICHARD C. WHITE

StarWarp Concepts
www.starwarpconcepts.com
New York, NY

A NightWolf Graphics Production

StarWarp Concepts
P.O. Box 4667
Sunnyside, NY 11104
www.StarwarpConcepts.com
Visit Richard C. White on the Web: www.richardcwhite.com

Library of Congress Control Number: 2026934491
ISBN: 979-8-9864432-3-2 (trade paperback)
ISBN: 979-8-9864432-4-9 (e-book)
First Print Edition: 2026

Front cover painting by Astor Alexander
Back cover photograph by Dorothea Lange, courtesy of the Library of Congress Public Domain Archive
Interior illustrations by Eliseu Gouveia and Rock Baker
Edited by Steven Roman
Book design by Aaron Rosenberg
Printed in the USA

This book is dedicated to Jack Kirby, Joe Simon, Bob Kane, Bill Fingers, Will Eisner, Martin Nodell, Matt Baker and all the other writers and artists who brought us the Golden Age of Comics.

ACKNOWLEDGMENTS

As with any project, there are a number of people who have been invaluable in helping this book come together:

Tommy Hancock, who originally sent me down the road of researching Golden Age heroes. Without your nudge, The Furies would never have taken flight.

Aaron Rosenberg, who stepped in to handle the cover and book design for us.

Astor Alexander, who created the magnificent cover for this book, and Eliseu Gouveia and Rock Baker, who did the interior illustrations.

Steve Roman, my long-suffering editor who has been working with me for over thirty years now—and still speaks to me, which says a lot for his patience. *grin*

And, of course, my wife, Joni, and the daughter-unit, who put up with seeing the back of my head for long stretches while I work on my various projects.

Honestly, without all of you, this book never would have happened. Thanks!

CONTENTS

THE CAT

MOUSE TRAP

"Cut! Cut!" Hawkes leapt from his director's chair, fanning himself with the latest shooting script. "This is not what the script called for. Who set up these lights? Why is that boom microphone so low? Can no one follow simple directions?"

Gina Baker watched her temperamental director walk off to find his chief technician, muttering about delays. She had done dozens of films for Ian Hawkes since he'd become her main director at Galaxy Pictures. He always fretted as if he were one step away from the precipice on every film until it was finally released, but this time it seemed his nerves were in sync with what was happening.

It was chancy shooting on location, even one as beautiful as Monaco. Whether it was the crew dealing with unseasonable rain, the locals crowding around the set to see the American film stars, or everyone getting used to the time changes—these were normal hazards. What she couldn't figure out was why they'd been having so many accidents.

Two stuntmen had been injured in the very first scene. Then the generator for the lights had caught on fire. Today was the first day they'd really had a chance to shoot, and now, the chief technician was not on the same page as Hawkes.

Literally.

"No, no, no! I said we needed softer lighting here. We're trying to set a mood. This is the first time Barry sees Gina. He's hurrying along, worried the Gestapo could be on his tail and then . . . he turns . . . there she is, this fragile flower against the barbarity of war . . . and then the crowd walks past and . . . poof, like a mirage, she is gone."

"Well, that's all well and good, Mr. Hawkes, but that's not what the script said. It says you want powerful lighting. 'Bring out the stark nature of the horror of war.' It's all right here."

Hawkes snatched the script out of the technician's hands. "No, that is not right. I know. I helped write this . . . What? What is this sacrilege? Who rewrote my scene? Who rewrote my pivotal scene?"

Hawkes sat back heavily against a crate as Gina walked over to talk to the two men. "Can I see your script, Pete?" she said to the chief technician. The burly man extracted it from Hawkes's hands and handed it to her. He stuck his hands down in his pockets as she flipped through the pages. "This is odd, Pete. Look here, this looks like it was typed with a different typewriter."

The big man looked over her shoulder and rubbed his chin. "What do you know about that. It sure does, Miss Gina. That's plumb odd."

"What? Let me see that."

Gina barely had time to react before Hawkes snatched the script away from her and compared the two. "Ah-ha! Sabotage! No doubt one of my rivals wants to see Ian Hawkes fail, but they shall not succeed. Come, Pete, we'll get this straightened out with the master script. Gina, please tell the cast we'll be back in a half hour and be ready to go. No dawdling."

"Sure, Ian."

She watched the two men disappear toward the trailers the cast and crew were living in on the set. A sudden noise behind her caught her attention and she spun around with her hands in a defensive position. The man who'd approached her scrambled backward, nearly tripping over a coil of wire.

"Cliff Steele, you should know better than to sneak up on me."

The handsome reporter balanced himself against a crane and then gave her a crooked grin. "Whoa! The way you spun around . . . for a second there, I thought you were The Cat. But that's impossible; she's back in Hollywood fighting crime."

Gina mentally kicked herself. Cliff didn't realize how close to the truth he was, because Gina *was* The Cat—the "other woman" in Cliff's life. Unbeknownst to him, the two women he was in love with were the same person and Gina loved to tease him about it. "Don't you dare compare me to that hussy, Cliff. Don't forget, I was a stuntwoman before I took up acting for real. I *can* take care of myself."

"I've never doubted it for a moment, Gina. You always seem to be so jealous of her. She's definitely not as cute as you are."

"So you say, you Lothario, but your eyes sure light up when you talk about her."

Cliff stared out into space for a moment before answering. "I know. There's a fire that drives her. Why, you'd never handle half of the adventures we've wound up on."

"So, maybe you should go look for her instead of spending time with me."

He held his hands up as if warding off a flurry of punches. "Now, Gina, don't be jealous. You're both special. Anyway, what's put a bee in ol' Ian's bonnet?"

Gina relaxed, realizing she'd gotten Cliff's mind off her goof-up. "He's trying to figure out what happened with that last scene. Someone switched some pages in the script and it messed up the shot. I swear, if I were the suspicious type, I'd think someone was actively trying to sabotage this film."

Cliff nodded in agreement. "It does seem strange. I've covered your films before, Gina, and I don't recall ever having these kinds of issues." His eyes looked troubled for a moment and then a smile crossed his face. "Still, it is quite an honor doing a movie about an honest-to-goodness war hero. It's too bad people aren't familiar with Nancy Wake and others like her. I mean, the whole setup—a beautiful redhead parachuting into Occupied France, having gun battles with SS troops, trying to keep her partisan group together when everything seemed dark. I only wish we could tell her real stories instead."

"I know, Cliff, but the British are sticklers for their secrets. We're lucky they're letting us tell this much of Nancy's story. It'll be years before the real story comes out."

"Still, the White Mouse . . ." Cliff's voice trailed off in an admiring sigh. "Heck, I guess it's a good thing The Cat isn't around. Wonder if they'd get along?" He grinned at his own joke.

"Again with the daydreaming about that hussy. I swear, Cliff, you've got to get your head out of the clouds. By the way, what are you doing *on* the set? As jumpy as Ian's been today, he'll skin you alive if he catches you here. You know there's no press allowed on the first few days."

"Hawkes? He'd faint at his own shadow. Besides, I have a part in this movie."

"You do? And you didn't tell me?"

"It's not a huge part. I'm supposed to stand behind Barry Grant and glower menacingly while he's being interrogated by Edgar Robertson. I think the script says I'm Guard Number Two."

Gina saw the look on Cliff's face and almost felt sorry for him. She'd talked to him before, but he never bought in that everyone enjoyed his company when he was just being Cliff. He felt her Hollywood friends still looked down on him for being just a reporter. "Still, congratulations. I think my first part in a movie was driving a car into a ditch. Luckily, I happened to be about the same size as Katherine Clayburn, so I drove into the ditch, they said 'cut,' and the next thing the audience saw was her climbing out of the wreck. I think I was on screen for about fifteen seconds." She laughed and walked up and put her hands around Cliff's temples. "Do you think they make hats big enough for you after this?"

"Aw, come on, Gina. Besides, it was Hawkes's idea. He said since I was coming along anyway, it'd be easier than hiring a local. Something about he was reasonably sure I understood his English."

"At least he's easier to understand than Fischer was."

Cliff's face darkened as he thought about Gina's first director. What he didn't know was Karl Fischer was the reason she had become The Cat in the first place. Even before the war, Gina suspected he was working for Nazi Germany but couldn't prove it at first. It was on a set where they were filming with a black leopard that she learned two things: Fischer was passing information about the United States Naval Yards to other Nazi Bund members; and he was deathly afraid of the big cats on the set. That's when she decided to become a cat-themed costumed hero to catch him in the act.

She ran into Cliff on that first case. He'd been tipped off about Fischer's organization and was hoping to expose the director himself. They bumped into each other going through Fischer's home to find evidence and had to help each other escape from the Nazi spies. Later that same evening, they busted the spy ring, but Fischer escaped the dragnet. Lacking evidence to pin the actions on him, they were forced to let him go.

I wonder whatever happened to Fischer? Cliff and I never turned him over to the authorities because we hoped he'd lead us to the mastermind behind the espionage and sabotage attempts on the West Coast. I guess they thought he fouled up one too many times. I suspect they'll find his skeleton out in the Mojave one day.

"Let's not talk about that creep, Gina. Although, I guess, I should thank him for one thing."

Gina's eyes widened. "What in the world could you thank him for?"

"If not for him, I wouldn't have started hanging around Galaxy Pictures and I wouldn't have met you or your father."

"Aw, Cliff, that's sweet."

"Plus, if I hadn't been checking out a tip, I wouldn't have run into The Cat either."

Gina's mouth pursed at that little tidbit. "Really, Cliff, can't you go five minutes without talking about her?"

Cliff ducked as she threatened to pick up a prop. "Sorry, Gina. I'll be on better behavior at dinner tonight. Your dad still joining us?"

She smiled before answering. "You're taking us to dinner at the famous Monte Carlo casino. I don't think you could keep Dad away with a herd of wild horses."

"I didn't think your dad was a gambler."

"It's not that as much as it's *the* casino. All of his friends told him about their experiences here before the war, but he never had the chance to visit. I suspect he's going to be reminiscing about his old friends as much as seeing the casino."

"All right, I'll see you and Rem around seven. Now, you better get back to the set. I suspect Hawkes is ready to start shooting again."

"Awk! Darn you, Cliff. If you made me late to the shoot . . ."

As he vanished into the clutter of crates and props lining the lot, his voice echoed back, "It's not my fault I'm so much fun to talk to."

I swear if he was as big as his ego, we could have used him instead of the boat to carry all the gear from Hollywood.

Gina hurried back to the set and rounded up everyone just before Hawkes came around the corner with a new script in hand. "Ah, thank you, Gina for having everyone ready. Now, listen up. We're only going to have the light for a bit longer, so everyone has got to hit their marks. So, let's get going. Places everyone. Lights? Good . . . and action."

Gina checked the mirror one more time to make sure everything was perfect before her dad arrived. Ciara Byrne, her personal assistant, walked up with her mink stole and slipped it over her shoulders. "Now, Gina, you need to calm down. Remember, there's likely to be a crowd of photographers at the casino, so be on your best behavior. The gossip magazines back in the States are bad enough; we don't need to start anything here. Why, next thing you know, they'll have you dating the Prince of Monaco or something."

"Byrnsie! Prince Rainier? He's cute and everything . . ."

". . . and rich . . ." Byrnsie broke in laughing.

". . . and rich. Still, I've never even met him and I'm not interested in that type. Why does everyone try to pair me up with some prince or the latest star? Maybe I'd prefer someone not in the public eye."

"Maybe like a certain reporter we both know?"

Gina spun toward Byrnsie, her hands on her hips. "Cliff? Only if he ever starts making moon eyes at me like he does that

Cat person. You should have heard him earlier today. He's like a schoolboy with a crush on the local cheerleader."

Byrnsie flumped down on the couch in Gina's apartment and rearranged the pillows until she was comfortable. "See, he's got it as bad as the average person has about you. It's why you're *in* the magazines to begin with, Gina dear, because, to most people, *you're* unobtainable. You're this beautiful woman on the silver screen and the average citizen has a hard time believing you're real. I'd bet most girls back in the States wish they were you, and if you marry a prince, then maybe they could too."

"If I find a prince, they can have him."

Byrnsie adjusted her glasses and put her hands up beside her face, imitating a young girl in rapture. "Why, Miss Baker, if you don't want him, can I have him?"

Gina laughed at Byrnsie and felt herself beginning to relax. "Now I remember why I keep you around. I don't have to worry about getting a swelled head with you here."

A sudden knock on the door grabbed her attention. "That must be Dad."

"You guys have a good time," Byrnsie called as Gina headed toward the door. "I'll ask you all about it in the morning."

Gina opened the door and found Remmington Baker and Cliff standing there. They made quite the dashing duo in their tuxedos, although Cliff kept tugging at his collar. Gina moved over and adjusted his bow tie.

"Now, stop fidgeting, Cliff. It's good for you to dress up once in a while."

"I can't help it, Gina. I'm not used to wearing these monkey suits. Give me a good old-fashioned sports jacket and tie any day."

Rem let out a soft chuckle before speaking up. "Now, Cliff, you're gonna have to get used to it. After all, if you're gonna be a movie star, you're expected to wear costumes like this. I mean, I don't have a lot of use for this outfit out on my ranch, but you don't see me complainin' about wearing it."

"Not where anyone can hear you, Dad. I remember teaching

you how to tie that bow tie when I was a kid, after Mom died."

"Your mother was always fussing at me to dress nicer. The problem was we never made much money back in vaudeville. I was lucky to rent the tuxedo I wore to our wedding. Everything I made back then went into buying stage costumes."

Cliff stopped tugging at his jacket long enough to turn to Rem. "You know, I've known you for quite a while, but you never talk much about being in vaudeville."

Rem shrugged as he herded Gina and Cliff toward the elevator. "That's because it never seemed important. Whenever we're together, we're usually on the set of one of Gina's movies or else we're involved in some dang-blamed scrape with that Cat filly."

"Oh, Dad, not you too. I hoped we could go one evening without that woman coming up."

"Now, honey, you have to admit, she's definitely crossed our path more than once."

Gina rolled her eyes, even though she was grinning on the inside. Remmington Baker was the only other person who knew Gina was The Cat. He didn't exactly approve of her extracurricular activities, but he had never told her not to do it either. Besides, he'd been instrumental to solving several of her cases and he seemed to get a kick out of the excitement.

When the elevator doors opened in the hotel lobby, a press of photographers surged forward to take pictures of Gina. "Miss Baker! Miss Baker, is it true you're dating Barry Grant? Can you tell us about the picture! Please look this way, Miss Baker!" The cacophony of questions and flash bulbs popping caught Gina off guard, but she smiled gamely as Cliff and Rem shielded her from the press of bodies.

One of the hotel managers came rushing over, trying to shoo the press away. "Go. Go on. Get out of here. This is my hotel lobby, and you should not be bothering my guests." A group of the red caps joined him and eventually they formed a human corridor through which Rem and Cliff were able to guide Gina into the waiting cab.

The manager leaned through the cab window. "I am so

sorry, *Mademoiselle* Baker. One of the bellboys let them know you were a guest here. Excuse me, one of our *ex*-bellboys."

"Now, Jacques, don't be too hard on him. I don't want anyone being fired on my account."

The manager looked dubious, but then he shrugged as he withdrew from the cab. "As you wish, *Mademoiselle*. Still, he shall be reprimanded fully for this indiscretion. Our guests deserve their privacy. Would you like me to move you to a new hotel?"

Rem leaned forward to look at the manager. "Let's see how it goes, Jacques. No sense in making a bunch of work for someone if we don't need it."

The cab pulled out and the press made a beeline for the street to flag down taxis for themselves. Rem glanced through the back window and chuckled. "Seems you're pretty popular here in Europe, Gina. 'Course, after what these people been through the last few years, I can't say I blame them. I imagin' they're just as hungry for something to distract them as people were during the Depression back home."

Gina looked out the cab window as they sped through the streets. Monaco hadn't been hurt as badly during the war as Italy, France, or Germany, but it still had been occupied just like many other European countries and had its own share of horrors. Some of the people on the film crew had apparently been *Marquis*, the French Resistance, and a few had the scars to prove it.

The trip from the hotel to the casino was quick and Gina and her two escorts slipped through the entryway of the casino before the first photographer's cab arrived. Inside the casino was alive with excitement yet still dignified. Everyone was dressed to the nines and as the staff led them to the salon where they were to have dinner, Gina swore she passed half a dozen people she'd only seen in the newsreels before now. Apparently the *crème de la crème* of Europe was out this summer to try and forget the nightmare years.

"Quite the spectacle wouldn't you say, Gina?"

"It's incredible, Dad. This is going to be some night." She

glanced around again and spotted a small disturbance near the doorway. She thought the photographers had gotten past Monte Carlo's fabled security at first, but it was someone accosting Tina Green, one of the actresses from the movie. She hurried over to see if she could help but by the time she arrived the man had disappeared and Tina was walking out.

"Tina, are you all right?"

Gina saw the anger in the tall brunette's face. "I can't believe what just happened. That man was . . . well, he was just rude."

"Are you going to be all right?"

Tina calmed down but Gina couldn't tell if she was upset or frightened. "I think so. However, I'm going back to the hotel. In the mood I'm in, I'm not going to enjoy tonight. I'll come back another evening."

"You let me know when you want to come back and Cliff and I will be happy to accompany you."

"Now, Gina, I don't need a babysitter. You and Cliff go enjoy yourselves. Don't worry about me."

Gina thought for a second. She only caught a glimpse of the man but something about him seemed familiar. "Tina, did you recognize the man who was bothering you?"

"No, I don't think I'd met him before. He was very unpleasant, with a thick accent. I think I'd remember him."

Gina glanced around one more time, but the man was gone. "Hopefully that's the end of the matter. I hope the rest of your evening is better than this."

"It can't get much worse."

Gina watched Tina make her way to the taxis out front. The more she thought about it, the more uneasy she felt. *Something's wrong. Why would someone just walk up to Tina and pick a fight with her? Hey wait a minute . . .*

Two men suddenly stepped out of the crowd and shoved Tina into an unmarked car. Before the footmen could react, the car gunned its engine and sped away.

Gina rushed out to the street and spotted a young man leaning against his convertible. "Someone just grabbed a friend of mine and drove off. Can you follow them?"

The young man glanced at Gina and then looked in the direction she was pointing. The car made a turn a few blocks down toward the ocean. He looked back at Gina, shrugged, and jumped over the side of his car into the driver's seat. "This better be on the up and up. Let's go."

They roared off. Gina glanced over her shoulder to see Cliff and her father rushing out of the casino, trying to flag down a taxi. They'd have to hurry, as her driver wove in and out of traffic with impressive skill, skidding around the corner the kidnappers had taken almost without slowing down.

"So, do you usually go chasing after cars with perfect strangers?" the young man asked, his mop of hair going every which way in the breeze.

Gina tried to keep her eyes on the taillights up ahead while she contemplated what to do if they caught them. "No, my friends don't normally get kidnapped where I'm from."

"Really? After all the Yank movies I've watched, I would think this was a fairly common occurrence." The young man skillfully downshifted and whipped past a slower-moving vehicle without losing an inch on the car ahead.

"You really shouldn't believe everything you see on the screen."

"I guess not. Anyway, I'm Stirling. Pleased to make your acquaintance." He whipped around another corner, still conversing like they were out for a Sunday drive in the country. "Not every day a beautiful woman jumps in my car with me. I think I could get used to it."

"Are you flirting with me, Stirling?"

"And failing miserably. I haven't even gotten your name."

"I'm Gina and you can't be a day over sixteen."

"Oh, now you're being mean. I'm almost eighteen. Just out for a spot of fun before I have to get back to work."

Gina found herself grinning in spite of the situation. "Your work?"

"I get my racing license in a few months."

He took another curve, narrowly avoiding two cars and slid

to a stop. "Here you go. They disappeared into that garage up there. Not sure what *you're* going to do, though."

"Listen, Stirling, I need you to find the police and let them know what's going on and where we are. I'm going to check things out and see if my friend is okay."

"What? Leave you here by yourself? I should think not."

"But you have to. I've only been here a couple of days and I have no idea where we are or what's going on. The way you drive, you'll be there and back in no time."

"I don't like it, but never let it be said I'd let a lady down. All right, but you stay low. I'll be back in a dash."

Gina slipped out of the car and Stirling expertly turned around and disappeared into the night the way they'd just come. *I was a damn good stuntwoman and there's no way I would have taken those streets like he did. I have a feeling he's going to have one heck of a career. But now it's time for The Cat to make an appearance.*

Gina slipped into an alleyway and a few seconds later, a shadow began making its way through the streets of Monaco. While the inhabitants of the small principality might not have recognized the classic silhouette, it was certainly well known in Hollywood. Clad in her traditional black one-piece suit, tights, boots, gloves, and mask, the female crime fighter known as The Cat made her way to the garage.

Gina gave the building a once-over and noticed there was only one light visible through a second-story window. A quick check confirmed the main door was locked as well as the side door. Continuing to move around the building, she spotted a window ajar in the back. Keeping low to avoid anyone seeing her, she eased the window open and crawled over the windowsill into an office. Letting her eyes acclimatize to the darkness, she made her way to the door and continued her search.

She climbed up a rickety flight of stairs and spotted light coming from under a door down the hall. Moving closer, she could hear a woman speaking with two men, but the words were indistinct. Gina thought she could hear Tina, but her voice sounded muffled. She decided to chance opening the door an inch or so. She couldn't see anyone but the voices became clearer.

One of the men had a whiny voice. "I still don't see what good grabbing this bird is doing us. It's not like she's got a big part. She probably don't know nothing about what we're after. She's just dead weight."

The woman's voice was an animalistic purr compared to the man's high pitch. "You don't see because you're thinking too small. If she doesn't reappear, they'll need someone to take her place. That's when one of our people will join the cast and we'll have free rein from there. You don't understand the stakes."

"But, what *are* you looking for?"

"Do you *really* want me to say it right here in front of her? After all, if she knows what I want, I'd have to kill her. Wouldn't that be a shame?"

Gina's blood ran cold. She'd dealt with some dangerous people in Los Angeles as The Cat, but this was beyond the pale. To discuss another person's death this calmly frightened even Gina.

"*Ach*. Look what you have done. The poor girl has fainted dead away. Really, you are much too cruel."

"And you're too weak, *Schweinehund*. I've picked up after your mistakes for nearly seven years. You were worthless then and if the Triumvirate hadn't tasked me to retrieve the information you possess, you'd be worthless now. Just pray you know as much as you claim. If you make one more misstep . . ."

"*Ja, ja,* I know. Still, this time I am right."

"All right. Now go, both of you. Get rid of that car too. We don't want anything to—" The sound of sirens in the distance stopped her in mid-sentence. "You fools! You must have been followed," she snarled at them.

"Impossible."

The sirens wailed again. "That doesn't sound impossible, does it? Get out of here. We'll meet back up tomorrow night."

"What about her?"

"She's no good to us now. No sense in leaving witnesses."

Gina decided she couldn't wait any longer and burst into the room. The men were just shutting the door behind them, leaving the tall blond woman, a German Luger in her hand.

"The Cat? Here? Impossible?"

Gina rushed the woman before she had chance to react. A quick judo chop against her opponent's inner arm sent the weapon flying. However, her opponent's leg sweep caught Gina off guard and sent her crashing backward into the table. She rolled to her feet, but the blonde paused as the sirens grew louder.

"We're not done here, Cat. I don't know what brought you to Monaco, but you will not be leaving . . . at least not alive."

Gina started toward the woman, who spun and dove head-first through the window. Gina ran to the window but her opponent was already partway down the alley.

There'll be another time. I have to take care of Tina first. Wait, what's this?

Gina stared at the window frame. She saw it wasn't glass at all but sugar glass—a hardened form of sugar movie companies used for stunt scenes. Apparently her opponent had prepared for a quick exit. However, that was a clue. Most people didn't know about sugar glass. Then Gina noticed the stack of mattresses strategically placed in the alley. Whoever this woman was, she either had been in the movie industry or knew someone who was.

And why did that small man seem so familiar?

Just then, the door flew open and the Monégasque police came charging in with Remmington Baker and Cliff Steele right behind them. Gina gave them a wave and followed her blond opponent's example, diving out the window to avoid being tied up all evening answering questions from the police. A quick change later, she reappeared at the front door, asking to see her father.

"Gina, what in the world were you doing running off?"

"I'm sorry, I couldn't wait. I was afraid they might get away. Luckily, Stirling was able to keep up with them."

Cliff stepped over, a look of concern on his face. "Stirling?"

Gina put her hand over her mouth and laughed. "Cliff, really, he was seventeen. He's quite a driver, though. If we need a stunt driver, I'd see if Ian would offer him a contract in a heartbeat."

Rem frowned at her before speaking. "Actually, we lost the both of you after the second or third turn. You'd disappeared into traffic and we had no idea where you'd gone. We saw the police headed this way and just followed. You gave us quite a fright, young lady."

"Yeah, you could have gotten into trouble. Good thing The Cat was around, although I can't figure out what she's doing in Monaco of all places."

"Cliff, honestly. The Cat? You mean you saw her here?"

"Only for a moment. Took a while to convince the police she's one of the good guys. I'm guessing there aren't many costumed heroes here in Europe."

Rem rubbed his hand on his chin to keep from grinning. "Well, I'll imagine not in a place like Monaco anyway. Always heard this was more of a rich person's playground than a hotbed for crime." After a few seconds, he seemed to sober a bit and spoke in softer tones. "Although, with the war, things could change. We forget this land was occupied by some pretty unpleasant people. No telling who's on the side of angels after such an experience."

I'm still curious why they kidnapped Tina. Why do they need to get someone on our set and who do they think they'd replace her with? It's not like Ian would hire just anyone, even for a small part like Tina's.

The trouble is, I can't tell anyone what I heard. Not unless I want The Cat to be the main attraction on this movie.

Cliff grinned at Gina. "Well, it was a good thing The Cat was here. I can't imagine you rushing into this building to take on the kidnappers."

"I have more sense than that, Cliff. I tried to flag down the police, but you all went rushing past me like I wasn't there. You were so intent on getting into the building first, if I had been one of the kidnappers, I would have gotten away scot-free."

Cliff's eyes got wide and he smacked himself in the forehead. "Wait a minute. Now that you mention it, there were a couple of guys standing in a doorway when we followed the police in. You don't think . . . ?"

"I wasn't there, Cliff. What do you think?"

"I think I'm going to pay a lot more attention from now on. Between what happened earlier and this, there's more than meets the eye here. I don't know if it's what we're filming, who's involved in the film, or where we're filming it, but since I don't have a big role, I'm going to do some snooping in my free time and see what I can figure out."

Remmington Baker patted him on the shoulder, "I'll do what I can to give you a hand, Cliff. Two sets of eyes are better than one, you know."

One of the policemen joined them. "*Mademoiselle* Green is feeling better. We have all the information we need from her now, although we may need to speak to her again at the Palais de Justice tomorrow. She has asked if we could take her back to her hotel, but would you like to speak to her before she leaves?"

Gina stepped forward. "I'd like to go along, if you don't mind. She might be more comfortable if someone she knows is with her."

"But of course, *Mademoiselle* Baker."

Gina called over her shoulder, "Dad, could you please pick up my stole from the casino? Maybe we can visit it again tomorrow night?"

Rem nodded his assent as Gina joined Tina in the police car. They rode in silence to the set and then Gina escorted her to her hotel room. Tina paused at the door before turning to Gina. "I appreciate everything, Gina, but I think I want to be alone, if you don't mind."

"I spoke to the police. They'll be supplementing the usual security here tonight."

Tina gave a wan smile. "Maybe I should have been a stunt-person like you first. I'm not used to actually being in danger. In the movies, when someone's trying to kill me, they're using blanks and rubber knives. I think I just want to lie down and have an old-fashioned cry . . . or maybe just an Old Fashioned. Good night, Gina."

Gina puzzled over the events of the evening as she walked back to her room. Maybe she could talk things over with her father later—he was notorious for spotting things she overlooked. She was so wrapped up in the puzzle, she didn't even remember going up to her room or Byrnsie helping her get undressed and into bed.

Ten minutes later, she fell asleep still mulling it over.

The next day's shoot went without incident, to everyone's relief. Ian was almost beside himself as he called "Cut!" as the daylight began fading. "Very good, very good. You all have made Ian proud today. Now, stay out of trouble and get a good night's sleep. We start shooting at eight in the morning."

Cliff made his way across the set to where Gina was coordinating with Byrnsie about getting tomorrow's script pages. "Hey, Gina, are you free for dinner this evening?"

"Thanks, Byrnsie. I'll get with you later. Yes, Cliff, but what's going on?"

Byrnsie gave Gina a conspiratorial smile. "Don't stay out too late, you two. You've got a lot of lines to memorize between now and tomorrow morning." She walked off, her laughter trailing along behind her.

Cliff watched her disappear, shaking his head in amazement. "That Byrnsie. How long has she been with you?"

"Long enough to know you, that's for certain. Anyway, what did you find?"

He got a mysterious look on his face before responding. "Since I didn't have to be on the set, I thought I'd check in with an old friend."

"So, you snuck off to visit with The Cat . . ."

Cliff let out a small laugh. "Tempting, but since I didn't know she was coming, I don't have a clue where to find her. No, I called a friend who works with United Press International.

He heard about the attack on Tina last night and has been checking into it. The police haven't turned up anything new, by the way."

"I didn't think you liked to share a byline."

"Normally, no, but Bob and I went to college together. He likes traveling the world more and I'm fond of a steady paycheck, so we went our separate ways. He's got connections here, so it makes sense to work together. If he was looking into something back in LA, I'd give him a hand too. He'll be in touch as soon as he hears anything."

Gina frowned. "I know we didn't come to Europe to get involved in another mystery, but after what happened to Tina, I think we're in one, whether we want it or not."

Cliff shaded his eyes from the late afternoon sun. "And speaking of mysteries, who was that Stirling guy you caught a ride with last night?"

Gina sat down on one of the prop cases and laughed. "Cliff, you're still worrying about that? I told you, he's barely out of high school."

"So you said. Our cabbie swore he was a Grand Prix racer the way he took those corners."

"Maybe he will be one of these days."

"I wouldn't jump into cars with strange men any more than necessary. This may be the Riviera but it's not one hundred percent safe. Bob tells me there's more crime here than they let on. It just doesn't make the news. Bad for the tourist business."

"I promise to be more careful, Mother Hen."

Cliff confirmed the time they were meeting for dinner and Gina headed toward her trailer to get some things she'd left while on set. She was making her way through the maze of props and crates when a soft noise caught her attention. It sounded like someone moving equipment nearby. None of that gear was scheduled to be used until the big fight scene at the end, so no one should be opening those packing crates. She crept closer to find three large men attempting to open one of the crates with a crowbar.

"You are sure this is the one?" said the smallest of the three.

His mannerisms and face reminded Gina of nothing so much as a weasel.

The largest of the men turned his head slightly to answer. "*Ja*. It has the marks we were told to look for. Now, be quiet. We do not want to be overheard."

A hidden fourth member spoke up then. Gina couldn't see who or where they were through the clutter of crates. "Trust me, this will ensure the finale of this movie is the finale . . . for all of them." He spoke so softly Gina could barely hear him. Still, something about his voice sounded familiar. She wondered if he was the same one from the night before.

Of all the times not to be wearing my Cat costume. I guess I'll have to handle this one as myself.

Gina spotted a pile of crates near the men and a few long boards. She picked out the thickest board to wedge beneath the crates and carefully dragged another crate close to use as a fulcrum. She heard something and realized the men had heard her. Before they had a chance to react, Gina jumped up on the crate and then on the end of the board. Her momentum and weight were enough to get the crates to begin leaning and then gravity took over.

She rushed behind another stack of crates to hide. She could hear the intruders shouting warnings to each other and then them diving to the side as the crates fell and splintered near them. From the cursing, they hadn't escaped completely unscathed.

In the distance, she could hear technicians and stagehands hurrying over to see what had happened. She heard the saboteurs picking themselves up from the debris on the other side of the crates.

"Get out of here. There'll be other opportunities later."

The sound of running feet was her cue and she followed them through the clutter and fragments gathered in the backstage area. She knew they couldn't afford to be spotted so she hoped they'd be too busy trying to escape to look back and see her following them.

With any luck, they'll lead me to their boss. Then The Cat can make an appearance later to get some answers.

The men headed toward a car and a cargo truck with a large canvas covering on the back—a leftover from the war, it appeared. The diesel engine roared to life, sending a plume of thick black smoke into the sky from the exhaust pipe.

Got to take this chance. If I miss this, I'll never flag down a taxi in time.

Gina took a long stride and jumped, hooking her fingers over the top of the tailgate, then clambered up and over the gate as it began lumbering down the street. Luckily, there was nothing in the back but some crates, so she settled in for the ride. She tried to keep track of the street signs as the truck cruised along. No one seemed to pay attention to the truck, which suited her fine; she wanted the driver to be relaxed. This way, he was more likely to take her to their hideout instead of ditching the truck.

The truck slowed down to pull onto a street near the docks. Gina spotted a sudden movement and ducked behind one of the crates as the car carrying the others pulled up close behind the truck. The truck slowed and she heard a metal door lifting nearby. The truck took a sharp turn and she saw they were pulling into a warehouse. She waited as they rolled to a stop and then the engine was shut off and silence fell in the large building.

She remained behind her crate as footsteps walked toward the back of the truck. The car had pulled in with them and three passengers got out. Unfortunately, the car's headlights were still on, backlighting the figures as Gina peeked around the edge of the crate. Still, a couple of the figures seemed to be the right shape and size of the people she'd encountered a few nights ago.

A door opened and closed off to the side. A familiar woman's voice cut through the silence. "You're back early. What happened?"

A deep voice answered, "Not sure. There was a noise and the next thing we knew, a stack of crates crashed down on our heads. We had to leave before we could finish the job. Still, we got most of it done. Won't be hard to sneak back in there and finish it up."

The woman laughed, but it wasn't a pleasant sound. "You idiots. Crates don't just fall by themselves. It's obvious you were spotted. They've either found the bombs by now or they've alerted the Monaco police, who know how to find and disarm bombs. Once again, you've managed to bungle a perfectly simple job."

The one man spoke up again. "Look, it's been some bad luck. There was no way to predict we'd run into one of those costumed American idiots here. I thought the agreement after the war was all those so-called superheroes were not to operate outside their native lands."

"Imbecile. Those treaties only apply to people who have unnatural powers. There's nothing stopping any of the so-called mystery men or women from traveling the world. They're no more super than you or me . . . well, me anyway. I'm pretty sure a mouse might be more super than you, especially in brain power."

Gina could almost feel the man wince at his verbal lashing, but he gamely continued. "Besides, there's always people wandering around on a movie set. Who knew they'd think we were up to something? I mean, we're there legitimately."

What did he mean by that?

"Enough!" the woman snapped. "There will be no more excuses. Our goals *will* be accomplished. Too much is riding on this. I don't care what it takes or how you do it. Just do it, because if I have to take a more direct hand, I think it's safe to say some of you will become redundant. And you don't want that to happen."

Another person spoke up then—the familiar voice—but again, Gina wasn't quite able to place it. "There will be no need for that. I know the set now. I guarantee there will be no slipups next time."

"You'd better, because you're the first one on my expendable list. I've taken the heat for your mistakes for years now, both in America and in Europe. I'm not losing my position because of your incompetence again. And if The Cat shows up again, I expect you to personally deal with her . . . permanently."

"It shall be done."

"Good. Now, get out of my sight. I don't want to see any of you before the meeting tonight at eleven."

The door slammed in the distance and one of the figures reached into the car and turned off the lights. It took Gina a few minutes for her eyes to adjust and then she saw a small light ahead as people walked through a door to the street.

She climbed out of the truck, trying to ensure she didn't make any noise. She didn't think they'd left anyone behind to stand guard, but there was no point taking chances—more than she already had. A few seconds later, she was out on the street and memorizing the address.

On her cab ride back to the set, Gina tried to make sense out of what she'd overheard. *The fact they want to stop the movie is clear, but I have no clue if they're working with another production company or what. And what did she mean by taking "the heat" for his mistakes in America and Europe? He didn't sound like an American. He sounded almost German.*

Gina sat upright, her knuckles white from squeezing the door handle. *No, it couldn't be him. That's impossible. He's dead.* She wasn't one hundred percent sure, but there was one person who would understand how a Hollywood movie set worked *and* how saboteurs could get in and out without being spotted.

Karl Fischer, her old director and Nazi bund member.

When Gina arrived back at her hotel, she went straight to her father's room. After he let her in, she flopped down in a chair. "Dad, I think I know who's behind all of this."

"That's great, honey. We'll be able to call the cops and get this picture back on schedule."

Gina bit her lip before continuing. "I don't think it's going to be that easy, Dad. I caught them trying to set an explosive in one of our prop crates and scared them off. Don't worry, I tipped off the police and let them know where it was. However, I didn't actually see who was doing it because I was trying to stay out of sight too."

Rem waved a hand at her. "Whoa. Slow down. If you didn't see them, how do you know who's behind it?"

Gina laughed nervously before responding. "I caught a ride in their truck when they took off."

"You did what?"

"Now, Dad, I was careful. Besides, it was the only thing I could think of at the time. I found out where they're hiding. That's where I heard the voice of one of the leaders. I'm pretty sure it was Karl Fischer's."

It was Rem's turn to let out a nervous laugh. "Fischer? We haven't heard or seen anything from him since right after Pearl Harbor. Are you certain, or could it just be a similar voice?"

"No, Dad, I'm not certain. However, if it is Fischer, he's going to have some bad memories because a certain feline is going to cross his path again. They're meeting at eleven o'clock tonight, and I plan on being there too."

"Just be careful, Gina. Remember, this isn't Hollywood. They're the home team here. They could be preparing a trap for you."

Gina nodded. "I'll be careful. Still, this might be the only chance we get to find out what's really going on here."

As night fell over Monaco, the nocturnal creatures were treated to an unfamiliar sight. Gina, now in her Cat garb, made her way across the rooftops toward the warehouse. She had to be careful since she was unfamiliar with the city. She and her father had planned out several routes she might be able to go to avoid drawing attention, but what looks good on a map doesn't always work in real life.

She had another concern—one she didn't normally have at home. The police around Los Angeles were willing to work with her even though she didn't have any official capacity. She wasn't sure the Monégasque police would be as open-minded, so she decided not to chance it, at least not until she had solid evidence against the saboteurs. The last thing she needed was to get arrested and have her secret identity exposed.

She cut across the top of a hotel and came to an alleyway separating her from the next building. She reached down and pulled a coil of rope off her belt. Quickly tying a lasso, she managed to snag a projection on the nearby rooftop. She tested it to be sure it would hold her weight before stepping off.

She landed feetfirst against the side of the building and pulled herself upward hand over hand. A few inches from reaching the roof, she heard a sharp crack and felt the rope growing slack. She pushed off with her feet and leapt upward, snagging the edge of the roof as the rope snaked past her. She clung where she was, trying to get her breath back and heard the sickening thud of something smashing against the pavement in the alley below. Taking a deep breath, she scrambled for a purchase and finally managed to get onto the roof.

"Not the most graceful entrance I've ever seen, but roof running is like flying a plane. Anything you can walk away from is a good landing."

Gina froze, trying to spot the person speaking. Finally, a man walked out from behind a chimney and nodded to her. "I think I've heard of you. You're The Cat."

She noted his handsome features and his lithe but muscular build. He blended into the night with his black clothing. Even his slightly graying hair served to enhance his looks. "I'm afraid you have me at a disadvantage. You know who I am, but I don't think we've met."

"No, I don't suppose we have. I've been out of the States for a long time. My name is John."

"Just John?"

A grin settled on his face, the kind a schoolboy gets when he gets caught doing something by the teacher. "Let's leave it at that. Maybe when I know why you're here and what you're after, we can exchange pleasantries. After all, I know you're The Cat, but I don't *know* who you are, true?"

Gina found herself grinning in spite of herself. "*Touché.* So, I assume you're not supposed to be up here either."

John glanced over her shoulder at the policeman walking down the alleyway and drew back farther into the shadows. Gina followed his lead, still keeping a wary distance. "I'm afraid not. In fact, there are some gentlemen in town who'd take a very dim view of finding me on these roofs."

"And what *are* you doing up here?"

"Sightseeing. I haven't seen Monaco like this since before the war. After that firework display the other night, I just wanted to see tonight's from a more familiar angle."

"And that's all?"

John held up one hand and crossed his heart with the other. "I promise you, I am doing nothing more illegal than you are. I am retired and plan on staying that way. That doesn't mean I don't enjoy getting some fresh air and seeing the heights from time to time."

Gina decided there was nothing to be gained by staring at John all night—not that it would have been a hard thing to do. If he was a criminal, he certainly was a lot better mannered—and better looking—than those she usually met. She hooked her grapnel onto a piece of twine and then fished the rope from the street. She coiled her rope up and hooked it into her belt while John watched with an amused look on his face.

"I've done a lot of roof running in my time, but I've never tried swinging from building to building like Tarzan. Is that something new back in the States?"

"I don't know how new it is, but it seems the easiest way to get from one point to another if you don't want to go down to street level."

He tossed his thumb over his shoulder. "Where are you going? Perhaps I can help you find a shorter and"—he chuckled—"safer way there."

Something about John's demeanor made Gina decide to trust him—up to a point, that was. She told him the address she was trying to reach, the route she was planning on using, but she kept the why to herself.

He nodded. "That's one way to get there. However, follow me. There's a quicker way if you know the city like I do."

He took off and she followed. He glided silently from shadow to shadow and with his black turtleneck, black slacks, and black soft-soled shoes, it felt like she was chasing a living shadow across the roofs. He seemed unusually familiar with this section of town and he pointed out obstacles and loose sections as if he'd lived here all his life.

The way he moves, you'd think he was part cat himself. Still, for someone who claims he's been out of town for a while, he must have spent a lot *of time in Monaco before he left. No one just spots those things in the dark. There's more to his story than he's telling.*

They were approaching a wide boulevard, but John showed no indication of changing directions. She glanced around, wondering how he was planning on crossing, when he angled toward the corner of the roof. She caught up with him and he pointed down. Three feet below their position was a flagpole leading out into the open air. Across a six-foot gap was another flagpole leading to the building across the way. Beneath the two flagpoles, sixteen stories down, were four lanes of traffic and a policeman standing in an island in the middle of the intersection directing traffic. She instinctively knew what John was going to do but couldn't bring herself to believe it.

He motioned for her to wait and watch as he lowered himself down to the four-inch-wide flagpole. He tested it a couple of times to ensure it was well secured and then, like a tightrope walker in the circus, he deftly stepped out onto the metal pole. She watched as it bent under his weight as he reached the end. Then, using the pole like a diving board, he bent his knees and leapt forward, letting the pole's own whipping motion drive him through the air. He caught the opposite pole and then swung himself up and walked to the next building. Once there, he sat down on the edge of the roof and motioned for her to join him.

She knew she shouldn't fall for his bait, but somehow she couldn't help showing off. She lowered herself to the pole and then ran out to the tip, feeling the metal sinking as she came closer and closer to the open air. She measured the distance with her eyes and as she reached the end, she pushed down hard with her feet. With the momentum from her rush, she was able to get more height on her leap than he had and then did a front flip, aiming for the adjoining flagpole with her feet. She landed on it and then let her knees and body bend, using the downward momentum to catch her balance. Once she had everything under control, she casually walked down the pole and joined him on the ledge.

He clapped his hands together gently and shook his head. "Do you ever get mistaken for a circus performer in that costume of yours?"

She frowned, trying to decide whether he was complimenting her or what. "Not generally more than once."

"I don't know what you do back in the States when you're not fighting crime, but I could see you now flying through the air on a trapeze. You'd make a fortune in the circus."

"I've done a lot of different things in my life, John. Still, you sound like you're familiar with that life."

He didn't answer for a bit, keeping his eyes on the traffic moving along the busy boulevard they'd just crossed. Finally, he lifted his head and stared out over the cityscape before speaking in a low, soft tone. "Spent some time there before the war. After that, I spent some time using those skills for something more profitable. Then using those skills to fight the *Boche* during the war. Now? Now I use my skills to deftly avoid bees and wasps while I'm tending my flower gardens and to open outstanding bottles of wine."

"Sounds like you miss the old days."

"Maybe just a bit." He swung around onto the roof and offered her a hand up. "But you have somewhere to go and the dawn isn't going to wait for us to sit and reminisce. Let's go."

A few minutes later, they arrived at the warehouse. John glanced around and then spoke softly. "I'd love to stick around and help, but I'd prefer the Monaco police didn't know I'm in town. They're notorious for holding grudges. Perhaps we'll see each other another time."

He pointed toward the warehouse and Gina looked down to spot the two guards lounging around one of the entrances. She turned around to say good-bye to John but he had already disappeared in the night. She hooked her rope to a cornice on the building and lowered herself into an alley near the warehouse.

She crept along, hugging the shadows until she reached the rear of the warehouse, where a small door was illuminated by a single glowing bulb above it. She didn't see anyone nearby but couldn't believe they'd ignore this door with guards out front. She pulled a simple sling out of a pouch on her belt and slipped a rock into the leather pocket. A quick twirl of her wrist and the rock shot out, shattering the light bulb and plunging the alley into darkness.

There was a small exclamation in German down the alley and the sound of running feet. Her eyes adapted to the dim ambient light, and she could make out his silhouette rustling around the doorway, trying to figure out what had happened. He checked the door and grunted in satisfaction, finding it still locked. He glanced up and down the alley and then shuffled off to the far end.

Gina waited until he'd gone far enough away, he wasn't likely to hear her and then approached the door. She pulled tools from her pouch and went to work on the lock. A few twists of her fingers and she felt the tumblers fall into place. She slid the door open and moved inside while the guard was still out of sight.

She glanced around until she was certain she was alone in the main part of the warehouse, then pulled out a small flashlight and cupped her fingers over the lens to minimize the glow. Moving cautiously through the cavernous space, she found the truck she'd ridden in earlier along with two other cars and a car made up to resemble a Monégasque cab. She scribbled down the license plates and other identification numbers in case she encountered them again. Once she had covered the main room, she crept toward the door leading deeper into the warehouse. She knew the woman she's seen the night before had gone this way.

Opening the door, she saw it was a dark hallway with several doors on either side and one at the end. The first couple of rooms were for storage, filled with tools and other things to support the vehicles out in the main area. However, when she reached the room at the end of the hall, she noticed this door was different—the others were old and ill-fitting, but not only was this new, it fit snugly into its frame.

No sign of anyone and it's eleven fifteen. I doubt the meeting got over that fast. They must be behind this door, but I can't hear anything. There has to be a way I can listen in. I'd really like to know what's going on and why they're showing so much interest in our movie.

She reached for the knob, but something didn't feel right. She played the light along the edges of the door and caught a small reflection of light in a minuscule gap at the top of the door. With one of her tools, and standing on her tiptoes to see, she pried at the gap until she could see two metal connectors.

Can't get in this way. I can pick locks, but there's not much I can do about that alarm, especially given how much time I have—if any—before their meeting breaks up. However, if they've gone to all the trouble to set an alarm, there must be something interesting in there. Let's see if I can find another way in.

Gina slipped back down the hall and into the storage area, opening the door just enough to peer out; there was no sign of the guard in the alley. She eased out into the open air and with a quick flip of her wrist lassoed a vent on the roof and scaled the wall with a minimum of noise. She recovered her rope and made her way to the far end of the warehouse, checking each step to ensure she didn't kick or trip over something. Along the ridgeline of the roof, she found a small skylight looking down into the secured room.

Strange, there's no light on and this is the end of the warehouse. Are they meeting somewhere else?

A quick check showed Gina there was no alarm, so she pulled out her tools and went to work on the window's lock. A few seconds later, she lowered the rope through the now-open skylight and let herself down.

Now, let's see what's so important in here.

Aside from the skylight, there were no windows. Gina felt more comfortable knowing she could use her light to examine the rest of the room. A large desk dominated the room and shelves lined two of the walls. Across the room from the desk was a large cabinet. She spotted what she assumed was a closet, but to her surprise, the doorway led to a small passage and stairs going down. There was a soft light at the bottom, and she could just barely hear voices ahead. She weighed going down versus searching this room for clues and decided she'd probably pushed her luck as far as she could for the night. She left the door ajar to listen for anyone coming up the stairs and began searching as quietly as possible.

A cursory search of the shelves revealed nothing of interest. The desk appeared to contain nothing either until Gina noted one of the drawers seemed to be sticking on something. She worked it out and discovered a small depression in the drawer channel. Reaching back into it, she found a folder. It took a bit to ease it out, but once it was free, she opened it up on the desk and played her flashlight over it.

Wait a minute. This is tomorrow's shooting script. How in the heck did they get this?

She glanced at the front page and noted a small set of numbers across the top: 45/50. Apparently, whoever had pinched this copy hadn't realized every copy of the script was numbered and that number indicated a specific individual. In theory, that was to prevent a rival studio or a nosy newspaper from seeing a script before shooting was finished. However, a shooting script is only issued the night before it was scheduled to allow the actors to rehearse their lines with the last-minute changes included. Plus, the chief technicians needed time to prepare their light scheme and microphone placement for the next day, as well as identifying what props or stunts needed prepping. These scripts were collected at the end of the shooting day and carefully accounted for. You couldn't draw the next day's script without returning the current one.

If I wanted to expose whoever's behind these "accidents," I'd just take this script. They'd have a hard time explaining where it had gone. At best, Hawkes would fire them for losing it. However, that would give away the fact I'd found their hideout, and we'd be back to square one. No, I know the number. It'll be easy enough to find out who was issued script #45 tomorrow from Cheryl, our script manager. Then I'll know who's leaking information and set up the proper place to try and find out why.

This answers one question, though. It had to have been Fischer's voice I heard the other night. This crew knows too much about the movie business. Somehow, I doubt he's reformed just because the war is over.

She slipped the folder back into place and returned the drawer to its original position. There was nothing else interesting in the desk, so she turned her attention to the cabinet. It was locked but it only took her a few seconds to pick the flimsy lock. Inside there was a small arsenal of weapons and explosives. While Gina didn't claim to be an expert on weapons, it wasn't hard to recognize the Schmeisser submachine guns or the Walther and Luger pistols arranged carefully with several boxes of ammunition.

I'm not going to jump to the obvious conclusions. These things can be found all over Europe since the war, but it's another clue that can't be ignored.

She relocked the cabinet and went around the room to ensure there was no sign she'd been there. Carefully shutting the door to the closet, she shinnied up her rope and secured the skylight before disappearing into the night.

"Gina, if you turn off your alarm one more time, I'm going to pour pancake batter down your nightgown. Hurry up and get out of bed. You have to be at makeup in an hour."

"Byrnsie, you're a cruel mistress."

Her assistant wandered in, her bright red hair tied up with a bandana. The wooden spoon she waved at Gina threatened to leave a trail of batter droplets in her wake. "Yes I am when it comes to ensuring you stay employed so I can maintain myself in a lifestyle to which I've grown accustomed."

Gina dragged herself out of bed and found a cup of hot tea waiting on her nightstand. The smell of batter hitting a frying pan helped clear her sleep-fogged brain and she stumbled toward the shower. A few minutes later, she appeared at the dining table dressed in a comfortable terry-cloth robe, a towel wrapped around her head. Byrnsie took one look at her and rushed to ensure the window curtains were drawn shut.

"It's a good thing we don't have any snoopy reporters around here. Can you imagine your fans getting a look at you sitting down for breakfast?" Byrnsie asked, setting Gina's plate down in front of her.

"What? I'm not allowed to look like a real person?"

"Gina, you know better than that. Of course not, because you're not. Maybe you were when you were still a stunt girl, but now? Now, you're an icon, a star. You're selling an illusion all around the world and it's important to maintain that image. Now, if you were out here in a diaphanous silk dressing gown with your hair immaculately coifed, *then* maybe some 'candid' publicity shots would be appropriate."

Byrnsie shook her head. "Sometimes, Gina, your head's in the clouds too much for your own good. You're a great actress, but sometimes I think you forget what it means to be a star."

"All right, Byrnsie. Maybe we should make you a star in my place?"

"Oh no, not me. I'm content being the invisible woman who pulls the strings from just off stage. You go out there and enjoy your cocktail parties and your soirees with European royalty. I'm quite content to be your girl Friday, as long as I get the occasional Friday off." Byrnsie grinned at her before returning to the stove to flip the next batch of pancakes.

"Ah, you're the Machiavellian power behind the throne."

"You know it."

There was a knock at the door and Byrnsie moved from the kitchenette to the living area of the suite. Gina listened as Byrnsie talked to someone and then her assistant called out.

"Gina, it's your dad. He wants some pancakes too. You haven't eaten them all, have you?"

"Come on back, Dad, or I just may."

Remmington Baker appeared in the kitchenette doorway. "You don't have to ask me twice to have some of Byrnsie's flapjacks. If I have to eat one more pastry for breakfast, I swear I'm not responsible for what might happen in the hotel kitchen. How're you doing this morning, Gina?"

"I didn't get a lot of sleep last night, Dad, but this is a great way to start the morning," she said, waving her hand over the food in front of her.

"Well, let me help myself here a bit and I'll just test out your theory."

Rem fell to, loading up a plate with the pancakes and added in a helping of fried potatoes and ham. The conversations came to a close as the three of them did justice to Byrnsie's cooking. Finally, Rem shoved himself backward from the table. "Whoo-whee, now that's a breakfast. Byrnsie, you could give that there five-star chef some pointers. Oh, he can make a fancy enough dinner plate, but nothin' beats a good ol'-fashioned breakfast. That'll stick with me for a while."

Gina wanted to talk to her father about last night's events, so she was trying to think of some way to politely get Byrnsie out of the apartment. Luckily, Rem must have recognized her distress, because he turned to Ciara before Gina could speak. "Hon, could I trouble you to pick up a copy of the paper for me? I plumb forgot to grab one before I came up here. I want something to read while Gina's sitting in the makeup chair."

"All right, Rem." Her assistant winked at Gina before turning and heading for the door. She'd been with the Bakers long enough to recognize when father and daughter wanted to speak privately, but she appreciated the subterfuge. She knew well enough Rem could have ordered a paper from the concierge desk if he really wanted one.

Gina waited until Byrnsie was gone before relating the events of the evening to her father. She went into her bedroom to change while Rem grabbed a cup of coffee and listened through the closed door. She couldn't tell if he was more interested in John or what she'd found inside the warehouse. She rejoined him and they went back to the kitchen table. He freshened his coffee, leaned back in his chair, and shook his head slightly.

"Now, Gina, I'm never gonna tell you what you can and can't do, but weren't you takin' an awful chance out there last night? What if this guy had been working for the people trying to sabotage the picture? He coulda led you right into a trap."

"It's hard to explain, Dad, but if he still lived back in the States, it wouldn't surprise me to see him putting on a mask and tights himself. There's no questioning his talent or confidence. He would have fit in with the other heroes I met during the war. You've got to admit, more people put on the tights to help fight the Nazis and the Japanese than anyone ever expected. Come to think of it, it might be nice to team up with someone from time to time."

Rem made a waving motion with both hands for her to halt. "Whoa, watch it now. You'll give poor Cliff a complex talking like that. He's already nervous enough about all the *stars* you hang out with. If you start socializing with other heroes, he's likely to just give up."

"Well, he's met most of them before. Of course, he didn't seem to appreciate me working with that one British superhero before he had to return to London. I think he was jealous over the Lancer's accent."

"Yes, but those were special occasions. Some of those are still classified too, you know. It'd be a bit different if you're hanging out with them all the time."

Gina glanced at the ceiling and let out a frustrated sigh. "Honestly, Dad, I'm never sure if he's interested in me or my alter ego. Whenever we go out, he spends more time talking about The Cat than he does me. It's flattering she's caught his fancy, but it's also frustrating. No girl wants to play second fiddle on her own date, especially when her date is dreaming about another woman—even if it *is* me."

Rem gave her a sympathetic look. “Well, there is a way around that.”

“Don’t think I haven’t thought about it, Dad.” She sighed. “If only Cliff wasn’t a reporter. I think I can trust him, but how can I be certain he can resist the lure of such a scoop?”

“Honey, if you have to ask that question, then you’re making the right decision. Personally, I think you’re misjudging Cliff, but you’re the only one who knows your heart. I’ll back you either way. Although I do agree—he does seem a bit more hepped up about The Cat than you at times.”

Gina started to reply but heard the door opening and Byrnsie’s footsteps. Her assistant nodded in approval, seeing Gina had already changed. “Come on, you two. If we leave right now, we may just get to makeup on time. Here’s your paper, Rem.”

Rem stood up and held Gina’s chair so she could get up easier. “Thanks, Ciara. I don’t know what we’d do without you.”

“Let’s hope Gina remembers her lines well enough that you never have to find out,” she said as she pointed toward the door.

The day’s shooting came to a close and Gina made her way over to visit with Cheryl Bradney, their script mistress. The middle-aged woman pushed her glasses up on her nose and shuffled through the stack of scripts sitting in a wheeled cart, fanning herself with her clipboard. “Looks like we got through today’s shoot without any issues, kid. That’s good to see. Ol’ Ian ought to be in a good mood today.”

“It was a nice change of pace,” Gina said, taking a seat on a small crate nearby. “Do you have the scripts for tomorrow?”

“Right here, sweetie. Hot off the press. I’m telling you, today has been good luck all the way around. Can you believe it? The script writers were able to get these done by noon and we had no trouble making the copies in time.”

Gina glanced at the set. Ian was busy talking to the technical crew, trying to set up the last shot of the day. She turned back toward Cheryl and smiled. "So, do you think I could go ahead and sign for tomorrow's script?"

"Sure, sweetie, as soon as you give me the one you have." Cheryl held her hand out expectantly.

Gina handed her copy over and then took the clipboard. She took her time finding the spot where she was to sign in today's script and then to the next page to sign for tomorrow's. She glanced down the list to see who had script #45. The name read Jo Page and apparently, she'd turned it in around lunchtime.

Hmm, I wonder who that is . . .

"Hey, Cheryl, I noticed a few names I don't recognize on the list. How many local people *did* Ian hire for the movie?"

"Sweetie, you'd have to ask Payroll if you want a specific number. I know we've got six people who get scripts who didn't come from LA with us. Three are actors Hawkes hired to add some local flavor beyond the usual extras we're gonna use for crowd scenes. The other three are technicians—a camera operator, an electrician, and a lighting guy. It was kinda odd. Ol' Ian is usually too paranoid to let just anyone see what we're working on, but we had a couple of guys get sick before we left the States. These guys had their certification with the French cinema from before the war, so the studio decided to take them on."

Gina scanned the list again as she signed for the script and then handed the clipboard back to Cheryl. "Hopefully things will calm down. It's been crazy the last few days with all the accidents."

"Tell me about it, sweetie. All these delays mean Ian and the writers are busy every evening trying to reorganize what shots we're going to do what day. It's all I can do to keep my script library up-to-date. I'm about ready to chuck the whole thing . . ." She paused and then looked conspiratorially at Gina. "And then I think about those beaches and all those rich guys running around down there and think, 'Maybe this isn't so bad after all.'"

Gina laughed with her and accepted the new script. "There

are perks everywhere if you just look," she said and gave the script mistress a wink.

"Speaking of which, you got big plans for this evening?"

"Nothing to speak of. Outside of studying these lines, I'm probably going to have dinner at the hotel with Dad. According to the schedule, Ian wants me on the set early tomorrow."

"Well, if you get bored, Trixie, Mabel, Trudy, and me are thinking about going to the casino. We bought all these fancy dresses and such when we heard we were coming to Monaco, but we haven't had a chance to go enjoy. Figure it might be better tonight than on the weekend. They're so darn crowded then."

The invitation caught Gina off guard. She didn't normally hang out with the crew off-set. Not because she didn't like them, but back in Hollywood, it felt like there were two separate worlds—one for the actors and one for the crew. She had been a lot closer with the stagehands and technicians when she was a stuntwoman, but when she started getting real parts, things changed. It might be nice to just relax for once.

"Let me check with Byrnsie. You may be the mistress of the scripts, but she's the mistress of my time."

Cheryl nodded in a friendly fashion. "We'd love to have you come, sweetie, but we know you've got a lot of responsibilities, both on-set and off." She looked around and gave her a conspiratorial look. "And trust me, hon, we wouldn't invite just anyone to come with us. You ain't as stuck up as a lot of the divas I've worked with the past twenty years. I've got stories I could tell you . . ." The matronly woman waved one or her hands dismissively and let out a low whistle.

Gina laughed in spite of herself. "If not tonight, I'll talk to Byrnsie about coordinating a special crew party at the casino when we get closer to wrapping up. They have special rooms you can reserve. It'll be my treat to you guys."

"Honey, you're all right. Well, we're going to head out about eight tonight if you get free. Hope to see you there."

Gina waved good-bye and took the script with her. Cliff seemingly materialized out of nowhere by her elbow as she moved among the crates of gear. "So, thinking about hitting the casino without me?"

Gina shook her head sadly. "I don't know, Cliff. I'm not sure you'd look good in a dress."

"What?"

"Cheryl invited me out with a bunch of the girls from the crew. I suspect it's a girls-night-out kind of thing, so if you're going to join us, you're going to have to look the part. Think of it as expanding your acting skills. You'll probably want to get started soon, though. It'll take a while for you to shave your legs."

Cliff made some sputtering noises and then turned bright red. Gina couldn't help but laugh at his attempts to stay composed. She patted him on the arm and then directed him back toward the actors' trailers. "Like I told Cheryl, I doubt I'm going to be able to go. This shooting script feels a bit heavier than usual. That means I'm likely to be up most of the night going over the scenes with Byrnsie and Dad. You are joining us for dinner, right?"

"I would be delighted, *mademoiselle*."

"Gina! Over here."

A young man waved at her from the far side of the set. She recognized him as Peter Roman, one of the up-and-coming junior directors that Hawkes had taken under his wing. He wove her way through the cables, boxes, and milling people preparing for the next scene until she reached the tall newspaperman. He finished his conversation with one of the cameramen when she arrived and turned toward her with an excited look on his face.

"What's up, Peter?"

"We're going to have to get ready. There's been a change to this afternoon's shooting."

"What?"

Peter rubbed his hand on his chin before responding.

"Yeah, I know. It's not like him. He's usually so meticulous, but the runner swore Ian handed these new scripts to her only a few minutes before she delivered them to me."

"New scripts? What's going on here?"

Peter shrugged. "Apparently someone came up with the great idea of a car chase between Nancy and the Germans. Since you've done stunt driving before, they want you to do the majority of the driving. They've rigged a car with cameras inside and everything. Says here once an actual stunt driver is available, they'll shoot the big climactic finish later. They just need you to do the basic driving today."

Gina glanced down at the script. "Wow, this will be an exciting scene. But I'm surprised. Ian is usually more conservative with his shooting. When I was still a stuntwoman, these sorts of stunts were usually prepared well in advance to get the timing down and ensure the equipment is ready. This seems kind of rushed."

"I know it's unusual, but apparently there's a time crunch and they don't have time to get a stuntwoman who looks enough like you to handle the driving. The runner said he'd just gotten permission from the French prefect of police and it's only valid for a few days. They don't want us tying up the roads too long. And besides, they're going to overcrank the film to make it look like things are going faster than they actually are. But, heck, I'm just one of the junior directors here. They don't always fill me in on everything that's going on." Peter looked around and then turned back to Gina with a smile. "It looks like a pretty easy drive for you. I've certainly seen you do more dangerous driving back in the States."

Gina nodded slowly. "It's been awhile since I've done anything like this, Peter. I hope my skills aren't rusty."

Peter pointed at the script. "The good thing is you don't have a lot of lines to memorize before we start shooting. It's mostly stage directions and shooting angles. From looking through the script, they'll be shooting from inside the car, they'll have a camera truck following you down the hill, and then they'll have cameras set up on various hills to get the scene from different angles. They'll shoot the dialog in the car mock-up back at the set later."

"It looks like Ian has thought of everything." Gina read through the script and her eyes narrowed the further she progressed. "Peter, are you *sure* these came from Ian?"

"That's what the runner said. Why?"

"This reminds me more of a script I filmed when I first broke in as an actress."

"What? Right before the war?"

"Exactly. Now, where is Ian? I'd like to ask him a few things."

Peter rubbed his chin again as he scanned the crowded set. "I don't see him. Jules is in the director's chair. I guess Ian went ahead to set up the afternoon shoot."

Gina felt that old familiar sensation she got when something was wrong. It wasn't that Jules Piper was at the helm. Jules was Ian's longtime second-unit director and occasionally filled in when Ian had a meeting he couldn't get out of with the studio executives.

No, this felt wrong because she thought she remembered this particular scene from a movie she'd made nearly ten years ago—a movie directed by Karl Fischer. Still, it wasn't unheard of for directors to lift scenes from earlier movies and put their own stamp on them.

"What time are we supposed to be on location?" she asked, eyeing the script suspiciously.

"The runner said we have to be there by one p.m. We're going to have to take off pretty soon if we're going to make it."

"All right. I'll meet you at the taxi stand in fifteen minutes. I want to get some stuff from my trailer."

Peter waved good-bye as Gina wove her way through the milling crew and left the noisy set behind. She glanced inside her trailer and was relieved Byrnsie wasn't there. She quickly put her Cat costume on underneath her dress and slipped the gloves, mask, and boots into a small carry-on bag. She shoved a change of clothes and some makeup on top for camouflage and then hurried to meet Cliff.

I'm not sure what's going on, but I have a feeling a certain masked heroine may be a surprise addition to the script today.

Gina walked around the Citroën Traction Avant, eyeing the low-slung car with some suspicion. The head mechanic came over, wiping some grease off his hands.

"Is there a problem, Miss Baker?"

"Hi, Bill. Well, I'm not real familiar with front-wheel drive. Is there going to be time for me to take this out before we start shooting?"

The mechanic checked his watch. "Well, not for a long drive, but if you want to take it out for a bit, this road leads to a village to the northeast of here. The road is pretty windy, but I suspect you can put the car through some paces and get a feel for how she runs. I know the motor is purring, 'cause I just finished tuning it earlier this morning."

Gina allowed herself a grin at that comment before moving over to the driver's side to take the wheel. *At least we're doing this in France. I'd be even more nervous if we were shooting in England. It's been a long time since I've driven on the left side of the road. I know I started as a stuntwoman, but I haven't practiced in a long time. Even running all over Hollywood as The Cat doesn't prepare someone for this.*

Before she climbed into the rigged car, she glanced over her shoulder. She didn't recognize the two men going over the touring car behind her. They were in costume already and had put their long coats and sunglasses on. *Guess Ian hired some new stuntmen. I don't think I've seen those guys around the set before.* She was curious who they were, but she needed to learn her own car's idiosyncrasies. She slipped into the driver's seat and started it up. Bill leaned in and pointed her in the direction of the village.

As she pulled out of the lot, she felt herself relax. The Avant was a lot more responsive than she had hoped. Soon she was pushing the car through its paces—powering through curves, rapidly accelerating and decelerating, as well as making abrupt turns and stops. Her confidence grew in the car and she found her reflexes snapping back into shape the harder she pushed the car. She reached the village in no time and stopped just long enough to buy a bottle of sparkling water and stretch before heading back.

On the return trip, she pushed her speed as soon as she reached the edge of the village. Her adrenaline began pumping as she imagined taking the car through this or that stunt. Approaching the set, Gina couldn't resist the urge to power-slide the car in the dirt into a parking spot between two large crates.

She bounced out of the car as Bill and Cliff came rushing over. "I think it'll do just fine, Bill. She pulls just a bit to the left, but that's easy to compensate for."

Bill looked the car over, and even though there was a frown on his face, Gina could hear the approval in his voice. "I said you could push it a bit. It looks like we should have discussed what 'a bit' means. I gotta get this washed quick and then get the cameras mounted. I'll be right back."

Gina tossed him the keys and Bill eased the car out of the tight spot she'd left it in. Cliff tapped her on the shoulder. "What the heck were you doing out there?"

"Testing out the car. I need to know what it can do if they want me to drive it."

"Yeah, but you could have been hurt."

Gina reached up and tapped him on the nose. "But I wasn't. Seriously, Cliff, I *was* a stunt driver, remember? I did a lot more dangerous driving than that before I stared acting full-time. If I'm going to do my own stunts, I can't guess what the car can do. I need to *know* how far I can push it before I get into trouble. Otherwise, I'll be tentative and either the stunt will look horrible or I'll flinch and wreck, which would be infinitely worse. There's a fine edge when it comes to driving and I need to know where it is." She paused for a second and then a mischievous grin appeared on her face. "Of course, if you're that worried, you can ride with me next time."

"Oh no. Mrs. Steele didn't raise a complete dummy. I've done some risky stuff to get a story—"

"—while chasing that costumed hussy you like so much."

"—when I was helping The Cat, yes, but that's different than taking chances just for fun."

Gina felt herself getting aggravated at his condescending tone of voice. "Cliff Steele, I'm not taking chances 'just for fun' or just to show off. If the script calls for me to dive off a building or jump through a window, then that's what I do. It's not like I sit around all day eating snacks and drinking champagne. I spend a lot of time working out with my trainers when I'm not on the set and you know that. I like being able to do my own stunts from time to time. Besides, I have to stay in shape with all these younger starlets gunning to take my place."

Not to mention, there's no way I could do the things The Cat has to do without training all the time too, but Cliff doesn't need to know that . . . yet.

From the expression on Cliff's face, she saw he knew he'd crossed a line and was trying to find a way to extricate himself from the situation. "All right, Gina. I just worry about you, that's all."

She gave him a quick hug. "That's all right, you big lug. I know you're just trying to look out after me. I'm sorry, I know shouldn't be so defensive. It's just tough because people used to look down on me because I was a stuntwoman. It's not an easy profession and I'm proud of what I was able to do. It's nice to see I haven't lost my touch."

"Well, just be careful out there."

She patted his arm and then went over to find Jules, going over some last-minute ideas with the camera crews. "Make sure you've got your cameras set up at these precise spots," he said. "We're not going to get many chances to do this shot and I'd like to get this done in one. It's a pain in the neck to try and match up backgrounds shots. Be certain we can get more than one camera on the bridge. That's where the big finish is going to take place. Watch your footing, there's some steep drop-offs out there."

The head cameraman nodded. "Roger, Jules. Give us about fifteen minutes to get everything set up and then you can start shooting whenever you're ready."

"All right, men. You've got your orders. Let's get to it."

Gina spread out the shooting map and examined it while Jules gave a few personal suggestions to the head camera operator. He then hurried over to join her. "Is there anything you're worried about before we get started?"

"Jules, where's Ian? I'm surprised he's not here for this. Not that I think you can't handle it, but he's usually such a stickler for doing things *his* way."

"Can't really say, Gina. I got a call this morning telling me Ian was sick and I was supposed to cover his shooting schedule today."

"Did you call the hospital? I've never known Ian to miss a day of shooting, even when he should have stayed in bed."

Jules motioned for her to follow him and they stepped away from the crowd. He glanced over her shoulder and then turned to her with a conspiratorial look on his face. "Look, Gina, I've known you for quite a while, so I'm going to give it to you straight. I really don't know why Ian isn't here, but I'm not going to waste time looking for him either. I've been Ian's backup for nearly six years. This is my first chance to really show him—and the studio—what I can do. I know I'm ready to sit in the big chair on my own picture."

He paused and looked Gina square in the eye. "Look, I'm not unsympathetic. I really hope he's just got a bad hangover or maybe he's 'testing' out some French talent. But this is my big chance, and I have to think of my career."

Gina's eyes narrowed, but she understood what drove Jules. Hollywood was definitely a "what have you done lately" town and it was tough to make the jump from second unit to director. Still, Jules seemed a little too focused for her comfort. "I understand, Jules. After all, I got my first chance because someone twisted an ankle on the set and I filled in while they recovered. That director recommended me for a bit part with another director and things went from there.

Still, I'm worried. This isn't like Ian."

"Would you feel better if I sent someone to go check on him?"

Gina smiled, but her eyes were still hard. "I think that would make me feel better . . . about you. After all, I need to make sure you're going to take as good care of my career as you are yours . . . if you know what I mean."

Jules smiled broadly at her. "I'll send Bernie to check up on him." He rubbed his hands together almost like a little kid getting ready to open presents on Christmas morning. "We'll make this is a sequence that'll take their breath away when it hits the big screen, Gina. With you behind the wheel, I can't fail."

"Thanks for the vote of confidence, Jules, but I better get into costume."

He made some shooing motions at her. "Good point. We'll be ready to go as soon as you are."

Gina hurried to the small trailer to get into her Nancy Wake outfit. While she was changing, she thought about her conversation with Jules.

I can sympathize with Jules. He's been in Ian's shadow a long time, but something is wrong. I can't put my finger on it, but this seems too contrived. It reminds me of the incident with Toby Howard when I had just gotten started both as an actress and The Cat. He hired a bunch of fake actors and used an actress's envy to stir up trouble on our set while he robbed a bank in the town we were filming. I'm getting that same feeling again, but I don't have a good reason to not shoot the scene. I just hope whatever happens, The Cat can handle it.

She reviewed her script one last time, then shoved it into the small bag with her gear and headed toward the car. She was impressed by the placement of the cameras. They were angled to capture scenes outside the car, inside the car, and out the front and back windows, but none of them obscured her vision. This setup was completely unfamiliar to her, but then again, she couldn't recall cameras this small before either. She glanced at them and noticed they were labeled in German, which surprised her.

Bill came to the window and leaned in. "All right, just like we talked about. You've got an idea what this will do, so just keep it under control. The guys behind you are going to be crowding you, but they're scheduled to miss a curve right after the bridge and crash. Just keep your cool and everything should go like silk."

"You've never steered me wrong before, Bill."

The mechanic screwed up his face at that bad pun and then became serious again. "Any questions?"

"No, if you say this stunt is safe, then it's safe. I wish I'd had some time to practice with the other drivers. This seems a bit rushed to me. Doesn't it you?"

"Yeah, but I guess Jules has his own system. Don't worry about it being too perfect. We're coming back tomorrow to shoot some extra footage with your stunt double to add in a few 'scarier' scenes." Bill blushed and paused for a moment, before continuing in a rush. "Not that I don't think you could do it, Gina, but our insurance agent insisted we use your double."

"That's all right, Bill. We're already tight on time due to all the delays. No sense in pulling me away from the main set to shoot and reshoot what's going to be a few seconds of screen time."

"Thanks, Gina. You were one of my best pupils back in the day. I know you can do this."

"Hey! I'm not that old and it wasn't that long ago."

Bill grinned and hurried away before she could say anything else. She looked in the rearview mirror as he went back to check on the other stunt drivers, then turned the ignition key. The Avant's engine purred like a big cat waiting to get started and she took that as a great sign. She maneuvered the Avant over to the starting line and waited for any final instructions.

Jules hurried over and leaned against the car. He pointed down the road. "We've got cameras all along the route, in your car, their car, and a camera truck is going to follow you. The camera truck should be back far enough they won't be in the scenes, but they should be close enough to catch all the action to splice in during editing. Now, be careful. There are a few places where the hill drops away just beyond the road, so be sure to hug the right side when you get near the bridge."

He flipped through the script and pointed at a page. "Remember, the 'bad guys' are going to crash at this point, right after you go over the bridge. There's a big enough spot where they'll be able to roll over a couple of times. Should be a great dramatic shot. You go down to here, then stop, get out and evaluate the situation, and then proceed back toward Monaco. There'll be a camera with a telephoto lens that'll zoom in to catch the expressions on your face. You're angry, you're scared, but you're also saddened by the futile waste of life this whole war has caused. Got it?"

"Just one question."

Jules looked at her with a surprised expression. "What?"

"Are you buying dinner if we get this on the first take?"

"You pull this off in one take and you can name your restaurant."

Gina watched as one of Jules's assistants came over with a walkie-talkie. Jules listened for a moment and then nodded. "All right, Gina. They're ready for you. I'll be following along behind the camera truck, but I'll be in constant contact with the camera crews with this."

Gina nodded and inched her car forward just a bit as the stunt drivers took their position. The script called for her to come down the road picking up speed. The other car would pull out of a hiding spot and begin chasing her down the winding road and try to force her off. She glanced at the stunt drivers as they drove past to get to their starting spot, but between their slouch hats, sunglasses, and turned-up coat collars, she couldn't make out their features.

That's odd. Maybe they're going to be walk-on extras later in the movie. That would explain their disguises. They can't "get killed" and then show up a few days later, unless we were shooting a horror movie.

One of the mechanics gave a wave with a white flag and Gina began her approach to the spot where the filming would start. She didn't push the Avant too hard yet, because she was supposed to avoid drawing attention to herself. She had just made the first curve when the touring car showed up in her rearview mirror. She glanced back at them and then gripped the wheel tighter as she accelerated slowly to keep some distance between her and them. As the touring car closed, she could see them waving at her, trying to get her to pull off.

That was Gina's signal to start the chase. She stomped the accelerator to the floor and the Avant leapt forward, raising a cloud of dust in its wake. A few seconds later, the touring car responded, bursting through the cloud in hot pursuit.

Per the script, they wove in and out of the two lanes as Gina tried to keep the bigger car from passing and cutting her off. Gina was a little surprised how aggressive the other driver was, but it wasn't anything she couldn't handle. They jockeyed for position through the first set of curves and then they entered one of the few long straight stretches.

Suddenly, the passenger in the pursuing car leaned out his window and fired a shot at her with a pistol.

Hey! That's not in the script!

The passenger fired again and one of Gina's windows splintered. She realized something was drastically wrong: those were real bullets! The hidden faces made sense now. They weren't stuntpeople—they were the saboteurs.

The touring car rushed forward and slammed into the back of the Avant, whipping Gina's head forward from the impact. She pushed her speed even more, trying to get some room between her and the pursuing car. Going into a sharp curve, she felt the Avant shudder as the trail car touched bumpers momentarily before the driver had to swerve to keep his own car under control. Even so, Gina could see the sharklike smile on his face.

Another ricochet bounced off her rear fender and then the touring car tapped her fender again. The Avant slid a bit in the loose dirt, but she managed to get it under control in time to make the next curve. She tried braking hard, but the touring car outweighed hers and he just took the opportunity to hit her one more time.

She could feel the Avant was starting to struggle under the beating it was taking from the heavier car. She swerved wildly, forcing them to back off a bit to avoid going off the road themselves, and then gunned the engine. She was going faster than she should on this dirt road, but there was no choice. If she didn't think of something soon, they'd eventually get lucky with a bullet or a shove. The sides of the hill were getting steeper as they approached the bridge—if she went off the road here, it was a couple hundred feet to the valley floor below.

Dodging their latest attempt to shove her off the road, Gina noted the cameras still seemed to be working. If she survived, this might qualify for an award for the best chase scene of the year. As another round shattered her rear window, she decided not to worry about the movie and concentrate on surviving to the bottom of the hill. Once she got onto flat ground, she'd have room to maneuver.

The next few minutes kept Gina's attention on the road as she whipped through a series of switchback curves and short straights. She glanced down at the speedometer and saw she was pushing 80 kilometers per hour on the straights and 60 kph in the curves. The Avant was struggling to hold the road, but Gina knew it was likelier to hang on than the touring car. The larger vehicle could keep up with her on the straights, but it had to brake harder than she did with these tight curves.

Gina saw the bridge coming into sight and knew that after this next curve, there'd be about a three-hundred-foot straightaway before she reached the bridge. That was going to be their last real chance to get her, so she tried to prepare for what was coming. She sped around the last curve and gunned her engine. With a roar, the touring car caught up and maneuvered behind her, despite her best attempts to swerve away. This time, there was only a small nudge as the touring car lined up its bumper with hers. Then there was as sudden jerk as her pursuers began trying to shove her car, picking up speed as they maneuvered to remain behind her. The Avant was rapidly becoming uncontrollable, and Gina could feel it beginning to lose traction.

They were trying to shove her off to one side of the stone

bridge and there was only one thing Gina could do to avoid going over the edge. The next time she felt the car start to swerve to the side, she slammed on the hand brake and turned the wheel savagely into the turn. The Avant executed a "bootlegger's spin" away from the pressure, rising up on two wheels, but then slowly settling back down on all four wheels.

With the resistance from the Avant removed, the touring car leapt forward, and a split-second later Gina heard the sickening sound of a crash. The touring car ran headfirst into the left wall of the stone bridge and then careened into the ravine. Gina jumped out of her car and rushed to the edge; to find the vehicle was a mangled heap in the shallow stream below and flames were beginning to lick around the passenger compartment. She drew back just as a small fireball went off, sending flame and smoke upward.

The camera truck came roaring up and Jules hopped out of the back. "Cut, cut! What the hell is going on here?"

"Jules, call an ambulance. The guys in the chase vehicle missed the entrance to the bridge and went into the ravine. I doubt anyone's alive, but someone needs to go check."

Jules blanched but immediately turned to the crew and had them pull the truck to the edge and hook a rope to it. Two men rappelled down to the flaming wreck. Gina watched, hoping against hope someone had survived. However, the signals from below dashed that hope. She swallowed hard and walked over to lean against her Avant, as Bill came rushing up with a wrecker.

"Gina, what happened?"

"Before I answer that, Bill, I want to show you something." She took the chief mechanic over to the rear of her car and pointed out the series of bullet holes.

"Wait, those are real. I know that car didn't have a scratch on it when I gave it to you. What's going on here?"

Gina took a deep breath before answering. "I don't think those were the real stuntmen. I think they're part of the group that's been trying to sabotage the picture. They shot at me and really tried to run me off the road."

"That's incredible. I'd heard you'd run into some strange

things on your shoots before, but this is the first time I've ever seen anything like this." He checked the interior of the car and whistled softly. "The one that took out the back window? It's lodged here in the headrest of your seat. It stopped just short of hitting you."

Gina felt the blood drain from her face. Bill rushed over and steadied her on her feet as Jules came running over. He stopped to make sure Gina was all right and then grabbed a technician, instructing him to grab the cameras out of the car.

"I don't know what happened here, but I swear this will turn out to be some of the best chase footage ever seen—if nothing was damaged, that is. Damn shame about those guys in the car, though. I'll try to get word back to their next of kin. Of course, now we're going to have to wait for the police. Might want to find a shady spot, Gina. You look like you could use a rest."

Gina was appalled at Jules's behavior, but then she spotted his hands shaking and realized he was trying to project a calm appearance for everyone else's sake. The rest of the crew slowly filtered down from their various sites and soon the sound of sirens filled the air. The French police showed up and began questioning everyone and taking pictures of the scene.

While everyone was distracted by the turmoil, Gina looked around and then grabbed Bill. "Hey, have you seen Cliff?"

Bill looked around before turning back to her with a shrug. "No, come to think of it, I haven't seen him since they started shooting the scene. I'd have figured he'd been over to check on you by now."

"Could you take me back to the temporary set? If the police don't need me anymore, I'd really like to change clothes."

"If they say it's okay, then sure, I'd be happy to, Gina."

A few minutes later, Gina got permission to leave, but the detective in charge insisted she report directly back to him as soon as she was done. Bill commandeered the camera truck and they drove back to the main camp. Gina went to change, but she paused and stepped over to the side of the dressing trailer. There were signs of disturbance and a small dark stain on the corner of the trailer. It looked like blood. There were also definite signs of someone being dragged away from the trailer and then tire prints going in the opposite direction of the bridge.

Someone had lost a fight here and she was pretty sure she knew who it was.

Gina was sitting down at her breakfast table when Byrnsie let her father into their suite. He pulled up a chair and turned to his daughter, a worried look on his face.

"Sorry, darlin', but I haven't found hide nor hair of Cliff this morning. Even got the maid to key into his room, but his bed ain't been slept in. No one on the staff remembers seeing him come in last night either."

She poked at her breakfast with her fork, trying to decide what to do. "The police won't take the situation seriously, Dad. They think the accident was a publicity stunt gone wrong: 'Mysterious attackers try to stop war movie.' They wouldn't even look at the spot where I think Cliff got jumped."

Rem took the cup of coffee Ciara offered him and took a sip before responding. "Well, I can't blame them, hon. It does sound awfully fishy. They don't have the advantage of knowing what we know. I heard Ian wasn't too happy when you all got back either."

"No, he wasn't. He had received a message to meet one of the ministers downtown about an upcoming scene. They kept him cooling his heels for three hours before someone informed him there must have been a mistake because there was nothing on the minister's schedule about meeting him. By the time he got back, we were already shooting the new scene. He had no clue someone had brought Jules that script and was livid when he heard how close I came to getting hurt."

Gina let out a small laugh before continuing. "Of course, now that he's seen the dailies, he's in love with what Jules did and he's adding those scenes into the movie. But he's shaken up that someone hijacked his movie."

Rem took another sip and leaned back in his chair. "You

know, someone's going to an awful lot of trouble to make sure this here film doesn't get made. Any ideas, there?"

Gina pushed her plate away and leaned forward onto her elbows. She saw Byrnsie had left to get something from the other room, so she whispered quickly while she had the opportunity. "The woman in charge has a strong German accent and if Fischer is involved, it has to be because we're doing a film about Nancy Wake. The White Mouse was one of the most hunted British agents in the war. It's possible someone still holds a grudge."

"That could be a problem, then."

Gina perked up at that comment. "What's up?"

"I heard from Ian while you were shooting yesterday Nancy is going to be on the set in three days. The studio is actually flying her in. She's going to do a walk-on for the finale of the film."

Gina felt the hair rising on the back of her neck. "Dad, we've got to solve this before she gets here. If they're determined to stop this movie, they'd stop at nothing to get to her." She glanced up to see Byrnsie walking over to her with a puzzled look on her face.

"Gina, this envelope was shoved under the door. I don't recognize who it's from, but it's addressed to you."

Gina took the envelope and glanced at it like she was holding a cobra. There didn't seem to be anything in it other than a piece of paper, so she gingerly tore off one corner, slid her hand down the short edge, and pulled the letter out.

Dear Fraulein,

Your reputation is not unknown to us. We know you know how to reach The Cat. We advise you do that soonest.

Have her wait by the changing trailers at 10:00 tonight. If she cooperates, your friend Mr. Steele will be returned to you no worse for wear. If not, I'm afraid he'll never see either of you again. A cat may have nine lives, but I doubt Mr. Steele does.

We do so hope you'll make the right choice.

A friend

"Dad, take a look at this."

Rem took the letter and pulled out his reading glasses while Gina scanned the envelope. While her name was carefully spelled out on the envelope, the return address was illegible. Whoever had written there had just made it look enough like writing to fool a casual observer. However, the language in the note left Gina with no doubt who had written it. "Byrnsie, can you go down and see if anyone delivered this message to our door and if so, who gave it to them?"

The redhead raised an eyebrow at Gina, but she kept her suspicions to herself and soon disappeared into the hallway. Gina waited a few moments to ensure they were alone before she turned back to her father. "What do you think I ought to do, Dad?"

"Well, honey, I'd say the last thing I'd do is go alone. However, since Cliff isn't around to backstop you like usual, I guess I need to find a good place to hang out down at the dressing trailers."

"Thanks, Dad, I was hoping you'd say that. I'm not worried about myself, but it could be awfully tricky trying to deal with them and rescue Cliff. Odds are they're not going to bring him to the meeting."

"Nope. I sure wouldn't. However, you did say they had a warehouse a few miles away? I'd say that's probably where they'll take you to once they're sure you're cooperating."

"Can you have a car standing by outside? Hopefully, I won't need anything more than a quick getaway."

"I can do better than that."

"What do you have up your sleeve, Dad?"

"Never you mind, darlin'. Just don't try to teach an old cowboy how to rope a steer. Things weren't always so cut and dried out on the ranch when you were too young to remember. I've had to fool a few rustlers and dry-gulchers in my day too."

Byrnsie came back to report none of the hotel staff had delivered that envelope as Gina had guessed. Apparently, the gang was taking no chances. Rem excused himself from the room and Gina finished preparing for the long day ahead of her. She knew Ciara was dying to find out more about the mysterious letter, but Gina took it and the envelope with her when she left.

Luckily, Gina only had a few scenes in the day's shooting, so she was able to get her lines down. There was a current going through the crew, though. Everyone seemed on edge after the events at the bridge yesterday. Gina caught people peeking up into the light racks and behind boxes just to be sure something wasn't lurking just out of sight. Even Hawkes seemed out of sorts. He was snippier than usual with the camera and sound crews, but eventually all the footage scheduled for the day was completed.

Gina waited until she was certain everyone had left and then slipped into her changing trailer to pick up a few things for the evening. Once that was complete, she walked off the set and began scouting around the area. She took careful notice of anything that seemed different or out-of-place from the past few days, but everything seemed normal. Still, she had a strange feeling someone was watching the set. She couldn't spot anyone, but there were too many hotel rooms someone could be watching the set from, hidden back in the shadows. She took a circuitous route back to the hotel, just in case anyone was following, stopping in a few places, where it might make someone think she was contacting The Cat. The long afternoon shadows seemed oppressive, and every noise practically made her jump.

Calm down, Gina. This isn't the first time you've been in a tight spot. The object is to be prepared when you go to the meeting. They will be expecting you to cooperate with Cliff's life on the line. You've got to make them think that too, until they drop their guard. That's when you'll have to make your move.

Back at the hotel, she visited with Byrnsie for a bit and then went to her father's room. While he kept watch, she opened the bag she'd brought from the set and went to work. She slipped into a plain pair of slacks, an oversized blouse, a dumpy jacket, and casual flats, before adjusting a blond wig onto her head and, for a finishing touch, slid an oversized pair of glasses onto her nose. She stepped back into the living area and knew she'd done a good job when even her dad did a double take.

"It's a good thing I saw you go into that room, Gina, 'cause I sure wouldn't have known it was you when you came out. Now you be careful out there. I'll be taking off in a bit."

"Thanks, Dad. *You* be careful, all right?"

She gave him a quick peck on the cheek and then once he signaled the hallway was empty, she slipped out and made her way down to the elevator. She tried to keep the smile off her face as the elevator door opened and three of her cast members moved to let her in without any sign of recognition. She avoided speaking on the way out of the hotel and carefully made her way deeper into the town.

Once she had shaken the feeling she was being watched, she found a quiet, dark alley and slipped out of her disguise, revealing her alter ego. She ensured her extra equipment was secured and then took to the rooftops. She almost hoped she'd bump into the mysterious John again but knew her luck couldn't be that good. Still, he would have been a great backup for the mission.

It didn't take her long to reach the dark set and scout the area from the rooftops. A familiar cargo truck rested in one of the alleys. She waited for a bit to see if anyone was lurking around it, but there was no sign of life nearby. She lowered herself into the alley and crept up on the truck. No one was in the back, and the cab was empty. She eased back to the rear and let the air out of the two rearmost tires. Once the truck was resting on its rims, she climbed back up and then made her way to her appointment.

She navigated through the piles of gear and cables with care. She was hoping to spot the reception committee she knew was waiting for her before they knew she was there. A small knock and some whispered curses alerted her to the gang's presence. She paused and listened carefully, identifying where at least two other groups lurked. She checked her watch, and the luminescent hands showed her it was only moments before ten o'clock. She made her way past an electrical generator when she heard a sudden rush behind her. Without thinking, she grabbed one of the outstretched hands and with a quick twist and a pull, she executed a *seoi nage* and sent the form flying over her shoulder to crash into a pile of crates.

That seemed to signal a general melee. Dark figures came boiling out from behind crates, spools of wire, and other large shadowy forms. However, her attackers were at a disadvantage since they had to be sure who they were hitting. The Cat did not have to worry about that.

Gina did her best to keep moving because she knew the simple press of bodies would sweep her off her feet. One person rushed toward her, and she grabbed him by his lapels and fell backward, instinctively going into a *tomoe nage.* Curling her body into a ball, she landed on her shoulders and shoved upward with her boot in his solar plexus, sending him careening into two other figures rushing toward the sound of fighting.

A woman's voice cut through the noise: "You fools! Use your lights!"

As flashlights were switched on around her, Gina slipped between two crates and headed for deeper shadows. The woman's presence changed some of Gina's plans. If Cliff was back at the warehouse, that meant only a couple of thugs would be guarding him. With their truck disabled, it would come down to who could get there first.

For the next five or so minutes, Gina played tag with her pursuers. While it was true they had an advantage by being able to see where they were going, she had the advantage of knowing where they were. She took advantage of her knowledge of the set to lure a couple of them into an ambush where she dumped a pile of crates onto them. A few seconds later, she used a length of electrical wire to trip others who were chasing her down a narrow passage between boxes. As the fight swirled through the darkened set, she realized they were scattered and disorganized. Now was the time to make her move.

She slipped deeper into the darkness and hurried down a dark alley toward a main road. She had just reached the street when she heard a shout and the sound of running feet. Gina knew they'd be heading for their truck, and she wished she could be there when they found what she'd done.

She burst out of the alley and dove into a nearby taxi. She called out the street address of the warehouse and ducked down in the seat. The cabbie stared into his mirror at her until she waved a handful of francs under his nose. He glanced at her, the money, shrugged his shoulders and the cab roared to life. Gina looked back to see two figures rush out of the alley and frantically start trying to flag down a taxi of their own.

She kept an eye behind her as the taxi lurched through the narrow Monégasque streets, but she finally began to relax as she recognized the streets leading up to the warehouse. She told the cabbie to stop a few blocks away and paid him extra to roar off as if she were still inside. She waited in a nearby alleyway until she was reasonably certain no one was lurking about and then made her way to the alley behind the warehouse. She scanned the area one more time before tossing her rope up to the roof with a gentle swing. The tiny, padded hook caught with only a small noise and she pulled herself upward hand over hand. Reaching the roof, she pulled the rope up after her and hurried to the skylight, trying to make as little noise as possible. Again, the lock fell before her determined assault and she lowered herself into the room. She knew it was time to check out where the stairs behind the fake closet door led.

She crept down the stairs and found her suspicions were rewarded. There was a faint light coming from beneath a door ahead. She found the door unlocked and two men inside the room, sitting at a small table playing cards. A third man sat stiffly in a chair facing away from them and in the dim light, Gina could make out Cliff's familiar form.

She crept as close as she dared and when she knew they had to sense her presence, she leapt forward. She landed on the table with both hands and then kicked out, catching the thugs with her feet. They went sprawling out of their chairs and Gina rushed them, never allowing them to get their bearings. A few well-placed judo tosses and the two men were lying at her feet.

She rushed over to the chair and found Cliff half conscious.

She cut his bonds and used the remains of the ropes to tie up the two thugs before they could regain consciousness. She eased him to his feet and pulled one of his arms over her shoulders to help guide him.

"I always knew you couldn't stay away from me," he croaked through parched lips.

"And I always knew you didn't have enough sense to stay out of trouble," she whispered back at him. "Now, concentrate on walking. We don't have much time before they get here."

"How'd you find me?"

"Trade secret. Now less talking and more walking, Mr. Steele."

The short walk to the door seemed to take an eternity, but there was nothing to be done about it. There was no other exit visible, and Gina knew if the gang got back before she got Cliff out . . . well, she didn't want to contemplate that.

She half pulled, half carried Cliff up the stairs into the office. She listened at the outer door. The main part of the warehouse sounded quiet, but she couldn't take that chance. She hooked her rope underneath Cliff's armpits and around his waist and then climbed up to the roof. She heard roaring engines and knew company was not far away. She hauled Cliff up out of the office a few inches at a time, straining to keep her feet secured on the sloping roof. Finally, he was able to get his arms over the edge, and he slowly got a leg out before Gina's strength gave out. She helped pull him out and just got the skylight back in place when she heard the door to the office slam open. She lay there, trying not to make any noise as she heard bodies rush in and then pound down the stairs.

The fresh night air must have helped as Cliff slowly shook his head and then climbed to his hands and knees. "Just point me in the right direction," he whispered. "I think I can make it from here."

"We shouldn't have to go too far. There's supposed to be a car waiting nearby."

"Then we shouldn't keep the driver waiting."

"If you're feeling well enough to make smart remarks, you're well enough to walk. Follow me."

She unhooked the rope from around him and made her way to the closest end of the warehouse. Even though she was tired from the fighting and then hauling Cliff out of the building, she did her best to step as lightly as possible. Although, from the sounds of shouting coming from beneath her, she wasn't sure anyone would have heard her stomping across the roof. Reaching the edge, Gina let herself down and then caught and steadied Cliff as he dropped the rest of the way. They slipped out of the mouth of the alley and started making their way down the street. A touring car ahead of them flashed its lights twice and the two made their way to it as quickly as they could. They ducked down behind it as a horde of men came boiling out of the alley and took off down the street in both directions. Gina eased the door open and they climbed in.

"Well, Miss Cat, it's good to see you made it. Gina said she was going to be looking for you."

"Luckily, I found the message she left for me. Thank you for having this car waiting, Mr. Baker."

"Not a problem. If you two will stay on the floorboards there, we'll get you home quickly."

That caught Cliff's attention. "'We'll'?"

"Sure. Gina's driving. I'm just along for the ride."

Gina did her best to hide her surprise. She wasn't quite sure how she was supposed to be driving since she was down on the rear floorboards with Cliff but now was not the time to ask what her dad was doing. The car pulled away from the curb smoothly and soon Gina could see they'd entered the casino district. They pulled up a few blocks short of the hotel to let her get out of the car.

She hurried into a dark alley, changed back into her disguise, and rushed toward the hotel. Approaching the door, she saw Rem helping Cliff inside as the car roared off. Gina waited a few minutes and then took a different elevator up to her floor. She saw her father helping Cliff into his room and then she slipped into her room once the coast was clear. She rushed to her bedroom and stripped out of her disguise and into some comfortable clothing.

A few minutes later, she made her way down to her dad's room. A quick knock and Rem let Gina in. "I saw Cliff in the hall. Did everything go all right?"

Rem's eyes twinkled as he played his part in the night's charade. "Yes. While you were hunting for The Cat, we were able to get a car and followed the gang back to their hideout."

There was a noise as the bedroom door opened, and Phyllis Taylor, Gina's stunt double, came out and handed Rem one of Gina's dresses and a red wig. Phyllis looked at the two. "I think this is the first time I ever pretended to be you when there weren't cameras rolling. I have to say, knowing the people out there might have real guns made it pretty exciting."

"I grabbed Phyllis, since she's almost as good a driver as you are, but I had her dress up like you because it would be less suspicious if you and I were out driving around town. I didn't figure it'd help Cliff any if people were looking for you while you were looking for The Cat."

"Quick thinking, Dad. Thanks, Phyllis. We owe you."

"I'll remind you of that when we get back to the States."

The next two days were quiet at the set, which seemed to relax everyone except for Gina. Instead, she found herself pacing backstage like a caged panther, trying to guess what the gang's next move would be. She knew the mystery woman had to be seething over how easily The Cat had escaped her trap and rescued Cliff. Her opponent's ego had been badly damaged that night and Gina knew whatever was coming next was going to be explosive. But what were they planning?

It's driving me nuts. I'm still not sure why it seems they've targeted this particular movie. Fischer trying to sabotage Ian makes sense. After all, Fischer never lacked an ego. This would let him get his revenge on the studio and Ian, and I can't imagine they want a movie made about Nancy Wake anyway. Or is it her *they're interested in? If so, how'd they know she was going to be here?*

I have to admit; Karl Fischer was a great director before the war. I have no idea what he's been doing the past six years, but it's not like he can just show up and get a job directing movies anymore. Everyone in America was convinced he was dead when he disappeared back in 1942.

In fact, until I saw him and heard his voice, I was one of them.

Still, while Fischer was a great director, he was a horrible spy. To be honest, he was a bumbler, which is why I always let him escape. I kept hoping he'd lead me to his boss. I came close several times, but he or she always stayed out of reach. No, he's a bit player in this caper too. Probably brought on because he knows the industry.

No, that woman is definitely the one in charge of this group. I wonder if she's his mysterious boss? And who or what was that Triumvirate she spoke about? No, Gina, don't go chasing butterflies now. Focus. What could possibly be her motive to stop this movie from being made?

"Hey, Gina?"

Startled out of her thoughts, she glanced over her shoulder to see the tall blond newspaper man approaching. "Oh, hi, Cliff. How're you doing?"

He leaned against a packing crate, rolled his shoulders, and rotated his neck before answering. "Not bad. I'm stiff, but the doc said there was no serious damage. I have to admit, those guys worked me over pretty good in that basement."

"I can't believe Ian talked you into not going to the Monaco police. I mean, this is twice someone associated with the movie has been kidnapped."

"Don't complain too loudly, kettle. Why didn't you go to the cops after your little escapade in the hills? I was just kidnapped. They tried to kill you."

She started to blurt something out and then caught herself and blushed. "We tried to, but they thought it was a publicity stunt that went wrong. They threatened to haul Ian up on charges for the 'accident.' Besides, he's afraid word will get back to the studio—some of them didn't think he's ready for an international shoot. This is his big chance and it's an important subject. I've never seen Barry or Edgar so focused. They really want to nail this picture, even with all the delays and strange happenings. This could really be the break Ian has been waiting for."

"I know, and the fact he's an excitable teddy bear doesn't make it any easier." Cliff paused for a moment and then glanced at the stage where Ian was giving directions to Barry Grant and two actors playing French Resistance soldiers about the next scene. "Gotta go change and practice my sneer. My big scene with Barry is right after this one."

"Go get ready. I'm sure nothing will happen before you get back."

Cliff grinned and hustled toward the trailers. Her gaze settled on a number of new faces around the set—faces she didn't associate with movie actors except when shooting gangster parts.

Hmm, did Ian hire some new security for the set? Maybe he's taking this more seriously than I thought.

She noticed she wasn't the only person who'd noticed the sudden influx of large and very professional-looking men. Ian looked up from his discussion with Barry and motioned his assistant over to him. Ian whispered something and the assistant rushed over to a dark-haired man. The newcomer listened to the assistant and then swung his hand around in a small circle over his head. The others nodded and pulled back to the outskirts of the shooting set. The dark-haired man stepped into the background away from the stage but positioned himself where he could observe everything without being too obvious.

She wasn't due for several scenes, so she decided to indulge herself and find out what was going on. She wandered over to the dark-haired man. There was something about him—he was no ordinary security guard. Gina decided to see if he was the talkative type.

She took a seat on a small crate next to him. "Good morning."

"Morning, miss. Can I help you?"

"Just noticed you and your team here today. Hadn't seen you before, so I was wondering if something was up?"

"You're Miss Baker, right?"

She started to say he could call her Gina, but from the way he held himself and kept his answers short, he wasn't there to make friends. "That's right."

"I can't go into details, miss, but I think you know you're expecting a VIP tomorrow. We're here to get the lay of the land in order to provide security."

"So which unit are you all with?"

The dark-haired man grinned in spite of himself. "I knew just growing out our hair wasn't much of a disguise. That obvious?"

"I've done enough USO tours to recognize a soldier when I see one."

The large man smiled before answering, "We're a mixed group, miss. I'm with the 101st Airborne, though." He extended his meaty hand toward her. "Captain Bill Stacey, but you can call me Bill."

Gina returned the smile and relaxed. "Thanks. Call me Gina. So, do you anticipate any issues?"

Bill's smile fled and he glanced around. "Gina, I always anticipate issues. I prefer to be pleasantly surprised than the other way. This is not a typical situation. The principality has given us some leeway for our mission, but we're supposed to keep a low profile."

He glanced around one more time, but Gina could see the smile beginning to reform on his face. His steel-gray eyes bore into her. "Our job is to anticipate what could go wrong and ensure they remain hypothetical. In actor talk, we're really good at ad-libbing."

Gina heard familiar footsteps, and she turned to see her father approaching. "Hi, Dad, have you met Captain Stacey?"

The captain took Rem's hand. "We've met, Gina, but I doubt your father remembers. I was just a buck sergeant when we saw the USO tour in England right before we jumped into Normandy. I never did get a chance to thank you and all the others for performing."

To Gina's surprise, Rem actually blushed at the compliment. "Aw, shucks, Captain, thanks. I just wish I'd been a bit younger so I could have volunteered to be with you boys."

Gina saw this was turning into a mutual admiration society meeting and excused herself. She spotted Ian going over some script changes with Cheryl and walked over to see him. He sent Cheryl to make the changes and then turned to Gina. "So now, Hawkes is not distracted enough, he must now suffer through soldiers stationed around his set. How do they expect me to finish this movie with such interruptions, I ask you? The fact I have not yet collapsed into a ball of nerves surprises even me. But, no, I shall persevere. Ian Hawkes does not bend to the whims of fate—Hawkes bends fate to suit his needs."

Gina gave him a mock clap. "Why, Ian, that speech will really wow them at the Oscars next year."

Ian began preening. "You really think so?"

"Absolutely. What could possibly go wrong?"

A heavy sigh escaped his lips, and he slumped against a nearby box. "Why, why are all of these things happening to my movie? I'm a nice man. I treat my actors and crew well. Why would someone want to make me fail?"

"Jealousy, obviously," Gina said, feeling the shadow of the ex-director Fischer hovering around the set. "It's a movie any great director would want to make, but the studio chose you. Personally, I think they made the perfect choice."

"All right, enough with the buttering-up. Hawkes will not give you more lines. You are already the star of the show. There is no more room for racing scenes or jumping through flames. I must return to the set."

Gina watched the pudgy director pretend to stomp away, but she could tell from the way he called out the next set of commands that he was in a better mood.

The rest of the afternoon sped by and both cast and crew took advantage of the lack of interruptions. Gina shot two scenes, one on the set and one walking down a street in Monaco, with Edgar Robertson and his men trailing her, not knowing she was leading them into a trap. The people of Monaco were great sports about the whole shooting process and were happy to serve as extras for the street scene.

Walking down the street for the third time, she went through her routine and then disappeared around a corner. There was some further movement and then she heard the words she'd been waiting for: "Cut! Print!"

She popped back out to see everyone gathering around Ian. From the expression on the portly director's face, she knew he was pleased with how today had gone. He glanced around to ensure everyone was looking at him before speaking to the crew.

"Very good. I cannot wait to see these dailies. Still, that is not the reason I am giving you the rest of the night off. As you may know, we have a very special visitor coming to the set tomorrow. I want you to get a good night's sleep. I don't want to hear of anyone wandering off to the casino or going out to any parties tonight. I want everything to go smoothly tomorrow. This is not a request. Am I understood?"

"Yes, Ian," came back the chorus of replies.

"Very well. I will see you all bright and early on the set tomorrow."

Gina went back to the set to ensure she had the latest script for tomorrow's shoot. Cheryl was sitting at her desk, looking over Gina's shoulder as if she was surprised no one else was there.

"Has anyone seen Ian?" the script mistress asked.

"He just released everyone a bit ago. I suspect the crew will be here soon to lock up the gear. Is there a problem?"

"There sure is. Why did he send a messenger with more changes to the script? I thought he and the writers had everything worked out earlier today."

"*Another* script change? That's strange."

"That's what I thought. Still, Jo Page showed up around half an hour ago with this new script. There's a big change to the scene with our guest star and Captain Stacey is none too pleased about it."

"Can I take a look, Cheryl?"

"Sure. Since you're the lead in most of the shooting tomorrow, you're in the changed scenes too."

Gina took a quick glance at the green pages, denoting the changed scenes. Her eyebrows rose. "Cheryl, there's no way Ian approved these changes."

"I was thinking the same thing, hon. Something's up. That's why I need to talk to him before I issue these changes to anyone else. Here's the other script. Take them both and if you see Ian before I do, let him see what's going on and ask why he sent Jo with those changes."

Gina left with both scripts under her arm, went back to her room, and began examining the scripts. The changes were subtle, but the main difference was the requirement for Nancy to be closer to the center of the square where the shooting was to take place.

. . . *Where the shooting is to take place* . . .

Gina froze as she realized what she was thinking. Of course, it only made sense. This movie was about the White Mouse, the one woman the Gestapo could not capture. However, if she were to follow this script, she'd be exposed, not expecting anything. There would be a thousand different ways they could try to capture or kill her. It wasn't as though they lacked for explosives or guns in that warehouse. She gathered up the scripts and headed down to Ian's room with a grim look on her face.

There will be a subtle change to the scripts tomorrow—one that includes an actress no one is expecting.

Ian walked around, guiding people to their places. "All right, we don't have all day. The good people of Monaco were nice enough to let us use this historic square for our scenes, but let's not waste time. We won't get it two days in a row. Look sharp, pay attention, and try to remember your lines."

Captain Stacey motioned Gina over. "Even though you've never met her, I suspect you're rather familiar with her work. Gina, this is Nancy Wake. Nancy, this is Gina Baker."

A beautiful redhead stepped forward and extended her

hand. Gina took Nancy's hand and felt herself shake more than she had for her first screen test. "Oh, my goodness. I'm . . . speechless."

Nancy winked. "Lord, I hope not. It'd be a damn short movie."

That broke the ice, and Nancy led them to a couple of chairs set in the shade of a few crates. "I understand you're playing me in the movie. I must say, I don't think I've ever looked so good."

Gina felt herself blushing all the way to her hairline. "I had heard you were the most beautiful agent the British had in the war. They did not do you justice."

"Oh, now, stop that or we'll be here all night complimenting each other."

Gina giggled and for the next hour or so, the two women visited like long-lost sisters. Nancy told her what she could of her adventures while Gina talked about some of the scrapes she'd gotten into back in Hollywood. Gina had never before been tempted to tell someone about her real adventures, but somehow, she felt Nancy would understand more than anyone else she'd ever met.

"I think my drill instructors could have taken lessons from your director friend, dear. All he needs is a swagger stick."

"Don't worry, Nancy, he has one. We just don't let him bring it to the set anymore."

The two women shared a soft laugh, while Ian frowned at them, not realizing he was the topic of their conversation. "If you two don't mind, could you move back until it's your time? I don't want the microphones picking up your laughter. This is a somber scene we're shooting here."

"Don't worry, Ian, you'll never hear us."

"My ears are not as sensitive as a microphone, Gina. Shoo."

Gina and Nancy took their chairs farther away from the main scene and the two found another shady spot near a large crate. "How are you enjoying your time here on set?" Gina asked, as one of the runners brought them each a glass of ice water.

"I have to say, it's a bit overwhelming. However, even among the chaos, I can see how everything flows together. It's a bit like a military operation, love. You plan, you prepare, and in the end, it all goes to hell anyway. You just adapt and overcome."

"True, but if we make a mistake, we get another chance to get it right."

A shadow passed over Nancy's face, and she nodded thoughtfully before her smile returned. "Right you are there. Luckily, more of mine went right than wrong, so I guess it all worked out for the best. I still can't believe you're making a movie about my escapades. There are so many others you could have honored."

"We were lucky to have someone who was a friend who worked with U.S. Army Intelligence, who has a friend who worked with the Special Operations Executive, who managed to get part of your exploits declassified. The British Home Office thought it might be good for the people to learn some of the stories about people who fought against the Nazis and their collaborators."

"Oh, pish, Gina. I only did what had to be done. The boys in the front lines were in more danger than I was most of the time. Besides, have you seen those Army rations? I think I'll take French food and wine over those canned meats any day."

The two women laughed again and then watched the current scene. Nancy continued the conversation. "Whatever you do, don't make me look too heroic, love. I was just doing my job."

"Nancy, I don't think there's anything I could do to make you look anything *but* heroic. After all, I've read some of the original debriefings and reports the writers used to create their scripts. You're way too modest. Riding your bike past German patrols to carry messages and spare parts, taking out a soldier with your bare hands, and then taking command of a Resistance unit when their leader was killed in an ambush? You were incredible. Sure, we're spicing a few things up for the audience, but I'm not sure they'd believe the real story. It's even more fantastic than this movie."

"Now, Gina, you're making the blood rush to my face. I heard a bit about your war exploits too. I'm not the only one with a classified file in London and Washington. You weren't even enlisted when you flew into Occupied France on your mission. Bravo, by the way."

It seemed like it was the day for Gina to blush. "Thanks. When they asked me, it never crossed my mind to say no."

"Then they picked the right woman to play me, because that's exactly what I would have done."

Gina looked around the set. Everything seemed normal but she was worried. Even without the bogus script, there were still two scenes Nancy had coming up, one right before the lunch break and one right after. Gina was with her in the first, but the afternoon one was primarily her, Barry Grant, and one of the other actresses. Nancy was supposed to walk over and set her purse next to the other actress and then, when Barry gave her the signal, she was to take the other purse and continue on down and catch the bus. She was supposed to then exit the bus, which would drive off. They would cut out her leaving the bus during the edits. It seemed like a simple enough scene, but it would require Nancy to be out in the open for a while. If the gang was really gunning for her, that's probably when they would strike.

Gina glanced around and saw Captain Stacey speaking into a walkie-talkie. From the expression on his face, he wasn't pleased about whatever he was hearing. She excused herself from Nancy and walked over toward him. He spotted her approach and tried to arrange his features into a more placid expression.

"Anything wrong, Captain?"

"Miss Baker, I know you mean well, but this is not a situation where civilians should be involved. Please do not worry about anything. We've got things well under control."

"Captain, I know you mean well also, but if you recall, I also have some experience with the Office of Special Services. I may not have been enlisted, but I certainly can pull my weight."

"Actually, we were briefed on your and Mr. Steele's actions during the war. Both of you are quite well thought of by the top brass. However, things are moving quickly and I really don't have the time—or authorization—to bring you up to speed. Nor do I have time to inform everyone if you get involved. So, please spare you and me a lot of trouble and don't get involved."

Gina recognized the look on his face and backed off. When Nancy left to go to Makeup and Costuming, she lurked in the area of the captain, but he made certain to keep his voice low as he coordinated with his men via the radio. After several attempts to eavesdrop on him, she finally gave up and started trying to spot the rest of his team. She noted most of them were scattered about the crowd watching the filming, but a few were noticeably absent.

She prowled around the set for a while, looking for anything out of place. However, the more she looked, the more it felt like any other day. She even spent time mingling with the crowd, signing autographs and having her picture taken. There was no sign of the gang and nothing out of the ordinary.

Something must be going on, though. If they want to strike at Nancy, this is their only chance. She flies out of Nice airport to London this evening on an RAF transport. No, there's something I'm overlooking, and I think the captain thinks so too. What are we missing?

However, answers were hard to come by and soon it was time for Nancy and Gina to do their scene. They were reenacting a situation that had actually happened in Nancy's life in Lyon. So, even though Nancy only had a few lines, Gina knew it was important to get this scene right. Thirty minutes later, Gina heard the director call, "Cut. Print," and finally relaxed. Nancy gave her a quick hug. "That was perfect, dear. It felt like I was watching a younger version of myself. It wasn't so much reliving the experience as seeing it from outside my body. Good job."

Gina felt a warm glow in her face at Nancy's compliment. "You were pretty darn good yourself, Nancy. If you had any interest in going into film, you'd be great."

"Oh, heaven's sakes, no. I think the government has more plans for me. Although it might be a good idea to visit some other parts of the Empire. Might be a tad healthier for me.

Apparently, there are rumors about some sore losers running around Europe. I might even look into visiting Australia or New Zealand. Now *that* would be a bit of a change of scenery."

"That's about as far away from here as you can get."

"It's just a thought. Hard to plan that far ahead, you know."

Captain Stacey came over and talked to Nancy for a bit. Ian called lunch break, which meant Gina had an hour before shooting started again. After visiting with some of the cast and the soldiers—who seemed to appreciate movie food from the way they dug into it—she returned to her trailer to wait until after lunch.

At least that's what a casual observer would think . . .

Changing into her Cat outfit, Gina slipped out a window and made her way to a rooftop overlooking the set. She wasn't sure why, but she knew something was about to happen. Apparently, Captain Stacey did too, because he was glued to his walkie-talkie and pacing around like a caged animal. The second scene with Nancy was getting underway and the captain moved as close as he could to the set without interfering with the shot.

From what Gina could see, everything was going well. The purse exchange went off perfectly on the first take and Nancy moved nonchalantly down the street, past the uniformed German soldiers, and boarded the waiting bus . . .

. . . which immediately took off with Nancy still inside.

Captain Stacey rushed forward, but the actors in the German uniforms pulled out their gas masks and tossed grenades at the crew and soldiers. A white cloud erupted from the grenades, and the pursuers coughed and choked from the tear gas. Gina hurried across the rooftops to follow the bus as it tried to gain speed in the afternoon traffic.

Gina glanced back to see some of the real soldiers wrestling with the phony actors. That worry dealt with, she concentrated on catching up with the fleeing bus. It slowed down for a moment to negotiate a turn, and Gina took the opportunity to leap onto the roof.

She landed heavily and then rolled to one side as a series of bullets tore through the metal where she had been only a moment before. As the bus bucked from one side to the other, she swung down through an open window to confront the shooter: a man who now tried to bring his submachine gun to bear on her. A quick judo chop to the wrist, though, made him drop it and a leg sweep took his feet out from under him. His head hit the metal floor of the bus with a solid thud and he lay still. She glanced toward the back of the bus and saw Nancy had taken advantage of the distraction—a second armed guard Gina hadn't noticed was lying crumpled in the seat beside the White Mouse.

Nancy picked up his Luger and waved The Cat forward. Gina rushed toward the front but ducked quickly as the driver snapped a shot over her shoulder, forcing Gina to drop to the floor. Before Gina could recover, the driver shoved something onto the gas pedal and the bus leapt forward, heading down a hill toward the Port de Monaco.

Gina moved forward, hearing Nancy coming up behind her. The driver looked back one more time, and Gina could see it was the woman who was the gang leader. A snarl formed on her lips before she spoke to the onrushing pair. "Not this time, Cat! Death to all the foes of the Reich!"

Gina and Nancy were forced to duck as she fired another shot from her Luger. Gina glanced up just in time to see her jump out the now-open bus door. The driverless bus careened down the hill, gaining speed and bouncing off parked cars.

Gina started to grab the wheel, but Nancy said, "Go after her. I'll handle the bus."

Gina didn't bother replying and dove out the open door. She hit the ground and rolled, coming up on her feet just in time to avoid a shot from up the hill. The bus's brakes squealed in the distance, but there was no time to worry about Nancy. Another shot clipped the wall near her head and Gina rushed forward, taking cover in a doorway. She glanced out and saw the woman rush into an alley. Gina counted three and then ran across the street and peered around the corner.

The woman ran toward a cross street, but as Gina tried to follow, the woman fired another couple of shots, and she was forced to duck behind a dumpster. By the time she reached the corner, she had lost her quarry, but Gina recognized where they were and broke off the pursuit to head to the warehouse.

She took to the rooftops and rushed across the city above the bustle and traffic, knowing the woman would have to slow down to avoid drawing attention. Gina also knew it was unlikely the woman would be looking up, so there was a good chance she'd think she'd lost Gina and let her guard down.

Soon, she came across familiar rooftops. With a well-placed lasso, Gina swung atop the warehouse. She spotted the woman coming down the street, trying to act nonchalant. The woman approached the front door to the warehouse as if nothing unusual had happened. No doubt she was congratulating herself on her escape . . .

. . . until Gina's boots caught her in the face, knocking her to the pavement.

Gina was tying the woman's hands behind her back when she heard sirens in the distance. A few moments later, two police cars pulled up, and Cliff Steele was the first one out of the car.

"Well, I wasn't expecting to see you here, Cliff."

"After the incident at the set, I thought they might try to take Nancy where they held me. So, I called the cops and luckily, I remembered how to get here. I should have known you'd have this wrapped up by the time we got here, though."

"Be careful going into the warehouse," she warned the officers as they approached. "There might be more in there and they've got weapons and explosives."

"You're not coming in with us?" Cliff asked.

Gina smiled at him. "No, I've got some other business to clean up. I'm sure I'll run into you again one of these days."

Before he could say anything, she rushed around the corner and returned to the rooftops, heading back toward the set.

I'm sure Nancy's all right, but I think Gina Baker needs to make an appearance soon, before Cliff or anyone else has a chance to ask any questions.

Gina finished her last scene for the day and was relaxing in her chair talking to her father. "I heard they picked up Jo Page this morning as she was trying to slip out of Monaco. It looks like they caught the entire gang except for Fischer. Seems like he always manages to slip away. He's got more lives than a cat, Dad."

"After this, I suspect he'll go into hiding again. It may be years before we see hide or hair from him. With any luck, he'll stay in Europe, and we'll be home soon. We've only got a few more days shooting here in Monaco. They'll finish the rest of the movie back at the studios at Galaxy Pictures."

"Well, I'm glad I caught up with you before you left," said a familiar voice.

Gina turned around to see Captain Stacey approaching. "Hello, Captain. I thought you were heading back to England."

"Good to see you too, Miss Baker. No, I have one more project to handle." He handed her an envelope. "I'll be seeing you at eight, I hope."

Before Gina could say anything, the captain saluted smartly and spun around heading across the set looking for someone else. Overcome with curiosity, Gina opened the envelope. Inside was an invitation to a private party on a yacht to watch the fireworks that evening.

Gina found herself getting caught up in the idea of the mystery party in spite of herself. The invitation did not name the host, but considering who had delivered the missive, she suspected it wasn't a trap. Even growing up in Hollywood, she still got starstruck from time to time. She always was amazed at the brilliant talents she'd worked with in her career.

She was still thinking about the invitation when someone cleared their throat behind her. Byrnsie stood there, script in hand. "Well, if you're going out this evening, you better get started on these lines now. Do you want a snack before we get started?"

Gina made a face before getting up. "You're a slave driver, Byrnsie."

"Gotta be, Gina. After all, if you don't work, you don't need a girl Friday. Then where would I be? I'm too cute to live in a cardboard box out in East LA."

"Can't have that hanging over my head. While I'm studying, can you lay something out for me to wear tonight?"

"Certainly. Maybe one of these days, I'll get to actually go instead of living vicariously through your stories."

Gina looked at her over the top of the script she was perusing. "Byrnsie, you're not exactly a wallflower."

"Gina, popcorn and the latest movie on Saturday night doesn't quite match soirees on yachts and mansions with those Hollywood dreamboats." Ciara got a dreamy expression on her face as she did a mock pirouette with an imaginary partner.

Gina fought back a laugh as she watched her assistant dancing around the set. "Byrnsie, you're wasting your time here. With your imagination, you should be acting or at least writing scripts."

"Maybe I will one of these days."

"All right. You write a script, and I'll show it to some agent friends of mine. If we can sell it, we'll ensure you get a part in it too."

"You're on. I wonder who you're supposed to be meeting tonight?"

"Well, if I can get some quiet time to work on my lines, we'll find out soon enough."

Byrnsie grinned at her and adjusted her cat's-eye glasses. "Understood, boss. I'll have everything laid out in the room by the time you get there."

Gina found Cliff, Rem, Barry, and Edgar waiting in the lobby of the hotel. No one had any more information on their mysterious host than Gina did. As more of the cast and crew made their way into the lobby, Gina realized someone had invited nearly everyone involved in the movie. At eight o'clock on the dot, a group of limousines pulled up in front of their hotel and Captain Stacey hopped out. He had the-cat-that-just-swallowed-the-canary look on his face as they drove through the town toward the Quai de Monte Carlo and refused to answer any questions.

After a short drive, they pulled up in front of a pier, at the end of which they were met by a couple of large men who looked very out of place in their jackets and slacks. There was a short conversation and then they motioned for a small skiff to pull up to the pier and assisted the stars down the wooden ladder. Other skiffs headed toward the pier to pick up the rest of the waiting guests.

"If I was casting a movie, those gentlemen would not be my first choice for flunkies," Barry said in his soft accent. "I think they're more soldiers."

"I agree, Barry," Edgar said, leaning back in the seat as the skiff hit a small wave. "Those boys are trying too hard to be inconspicuous. They remind me of new actors. They're trying so hard to get into character, they're more stereotypes than actual people. Makes me wonder what we're getting into?"

The skiff maneuvered around some smaller craft and headed toward a huge yacht floating in the harbor. Even at this distance, men could be seen running around on deck, getting things ready. Gina noted men obviously posted as sentries, keeping a close eye on all the other nearby boats, and turned to Captain Stacey. "If it was anyone other than you, I'd insist this boat turn around right now and take us back to shore. This doesn't feel right."

"Now, Gina, you wound me. Trust me, you're going to have a great time." He turned back toward the prow and yelled, "Ahoy the yacht! Six to come aboard."

With that, a small set of stairs swung over the side. Gina was given the honor of being the first up the stairs. Once again, her former stuntwoman training came in handy as she deftly handled the rolling motion of the yacht, eliciting an appreciative whistle from someone on deck above. She felt her cheeks flush for a second and then concentrated on the rest of the stairs.

Reaching the top, two sailors offered her a hand onto the main deck and soon, the five men from the skiff joined her. Cliff looked around anxiously, but the ship's captain quickly stepped forward. "Ah, Captain Stacey, we're glad you and your guests could make it. Gentlemen, and Miss Baker, thank you for gracing us with your presence. Your host and his other guests are waiting in the main lounge. If you'll follow me?"

Gina and the other actors glanced at each other and then let themselves be led into the lounge. The room teemed with young, and not so young, clean-cut men in tuxedos and military dress uniforms who quickly formed up around them to shake hands and talk to them. Gina quickly noted it was an international smorgasbord in the lounge. She recognized American, British, French, Canadian, Australian, Scandinavian and Eastern European voices but they blurred together in the overwhelming cacophony from their admirers.

A sudden ringing caught everyone's attention and the captain's voice cut through the noise. "Please, gentlemen, there will be plenty of time to visit with our guests. However, there are some others who would like to speak to our guests, if you don't mind."

Almost as one, the crowd around them parted and Gina and the others were escorted to the far end of the lounge. Gina felt a little flush when she realized who it was waiting to meet them, and she heard Barry take a deep breath in surprise.

"Good evening, Miss Baker, Mr. Grant, Mr. Robertson. I can't say how much I've looked forward to this opportunity."

Gina finally found her voice. "Thank you, General Eisenhower. I must say, this is a surprise."

A smile spread over the older man's face. "I hope you'll pardon the cloak-and-dagger routine, but my security detail insisted. And now, may I introduce someone you may be familiar with." He motioned to a young woman standing nearby who stepped forward to shake Gina's hand.

"Nancy. I thought you had left already?"

"Sorry for the small deception, Gina. This party had been scheduled for a while, but we couldn't tell anyone for security reasons. I know you need to circulate, my dear, but do look me up when you get a chance. I've got a little something for you." Nancy shooed her off with a wave. "Oh, go on, love. Besides, I think I'd like to visit with that Barry fellow you brought with you. Now *there's* a handsome cut of man."

The rest of the evening was a bit of a blur for Gina. She met members of almost every allied country and organization—RAF pilots, Special Air Servicemen, U.S. Rangers, French resistance fighters, Free Czech and Polish airmen who'd fought in the Battle of Britain and a host of others. She was lost in a whirlwind of voices and faces all wanting to speak to her. When the captain announced it was time to go on deck to watch the fireworks, it was actually a relief.

She found herself standing near Edgar as the first set of fireworks went off high in the night sky. "I thought I was used to parties back in Hollywood, but this is a bit overwhelming."

"I know what you're talking about, Gina. I can play a hero on screen. But here"—he waved his hand to encompass the entire group—"here we have the real thing, and I don't think I've ever met a humbler bunch of guys. Every time they told a story, it always was the other guys in their group who did the right thing at the last possible second to save everyone or to accomplish their mission. Almost makes me sad I'm playing the German in this picture. Why, these guys alone have a couple hundred movies we could be made out of their experiences."

"Don't worry, Edgar. If I know agents, they'll have people combing the woods hunting these guys down. I'd wager half the crew of my last picture was returning vets who'd just been released from their units. Ian had the writers for this picture meet with them. They had several good ideas to make the fight scenes more realistic."

"Good. I'm glad to hear it. After all, what those boys"—he paused and glanced at Nancy—"and gals went through over there, we should give them every chance to tell their stories."

The fireworks went on long into the night. Soon though, a young soldier came over and told Gina that Nancy wanted to speak to her on the upper deck. Gina made her way through the crowd and found Nancy standing against the rail by herself.

"Not enjoying the party, Nancy?"

"No, it's a wonderful evening. I'm going to miss these guys when I leave, but I wanted to get a chance to say thanks."

"Thanks? For what?"

Nancy turned and gave her a wink. "Why, for saving my life on the bus."

Gina tried to keep her features calm. "I thought The Cat saved you. I was back in the trailers."

Nancy reached over and patted her on the hand. "Of course you were—and that's the story I'll tell anyone who asks. But, love, don't try to kid a kidder. I recognized you the second I saw you on the bus. I spent years spotting people in disguise and disguising myself. But don't worry, your secret's safe with me."

"That makes things easier," a soft voice from the shadows caused the two women to spin around as a tall blond woman in a blue cocktail dress stepped into the light. Gina and Nancy immediately took defensive positions until the woman spoke up quickly. "I'm surprised, Gina. I figured you would recognize me, even without the usual red, white, and blue uniform on.

A puzzled tone crept into Gina's voice. "Miss Victory? What are you doing in Monaco? I thought you weren't supposed to travel to other countries?"

The blonde gave her a mischievous smile as she tipped her champagne flute at the pair. "Oh, I can travel in an unofficial capacity, I'm just not allowed to actually get involved in anything, which is specifically why I'm here tonight." Miss Victory smiled for a second, apparently enjoying getting one over on Gina, but then her expression hardened. "Normally, I wouldn't approach you so openly, but since Nancy already knows who you are, there's no time to waste. Something has come up. I'm recruiting a team to stop a threat that could make the last war seem like a football scrimmage."

Nancy spoke first, "That bad?"

"Maybe worse." She handed Gina a card. "When you get back to the States, call that number. Hopefully, I'll have the team assembled and I can tell you the whole story. However, if you call, you're committed. If you're not comfortable with that, I fully understand."

Gina nodded. "If it's important enough for you to come all this way to talk to me, I'll call as soon as I can."

Miss Victory relaxed slightly. "That's good to hear." She

smiled at Nancy. “I’d love to invite you along too.”

“I’m not hard to find, Miss Victory.” she said before continuing in an almost perfect Bacall imitation, “If you need me, just whistle.”

Miss Victory stepped back into the shadows. “I’ve taken enough of your time tonight.” And as soundlessly as she arrived, she was gone.

Gina stared at the spot Miss Victory had been in and then slowly leaned against the rail. “That was intense. Still, it’s nice to be able to be myself for once.”

“You heroes lead the most interesting lives. But the reason I asked you to stop by was to give you this.” Nancy handed her a small box and Gina undid the ribbon holding it shut. Inside was a small diamond pendant in the shape of a mouse on a silver necklace.

“Oh, Nancy, I can’t take this. It’s too much.”

“Nonsense. Consider it thanks from a White Mouse to a Cat.” Nancy reached up to her neck and pulled out a matching necklace, except her pendant was cat shaped. “After all, we have more in common than most people think.” A large explosion of fireworks went off and they both turned to the rail to watch.

“Yes,” Gina said softly. “Yes, we do.”

BLACK VENUS

THE BURNING CAULDRON

The clank of cups being set back onto saucers and the murmur of the waitresses and diners did nothing for the nerves of the young woman sitting across from Mary Roche. She jumped at every new sound. Mary wondered how long this interview would take if Sheila Harrington couldn't settle down and focus.

Mary stirred her coffee slowly, trying to keep her voice calm. "Now, Miss Harrington, there's nothing to be worried about. When you came to the Veterans Office, you said you were concerned about your fiancé, Rudy Thompson, but you didn't want to discuss it there. Do you feel up to talking now?"

Sheila looked around nervously, then looked down at the table. "I don't know. Perhaps I'm being silly, but I've had the strangest feeling that something's wrong. Even when Rudy was in the service, he never went this long without writing. I tried contacting him, but nothing seems to work and the company he's with claims his letter must be lost in the mail."

"What company is this?"

"Cauldron Enterprises. They were looking for men to help rebuild towns and cities in Europe. So many people lost everything during the war. Governments are hiring contractors to rebuild houses, hook up electrical lines, rebuild dams, and so on. It seemed like a great job. He would be gone for three years, but with what they were offering, we could get married as soon as he returned."

"Isn't it possible they're right about the mail? After all, they're still getting things organized over there. The U.S. forces in Europe report things going astray from time to time. I can't imagine American civilians are any better off."

Sheila glanced around again and lifted her cup, hiding

her mouth. "Yes, I've considered that. The strangest thing is, ever since I went down to the Cauldron building, I've had the strangest sensation of being watched. That's why I didn't want to talk to you at the Veterans Building. Maybe it's just my nerves, but something tells me Rudy's in trouble."

Mary scribbled some notes before responding. "Have you seen anyone? Can you describe them?"

"No, like I said it's more of a feeling. Oh, it's little things—a man walking through my neighborhood who doesn't live there. Hearing someone join the party line without identifying themselves. Why, I swear I saw someone at a distance when I came to the Veterans Building and I'm sure he was still across the street when we came out, but he left when we came in here."

Mary glanced around but saw nothing unusual. "Do you see that person now?"

"No. At least I don't think so."

Mary finished her coffee while Sheila glanced out the window. This was a far cry from her former role as Black Venus during the war, piloting a black P-38 Lightning and going toe to toe with Japanese Zeros. Still, helping protect veterans from criminals and shady characters was just as satisfying. *Just not as exciting*, she admitted to herself. Once Sheila was convinced the person she'd seen wasn't lurking around, Mary closed her notebook and stuck it back in her handbag. "I don't know if it will help, but we'll certainly contact Cauldron Enterprises and see if we can determine what's going on. Do you know where Rudy was sent?"

"Somewhere in southern France. He was a SeeBee in the Navy, and he was supposed to be helping restore water to a village. They didn't have all the details when he left. He said he'd write and let me know when he arrived."

"And he left eight weeks ago?"

"Yes. Even allowing for the mail coming across by a ship, I should have heard something by now. Since I don't have his address, I give Cauldron Enterprises my letters for delivery."

"I see."

Mary really didn't see, but the more she heard about this, the less she liked it. Sheila's story was starting to smell like some other shady deals she'd dealt with lately. There were days when she wondered why they'd wasted all those lives and time in the Pacific if the people back home were just going to take advantage of them now. Sheila continued talking, but after a while, Mary knew she'd learned everything she could.

As the two women moved toward the exit, Sheila became more nervous. "What if that man is waiting where I couldn't see him from inside?"

"I'm sure you have nothing to worry about, but, I'll walk with you and you can tell me if you see him. Once I report back to my office, I'll swing by Cauldron Enterprises and see if they're more forthcoming to an official visitor."

"Oh, if you would, that would make me rest easier."

Mary and Sheila left the café and paused in the doorway while Sheila glanced around nervously. After a few moments, Mary saw her companion's shoulders relax. "I don't see him. Perhaps it was just my imagination."

"I'm sure it was nothing. Now, just go home and relax. I'll call you as soon as I find out anything."

"Oh, thank you so much, Mary. I've been so worried lately; I guess I'm jumping at shadows."

Mary watched as Sheila walked down the street toward the crosswalk, scanning the crowd to see if anyone took a particular interest in her lunch date before turning to go back to the Veterans Building. *I'll have to ask Tom about Cauldron Enterprises. I don't recall hearing their name before. If they're specifically hiring veterans, we should have something in the files.*

She'd taken no more than two more steps when she heard the screeching of tires, the sound of an impact, and screams. Spinning around, she saw a black sedan racing down the boulevard and a crowd gathering at the corner. She rushed over to find Sheila lying in a heap near the sidewalk.

She shoved through the gawkers and pointed at one man. "Go call a doctor right now." He started, his eyes refocusing, then bolted to the nearest store. Mary began administering first aid to Sheila, as she heard the crowd murmuring around her. Finally, an onlooker jumped in and began checking Sheila's extremities and pulse.

"No broken bones that I can spot. Her pulse is weak, but steady." He opened Sheila's eyes and glanced at them. "Pupils look responsive to light, but that's a bad bump on the back of her head." He turned to look at Mary. "Sorry, I was a medic in the Eighty-Second Airborne. Old habits die hard."

Mary smiled at him. "I appreciate the help." She glanced up at the crowd. "Did anyone see what happened?"

A wizened older man spoke up. "Yeah. She'd just started across the street when this big black car swung out from the curb and hit the gas. Ran that red light bigger'n Dallas. I mean, if she'd taken one more step, she'da been hit square on, but luckily, it only clipped her. The driver didn't even slow down. Jest kep' right on goin'."

"Did you get a look at the driver or the license plate number?"

"Sorry, missy, he had his hat pulled plumb down almost over his eyes and, well, things happened so fast, I didn't see the license plate."

The rest of the crowd verified the old man's story, but no one could add any more details. The police and an ambulance arrived soon after and took over. Mary gave her statement to the police and stepped aside to lean against the nearest building.

The medic moved over and stood beside her. "I thought I'd left all that behind over in Germany. Didn't realize how practical it would be for city life."

"Thanks for helping back there. I had some basic Red Cross training through the USO, but it was mostly theoretical. Not many people got injured at the canteen or at the clubs."

The man smiled wryly. "I guess you weren't at any clubs the Eighty-Second frequented. If those guys weren't fighting Germans, they'd find someone in another company to take on after a couple of beers. I'm Joey Baker, by the way."

"I was mostly stationed with the Army Air Corps in the Pacific. I'm Mary Roche," Mary replied, extending her hand.

Joey gave her a hearty handshake, before blushing slightly

and turning her loose. “So, what do you do when you’re not helping accident victims?” he asked, staring at the sidewalk.

“I’m a troubleshooter for the Veterans Bureau—and I’m not convinced that was an accident.”

Joey looked up quickly, his eyes wide. “What?”

Mary started to tell Joey about Sheila’s feeling of being watched, but a familiar caution crept over her, and she changed what she was going to say. “If it was an accident, why didn’t the person stop? They only made it worse by fleeing.”

Joey shrugged and shoved his hands down into his pockets before responding. “Hard to say. People do strange things when they get scared. Did she say something to you to make you think she was in trouble?”

“We’d just had a cup of coffee together a bit before the accident.” *Wait a moment. How did he know we were together earlier?* Mary kept her expression neutral but chose her words a bit more carefully. “She seemed fine. Just talking about work.”

“I didn’t know you two were friends. Gee, that’s gotta make this worse.”

This is different from when the Japanese caught me, but it’s an interrogation just the same. Let’s see if I can’t turn the tables. She reached up and touched him gently on the shoulder. “I’m just glad you jumped into help. I was afraid I was going to make things worse. I just couldn’t leave her lying there with everyone just standing around staring.”

Joey looked embarrassed again but then he grinned at her, recognizing a fellow comrade in arms. “I guess it’s different for civilians. After a while, you got used to it. You just sorta turn off your feelings and your mind and muscles react out of sheer repetition. I hated working triage. It seemed like for every two you saved; there were three more you knew wouldn’t make it. All you could do was try to make sure the guys with the best chance got to the docs first.”

“That’s got to be tough. Most of the pilots we lost were shot down over the sea, so we never saw the bodies. About as close as I got to the real thing was helping the flight surgeon do inventory and rolling bandages during our downtime.

Anyway, thanks again for jumping in there."

"Glad to help. So, what do you do for the Veterans Bureau? You said you were a troubleshooter?"

Mary gave him the standard line about checking on businesses catering to veterans and ensuring veterans were getting all their benefits. He nodded knowingly but didn't seem fully convinced. He started to bring up Sheila's visit with her again, but Mary cut him off.

"I'll stop by the hospital this evening to check on Sheila. I hope she'll be all right."

"I thought you'd head down there right away," Joey said, nodding toward downtown.

Mary shook her head. "I should get back to work. I'll swing by this evening to see how she's doing. I'd just be in the way now."

He stared at the corner, a grim look on his face. "I hope they catch the bum who did this."

"Me too. Well, I'll see you later . . ." Mary let her words trail off. *Maybe Joey's all right, but I spent too much time in the Pacific to let my guard down now. It's just a feeling, but he knows more than he's saying. For all I know, he could be the guy who was tailing Sheila earlier.*

Joey said he'd stop by her office sometime and disappeared into the crowd. Mary paused at the next store and glanced in the window as if checking out the display, but she kept her eyes on Joey. He walked down the block, but then she saw him cross the street and come back her direction, mingling with the people waiting for the bus. She recognized some from the crowd around Sheila, but relaxed when Joey got on the bus, and it left.

Maybe it's my imagination, but something felt off there. He seemed a little too *interested in what I did and what I thought had happened. I'll see if Tom can run down some information on one Joey Baker later. But now, it's time to go visit Cauldron Enterprises.*

The Cauldron Enterprises offices were an old Quonset hut down near the docks. The docks swarmed with workmen, as the tugs guided another freighter into its berth. She watched cranes lift large boxes from inside the ships to the docks, and trucks lined up to load all the goods coming ashore. Mary had to knock several times before anyone came to the door and let her in.

A large redheaded man guided her past several other men busy typing and pointed her to a chair across from his desk. His arms bore tattoos signifying his time at sea and his thick neck and muscles showed he wasn't long removed from being one of those dock workers himself. The sign on the desk read Oliver Anderson, Owner, and his chair protested his weight as he eased into it. He gave it a dirty look as if it was critiquing his bulk. He offered Mary a drink of water, but she politely refused. He poured one for himself and pulled a bottle of aspirin from his desk. "Sorry for making you wait out there, lady. When a new ship comes in, I can barely hear myself think, and that's not counting this headache. What can I do for you?"

She waited until he finished swallowing his aspirin before starting and handed him a card. "I'm Mary Roche from the Veterans Bureau. I've recently learned of this project you're hiring men for, and I'm interested. We keep tabs on men returning from the war and try to help them find jobs. We noticed you hadn't registered your company with us . . . not that it's mandatory, but we do have quite a list of men looking for work these days."

Anderson got a big smile on his face and pulled a brochure out of his desk to hand to Mary. "Gee, that's swell of you guys. We've only been in this town about a month, moved down from Boston after our last assignment wound down. My partner scored a sweet deal over in Europe a few months ago. We're hiring construction workers, plumbers, electricians, and communications guys as fast as we can find them. While the big companies are helping rebuild the cities, we've teaming up with local construction companies in different countries to provide expertise and manpower to help with smaller places—villages, towns, hamlets; the smaller the better. We find a small place is perfect because we can concentrate our men, get in, get out, and move to the next one instead of being tied up with all kinds of regulations and paperwork."

Mary glanced up over the edge of the brochure at him and smiled. "This is all very interesting. So, how have you been recruiting your crews?"

"Oh, we've got guys in different cities on the East and West Coasts. We've been trying to identify and hire guys before they get a chance to scatter all over the country. It saves a lot of time and money. The way I see it, it's win/win for everyone."

Mary wasn't certain how much was fact and how much was sales pitch, but from Anderson's comfortable manner, she knew he'd given this speech to government types many times before. She asked several other questions that Anderson could give the same style of glib answers that used a lot of words to say basically nothing. Finally, Mary thought he was relaxed enough to come to the heart of the matter.

"The main reason I'm here is to inquire about one of your workers, a Mr. Rudy Thompson. I understand he's currently on assignment to Southern France?"

"Phillips, go pull the personnel files. See what we have on a 'Rudy Thompson.'" Anderson shifted in his seat as one of the other men quit typing and went to a file cabinet in the back of the hut. "We'll have to look into that, Miss Roche. With a company as big as ours, I can't keep all our employees straight in my head."

Mary smiled innocently at him. "Why, Mr. Anderson, I thought you'd be familiar with Rudy. You've been accepting his fiancée's letters and forwarding them. I'd think you should know exactly who he is and where he's located."

"Well, I wish I could take credit for that kind of memory, Miss Roche," Anderson said without a pause. He pulled out a stained handkerchief and wiped his forehead and neck before he waved a big thumb over his shoulder to the file cabinets. "See that one in the corner? It's filled with letters to be shipped all over Europe as soon as our next freighter finishes loading equipment and new employees. Once it arrives, one of our guys over there is going to have to sort it all out and ensure it gets delivered to the right places. Wouldn't want his job, nosiree." Anderson paused for a second and then smiled his overly broad smile at Mary. "To be honest, the name Thompson does seem to ring a bell, though. You say his fiancée spoke to you?"

"Yes. She's very worried that he's gone so long without writing."

"Let me think. Pretty little thing, brown hair, glasses, kinda pixie-looking? Would that be her? Seems I remember her stopping by the other day. Might have been asking about this Thompson guy. I apologize, I've got so much on my mind these days, if I didn't write it down, I'd forget before I got up from my desk."

Mary felt several sets of eyes on her, but she focused on Anderson. "Of course, I'm sure it's very difficult running a big company like this."

"That's true, miss. I mean, we're constantly busy adding new employees, dealing with some of the guys who've been with us for years. Heck, most of the guys in here started out on my first couple of jobs and stuck it out with me. Why, I'd be lost without most of them. Take ol' Pete there. Why, he's an architect's architect. Man can put down a set of blueprints faster and cleaner than a designer can dream them up."

"That's all interesting, Mr. Anderson, but we were talking about Rudy Thompson."

Anderson ran his hand down his face and fixed a cold stare on Mary. "Miss Roche, I don't know if you've been to Europe since the war ended, but it's not quite as simple as things here in America. Everything's got to be shipped in, sorted, and coordinated. If you're a new guy, it's easy to get swamped under—a new job in a new country. He's probably just too busy to respond. I mean, I doubt he's doing anything he's not supposed to, having a fiancée and all."

Phillips dropped a folder on Anderson's desk and walked back to his typewriter without saying a word. Anderson flipped it open and poked at the paper with his thick fingers. "Ah, here we are. He's in the town of Saint-Ciers, not too far from Rochefort . . . heh, near Rochefort, Miss Roche. Kind of a whimsical coincidence there, wouldn't you say? Anyway, that area was pretty chewed up by both the Germans and Allied bombing. We only opened that area up a month ago and we're still getting established. Not surprised mail is still messed up. But if it means that much to his fiancée, we'll do our best to get some word to her as soon as possible. Can't ask for more than that."

Mary put the brochure in her purse and snapped it shut with a decisive click. "No, I guess not. Hopefully, you'll swing by the bureau and register. We've got a list of men looking for work. We might be able to provide you with all the men you need."

Anderson visibly relaxed and smiled broadly at Mary before standing up. "That'd be right friendly of you all. Much appreciated, Miss Roche. However, I'm afraid I'm going to have to cut this short. I've got a meeting in a few minutes. Thanks for stopping by."

He came around the corner and offered her a hand. Mary knew she was getting brushed off but let him think she hadn't noticed. She thanked him for his time and allowed herself to be escorted to the door. It shut with a resounding thump behind her, implying they'd seen all they'd wanted from her, but that only brought a smile to her face as she walked to the end of the dock and caught a cab back to her office.

I can't point to any one thing, but there's more going on there than just arranging for workers to go overseas. He had too many pat answers to my questions . . . almost like he was expecting someone to stop by after Sheila's visit. I'm going to check in on her at the hospital and then I think I'll have to pay them another visit tonight. They might not have appreciated Mary Roche's visit, but I have a feeling they're going to like a visit from Black Venus even less.

The evening sky was just turning dark as Mary reached the hospital. She paid the cabbie and went into admissions. After waiting behind a couple who were obviously expecting and a mother trying to corral two young children and check on the status of her husband, Mary finally reached the receptionist.

"And how may we help you?"

"Yes. I'm here to see Sheila Henderson, please."

"Are you a relative?"

"No, but I was one of the people who helped take care of her after the accident until the ambulance arrived."

The receptionist glanced up at Mary and then down at a list of papers. "Miss Henderson is in recovery. Dr. Steven Peters is the attending physician. You can call him tomorrow between seven a.m. to three p.m., which is his next shift. If you're not a family member, we can't give out any more information than that."

"Can you at least tell me what room she's in?"

The receptionist's mouth set in a firm line. "I'm sorry, but again, that information is only for family members. Now if you'll excuse me."

Turning, Mary spotted the two kids running around their mother again and got an idea. Moving slightly, she let one of them brush up against her and sprawled backward against the receptionist's desk, upsetting a flower vase and dumping the water onto the receptionist.

"Oh, my goodness. I'm so sorry," Mary said, as the harried mother caught her two children and held them, apologizing profusely. Mary grabbed a handkerchief out of her oversized purse and came around the counter to help mop up the water.

The receptionist ran her hand down the front of her uniform and then pushed as much of the water off her desk onto the floor. "Oh, never mind. I'll be back in a second."

Mary mopped up some of the water from the desk while glancing at the receptionist's book. According to the records, Sheila Harrington was in room 624, but that was all the information she could get before the receptionist returned with a towel and a worse disposition. Mary apologized again, then took her cue to get while the getting was good.

Slipping around to a nearby alley, Mary removed her Black

Venus uniform from her oversized purse and slipped into it. It was a black catsuit, based on the original costume she wore when she was a featured dancer back in Paris. She had modified it over the years—first, with goggles and flight gear while flying in the South Pacific, and more recently a domino mask she'd added. Normally, she would have simply worn her flight goggles, but unlike the jungles of the South Pacific, she needed something more substantial to help hide her identity from reporters and thugs. Moving to the rear of the hospital, she made her way to the sixth floor via the fire escape until she found a darkened room.

Pulling a small flexible piece of metal out of her pouch, Mary worked the lock open and slipped inside. Luckily, the room was not only dark but deserted. She inched the hallway door open and noted the room number across the hall: 619. She waited a few more seconds to ensure the hallway was clear and then crept down the hall to room 624 and let herself inside.

It was a multi-person ward, with a couple of patients sleeping in the beds near the doors. She found a semiconscious Sheila lying in a bed farther back with the privacy curtain drawn. Mary moved around the curtain and pulled a chair up next to her bed. After a few minutes, Sheila realized someone was in the room with her and spoke up.

"Nurse?"

"No, Miss Henderson, I'm Black Venus. Mary Roche contacted me after your accident and asked me to investigate."

Sheila's eyes widened as she focused on Mary's face. "You're that crime fighter. Why are you interested in me?"

Black Venue pitched her voice low and motioned for Sheila to do the same. "Mary isn't convinced it was an accident. Didn't you tell her you thought someone might have been following you? I'm trying to get to the bottom of this for both of you. How're you feeling?"

"I'm a little groggy. The doctors have me on some pain medicine. I was lucky. If that car had been a bit slower, I'd have been right in front of it. As it is, the doctor thinks I can get out of here in a couple of days or so."

Mary felt a wave of relief at that statement. "Have the police been here?"

"Yes, but I was still unconscious. The nurse said they would stop by when I felt better. They had some questions about the accident."

Black Venus heard the door at the far end open quietly as she asked her next question. "Can you remember anything about the accident? Anything that might help identify who hit you?"

Sheila's forehead wrinkled as she thought, but after a bit, she shook her head. "No, it all happened too fast. I couldn't even tell you what kind of car hit me or what color it was. No, wait, there was something. The driver, there was something about the driver I saw just before . . . what was it?"

Mary heard the footsteps approaching the curtain and glanced around, looking for a place to hide. Suddenly, a gunshot rang out, plowing up the pillow only inches from Sheila's head. Mary yanked Sheila off the bed as two more rounds tore into the mattress where she'd been only seconds before.

The sound of running feet and shouts from the other patients spurred Mary to spring from behind the curtain and chase after the would-be assassin. She got to the door, but ducked back quickly as the gunman, wearing a doctor's jacket, snapped a shot in her direction. She rushed out to see him heading toward the elevators. Knowing she'd never catch him before the elevator doors shut, Black Venus rushed to the nearest stairwell. Half running, half leaping down the stairs, she reached the ground floor in time to see the gunman running across the lobby toward the front door. Spotting a heavy ashtray on one of the nearby magazine tables, she picked it up without breaking stride and threw it sidearm like a discus thrower might.

Her improvised projectile curved slightly but caught the gunman in the middle of his back as he reached the revolving doors. He stumbled face-first into the glass panels as his gun went flying to the side. Mary slammed into the door just as he climbed back to his feet and sent him sprawling onto the sidewalk. Using the momentum from the door, she leapt, landing in the middle of her quarry's back, driving the wind out of his lungs. Before he could catch his breath, two security guards rushed up.

"Hold this man for the police. He just took some shots at a patient upstairs."

One of the guards drew his pistol, but he aimed it indecisively between the two. The other moved authoritatively in front of her and motioned for her to step back as he kept his pistol carefully trained on the man on the ground. Mary moved with deliberation to ensure the guard didn't take his eyes off the gunman, who slowly raised his hands and climbed to his feet as the guards took him into custody.

Mary pointed back into the building. "His gun's back in there off to the right. You might want to get it before someone else finds it."

While the first guard went to secure the loose firearm, the second smiled. "Thanks, Black Venus. Heard about your exploits back when I was in New Guinea. I knew you were hell on the Japanese, but I didn't know you'd taken up crime-fighting in this town. Kind of a step down, ain't it?"

"Oh, I don't know. I'd like to think I'm still on the side of angels. Anyway, he took a shot at Sheila Henderson, room six twenty-four. When the cops get here, she'll be happy to talk to them."

The guard nodded and then hustled the gunman inside to wait for the police. Mary heard sirens approaching and knew she'd have to talk to Sheila another time. If she'd had any doubts about Sheila's accident being deliberate, they had vanished at the first shot. Slipping into the shadows, she hurried back to where she'd left her regular clothes.

"That was an impressive takedown, Black Venus."

Mary spun around and spotted a man standing in the shadows. He lit a cigarette, and she could see in the match's flame it was Lt. Bruce Mathewson from the city's Homicide squad. Mary watched him snap the wooden stick in two before tossing it over his shoulder.

"Better be careful, Lieutenant. A habit like that could make it easy for someone to recognize you if you went undercover."

He stopped and stared at her. "You been talking to Captain Hastings again?"

Mary walked over and joined him in the shadows as they watched the squad cars pull up and four uniformed officers rush inside. "Should I?"

"Nah, never mind. Guess I got a guilty conscience or something." He rested his shoulders against the brick wall and let a smile toy with his lips before they settled into their normal frown. "I'm surprised you didn't stick around to give the boys a report. You've always been cooperative before."

Black Venus shrugged. "It's a pretty cut-and-dried case. The victim will give a good report. I didn't think I could add anything more. Plus, I need to check up on something."

"Such as . . . ?"

"Such as, a friend of mine was a witness to this incident. She told someone she didn't think it was an accident and then a few hours later, someone took a shot at Sheila. Now I'm convinced my friend was right and if they went for Sheila, they may go after her next. I want to get over to her place and make sure she's safe."

"But you aren't going to involve the city's police force," Mathewson said, pushing his fedora up and wiping his brow with his sleeve. "You know, some of us were doing this before the war and we didn't forget everything we learned while storming beaches and driving trucks."

As much as Mary would have enjoyed hanging out with Bruce a bit longer, there was no way to explain that the person she was trying to protect *was* herself without disclosing her secret identity. "I know, Lieutenant, but I'd feel awfully dumb if I dragged you along and it was just an overactive imagination. Right now, I'm betting a hunch, but I'm trying my best to come up with something. If—and I mean *if*—I find anything, I'll turn it all over to you. Deal?"

"Just don't take too long. One thing I learned with the Rangers is info is perishable. If you wait too long, things aren't the same by the time you get there. Same goes for clues to crimes and enemy positions. You flew in the Pacific. You know what happens if a plane is late getting to a rendezvous point."

Black Venus nodded grimly. "Better than I like to admit. Point taken, Lieutenant. As soon as I find anything, you'll be the first to know."

Still in her Black Venus garb, Mary prowled outside her apartment building trying to spot anything unusual. Deciding she'd seen everything she could from street level, she hurried up the fire escape to her apartment and pressed the hidden latch, unlocking her window from the outside. She had made it halfway across the room toward the light switch when a table lamp suddenly snapped on.

"Well, not quite who I was waiting for. What's *your* reason for being here, sister?"

She turned slowly to see a young man, maybe in his early twenties, sitting in her chair. It was obvious he'd been waiting a while. His body relaxed and he smiled, but the .45 automatic in his hand never wavered. "You haven't answered my question. That's awfully rude, don't you think?"

"I thought this place was empty. Seemed like a good place to pick up some loose change."

"Uh-uh. I'm not buying it. This ain't some high-class joint with a wall safe. I should know. I checked. Plus, you're not dressed like a common second-story thief. They want to blend in as soon as they pull a job. You are either really damn dumb or you ain't no thief and I'm betting on the latter. Nah, you're probably one of those costumed heroes who've been popping up since the war stopped. Ain't got no Germans or Japanese to kick around, so you're busy putting guys like me in their places."

Mary fought down the instinct to smile at the gunman. He was smarter than most and cockier too. "All right, since you have all the answers, who am I and why am I here?"

He smiled at her and then snapped his fingers. “I got it. You’re that Black Venus dame who’s been butting in on rackets all over the joint. You were some kinda hot-shot flyer, but there ain’t no Zeros or Betties flying above this city, so I guess you’re just bored.”

“You’re half right,” she said, keeping her hands in the air, but taking a step forward. He tensed up, but she motioned to the chair with a stool across from him. He gave the gun barrel a quick wiggle toward the chair and she sat down daintily. She carefully set her arms on the arms of the chair so he could keep them in sight. “I *am* Black Venus but trust me: guys like you who prey on returning veterans keep me way too busy to be bored.”

“Is that a fact? Lady, guys like me don’t care if you were 1-A or 4-F, a pilot, a dogface, or a factory worker. See, I get paid because I’m really good at what I do, which is kill people and don’t leave evidence behind. This was going very well until you decided to stick your nose in where it wasn’t wanted, so now I guess I’m going to have to get paid double for this.”

Mary tensed slightly, watching his eyes closely. “Aren’t you worried someone will hear the shot? I mean, these walls don’t look that thick. Might be hard to get your other target with the cops investigating my shooting.”

His smile grew a bit bigger. “I guess I’ll have to take that chance.”

She saw his eyes tighten even before she saw his finger start to move. She kicked out, catching the stool with her left leg and launching it toward him. He instinctively flinched as the stool caught him in the chest and face. The gun went off, sending a bullet harmlessly into one of her walls. She bounded out of the chair and leapt, taking him over backward. The table lamp went flying and the bulb burst, plunging the room into darkness. She heard the gun land somewhere on the floor, and then it was just her and him going at it in the dark.

There were no Marquis of Queensbury rules in this fight. Mary scored a couple of solid hits on her opponent before a foot came out of nowhere and caught her in the midsection.

She felt all the air go out of her lungs as she flew backward and crashed into a book cabinet. It rocked forward, dumping a shower of books onto her.

Her opponent decided discretion was the better option and before she could untangle herself from the pile, she heard running steps and saw her door open and close. She climbed to her feet but by the time she reached the door, he was out of sight. Still gasping for breath, she decided a tie was as good as a win this time. Locking the door behind her, she flipped on the overhead light and went to the phone.

After a couple of transfers, she got ahold of Lieutenant Mathewson. "Lieutenant, got something else for you. I'm at the Stanford Apartments, room three-nineteen. Someone was waiting here for my friend. I surprised him or he surprised me, take your choice. Luckily, the damage was limited to a hole in the wall, a broken lamp, and a messed-up room. Unfortunately, I couldn't catch this one, but he left his gun behind. I'll bet dollars to doughnuts, it's hot."

"No bet. And another gun? You starting a collection?"

Mary grinned in spite of herself. "Well, if the police force isn't collecting them, someone has to."

"Droll, very droll. Will you be there when I arrive? Will anyone be there or am I going to have to piece all this together from scratch?"

Mary felt guilty about ducking out, but she couldn't afford to get tied up downtown, plus, they might ask her to produce her "friend," which would be tricky. "I'm helping my friend find a new place where she'll be safe. After that, I've got one more stop to make before I call it a night. I'll come by the precinct when I get done there. Give me a couple of hours."

"My shift is supposed to end at midnight, but at this rate, I may be here until morning."

"The joys of public service," she said before giving him a description of the gunman. The lieutenant said they'd put out an all-points bulletin on him, but he wasn't holding his breath on catching the guy.

"Oh," he said, catching her just before she hung up. "The

guy you caught down at the hospital is refusing to talk. The odd thing is that some high-priced lawyer showed up and tried to spring him on bail."

"You didn't let him go, did you?"

"Not yet. The judge turned down the bail request, but this lawyer didn't seem too perturbed. Just told his new client to say nothing and he'll see about getting an injunction first thing in the morning. How some two-bit punk like that rates that kind of legal representation raises more questions than it answers. It's obvious whoever sent the guy to shoot Sheila is also behind the lawyer but knowing it and proving it are two different things."

Mary twisted the phone cord in her hand as she glanced out her window. "It should be a pretty cut-and-dried case, isn't it? I mean, he was there, I chased him out of the room to the elevator, and he had the gun when I caught up with him. Plus, the ballistics on the bullets taken from Sheila's bed and that gun should match up."

"Unfortunately, not according to this attorney, since after all, you didn't actually *see* him fire the weapon. Sheila said he was on the other side of the curtain, so neither of you saw the shooter. Even with ballistics, he could claim someone else handed him the gun in the hall or the elevator. Sure, it's a thin alibi, but all it takes is one juror to buy it and we're sunk. Nope, the best thing we could get for a conviction is a confession, but between whatever he's getting paid and that lawyer, he's dummied up completely."

"It seems someone's worried about what Sheila and my friend think. From what I heard, this all started because Sheila's fiancé had a new job in Europe and hadn't contacted her since he arrived. This seems like an overreaction to a simple inquiry."

"Well, whatever's going on, someone's playing for keeps. Keep your head down. After stopping two of their hit men, they may decide you're more of a threat than anyone."

Mary grimaced, but he was right. "And on that cheery note, I'll talk to you later, Lieutenant."

It was nearing midnight as Mary climbed down from the roof of a nearby warehouse into the shadows below. She watched as the night watchman made another circuit of the docks near the Cauldron Enterprises building. Checking her watch, she knew exactly how much time she had to get into the building without being caught. Hours spent avoiding Japanese soldiers in the Pacific had honed her technique and her black catsuit helped her blend into urban jungles as well as the tropical ones.

Hurrying through the shadows, she reached the side of the Quonset hut and peered through the window. Seeing nothing moving inside, she slipped a small wire through the edge of the frame and hooked the latch. A couple of quick tugs later, the window was open and she was inside. She'd just put the window back down as light washed across the spot she'd just been, and she heard the watchman's feet receding into the night.

It could be a coincidence, but everything started happening after first Sheila's and then my visits here. Maybe I can find enough evidence to go to Bruce with because I know *something is wrong here. Let's see if Mr. Oliver Anderson is as dependent on taking notes as he claims.*

Taking out a small flashlight, she cupped her fingers over the lens, only letting a small stream of light trickle between her fingers. Locking the window behind her, she headed toward the file cabinets looking for the personnel files Anderson had helpfully pointed out this afternoon. *Seems like the most logical place to start.*

After a bit of a search, she finally found Rudy Thompson's file. She gave it a thorough going over and quickly realized Anderson had lied. There was nothing in the file about a job in Saint-Ciers. In fact, there was no mention of any city or town in France, so how did he know where Rudy was supposedly working? Skimming through a few other folders, she noticed none of them had any actual job sites listed.

Given the number of folders in the cabinets and the dates

on them, she realized Cauldron Enterprises had been on a hiring binge. They'd recently employed nearly three hundred workers, and almost all of them were former veterans. Along with engineers and SeeBees, Cauldron had administrators, communications people, radio technicians, mechanics, medics, and quartermasters. Still, even though she had names and occupations, that's all she knew.

Going through files in the next cabinet, she found the dates each group of recent hires shipped out, but none of the records listed their ultimate work assignments or even the ports of call for the ships. *Now, that's weird. While they may not assign people to a specific job until they get into country, they should have a centralized location for all new hires when they first arrive. I'm sure Anderson knows it. Still, it's strange that it's not annotated in their records.*

Continuing to check through the files, she realized there weren't any temporary work visas either. France might be grateful to get help restoring the countryside, but Mary didn't believe for a second that they'd just let hundreds of Americans in without the proper paperwork. She certainly had to have her passport and visa when she was dancing in Paris before the war.

Seems France is not a great place to have a fiancé. Sheila's Rudy is missing somewhere and my Jean was killed thanks to that bastard Colonel Yomata. If he hadn't been a damn attaché to the Japanese Embassy . . . they got him out of France before I could do anything . . .

Focus, Mary, you dealt with Yomata years ago. Let's see what you can do for Sheila.

Glancing back through the files, she realized something else was missing. None of the files listed any payroll information—no payment records, no tax withholding, no social security payment records, nothing. It was one thing for there to be two sets of books . . . she's heard of those shenanigans before, but *no* sets of books? Unless Anderson took them home every night instead of keeping them at the office, but that made no logical sense.

What is going on here?

She put all the files back and moved over to Anderson's desk. still keeping her light shaded. A quick twist with a hard piece of wire and the tumblers holding the desk drawers shut slid open. Most of the drawers just held innocuous information, but in the bottom drawer, hidden inside an envelope, there was some correspondence from one of his field agents. It addressed some snags in construction at one of their sites, called appropriately "The Cauldron." They were running into issues clearing trees for a new runway long enough for their supply planes to land. The agent was specifically requesting Anderson secure specific trades and occupations to get the new site operational as soon as possible.

Building their own runways? There are airfields all over France—I should know, that's where I learned to fly before the war. What would necessitate them having to construct their own runways?

Mind filled with more questions than answers, Mary was about to check out the other desks when she heard the click of a key. Slipping the papers back into Anderson's desk drawer, she shut it and ducked beneath one of the desks facing the wall. She had just turned off her flashlight when the door opened. The overhead lights flicked on, and she saw two sets of legs walk through the room.

A familiar bass voice told her Anderson was one of the men. "You had one job this evening, Sid—take care of that Roche dame. Bad enough Harrington got to her, but Roche showing up here with no warning?" Anderson shook his head and continued his harangue. "I thought it was just a routine visit, not that she was here investigating what happened to Harrington's boyfriend. They spent a half hour talking together, for God's sake! Who knows what else Harrington tipped her off about?"

The voice of the gunman she'd faced in her apartment still sounded cocky. "Look, who knew Black Venus might be involved? It was supposed to be a simple hit. She opens the door . . . pop, pop . . . and she ain't investigating nothing again. It was just pure dumb luck that do-gooder showed up.

Next time, I'm shooting on sight. I don't care what she knows or who she's told. I owe her for this crooked nose."

Mary smiled, knowing she'd scored one good hit in that fight. Still, Sid was someone she'd have to keep an eye out for in the future.

"Great. That's all we need. Bad enough, the Veterans Bureau is nosing around, but I guess we can learn from this incident. Get Willy to generate some innocuous letters . . . no, better yet, make them telegrams, that way they won't have to be signed. We'll send them to some of the wives and sweethearts to tide them over . . . Hey, Sid, look at this!"

"What's up, boss?"

"My desk is unlocked. I know damn well I locked it before I left. Check around."

She heard shuffling feet and then Sid called out, "Two of these file cabinets are unlocked too."

Anderson swore. "All right, we can't take any chances. We're wrapping up here. We've got enough suckers lined up for this trip. Get the boys and break this down. We'll move everything aboard the ship tonight and sail as soon as we can get clearance. Bring the workers to the docks at 0630. They're used to reveille; they won't think anything's odd until the ship turns south. By then, it'll be too late."

Mary held her breath as the two sets of legs paused in front of the desk she was beneath, but after further conversation, the two men turned out the lights and left, locking the door behind them. Playing a hunch, she remained in place and was rewarded when she heard the lock turn and the door slowly open.

"Must have been my imagination," she heard Anderson mutter as he shut the door and relocked it.

Mary waited a few more minutes just to be certain and then made her way back to Anderson's desk. In the top drawer, she found what she was looking for—the manifest of the S.S. *Bakersfield*, an old Liberty ship bound for not La Rochelle or Brest or anywhere in France, but for Cayenne, French Guiana. With that last bit of information, she eased out the window after ensuring the coast was clear and faded into the night.

Anderson didn't know it, but Black Venus would be waiting for him in Cayenne to see just what *was* going on.

Mary stared out the window of her hotel room with her binoculars, scanning the port of Cayenne. Men rushed around the busy docks, loading and unloading the waiting freighters. There was more shipping traffic than she'd been expecting, but only a few ships were in port this morning. Her cover as a shipping agent had helped in making contacts with the port authority. One had mentioned that the S.S. *Bakersfield* was due today, so she was paying careful attention in anticipation.

She thought back to her last few days before heading south. Lieutenant Mathewson hadn't been kidding about that lawyer. They'd done everything they could to keep the gunman in jail, but the lawyer must have had *some* connections because after a phone call from the state capital, he and his client waltzed out the door. Four days later, the suspect failed to show at his arraignment and the lawyer surrendered the bail money and walked out, leaving Mary and Bruce fuming. Even though they put out a dragnet, they still hadn't found the gunman before Mary had left to meet the *Bakersfield*.

Prior to her departure, Mary spent quite a bit of time fuming because she couldn't take her own plane to Cayenne. She had been allowed to keep her acquired P-38 Lightning after the war's end as a reward for her service from the U.S. government. She had used it several times against criminals who had acquired military weapons of their own in fact. Still, the State Department was concerned about a diplomatic flap if she flew a fully armed fighter into a foreign country—even a former ally's territory—as a civilian. Something told her that her plane would come in handy, but the State Department made it very clear if she took it to French Guiana, there was a better than even chance it'd be confiscated when she returned, so she resigned herself to flying commercial to Cayenne.

A smudge of smoke on the horizon caught her attention and she adjusted her binoculars to get a better look. The incoming vessel was still quite a way from port, but it certainly looked like an old Liberty ship. She guessed it would be a few more hours before the ship arrived, so she left her hotel to find a better place to inconspicuously observe the docks.

Almost immediately, she was swarmed by young boys offering to escort her to this tourist spot or that, but she managed to extract herself with some deft dodging. Halfway down the street, she noticed one of the urchins was tagging along, not quite catching up, but doggedly keeping up with her. She guessed he was about thirteen, but he stared at her with eyes that belonged to someone much older. She decided to stop in a store for just a moment and browsed the shelves before stepping back outside. The young man was still out there, looking in a store window as if fascinated by the items on display.

Reentering, Mary approached the store owner and spoke to her in French. "Pardon me, *madame*, but there's a young man outside who's been pestering me ever since we met at a party the other night. I don't want to make a scene, but I'd rather he didn't follow me all day. Is there another way out I could use?"

The older woman looked Mary up and down before grinning. "Ah, *mademoiselle*, I would think it strange if you were not being followed." Mary blushed slightly at the compliment as the woman went on. "Still, one should not be *too* available. I think I can help you. Follow me."

She led Mary to a crowded back room. Motioning for her to stay still, the shopkeeper opened the door and casually took a wastebasket to dump in the can out back. After a few seconds, she waved Mary toward the door. "There is no one out here now. Follow the alley to the left and it'll take you to the boulevard. Turn right and it goes to a local park. If he's still looking for you, it'll be hard to find you in the crowd."

Smiling her gratitude, Mary reached into her purse and handed the woman a handful of francs, insisting when the shopkeeper tried to protest. Taking the francs, she wished Mary luck and went back into her store.

Mary waited for a few seconds to ensure sure no one was watching before heading to the mouth of the alley. Once there, instead of turning right, she turned left back toward the street she'd just been on.

The young man was still there, but he was getting more and more impatient waiting for Mary to reappear. Finally, he walked across the street and peered through the smudged windows into the dim store she'd just left. When he didn't see Mary, he went inside but was shooed out a few minutes later by the owner. He glanced up and down the street, obviously wondering how she had gotten out of the shop without him noticing. Shrugging, he finally began walking toward the docks. Mary let him get a few stores down the street, then began tailing him.

Maybe he just wants to earn some money carrying packages or playing tour guide. Still, Anderson could have people down here on the lookout for Americans getting to close to his operations. No sense in being careless with the Bakersfield *arriving soon. Let's see where my little friend is heading.*

The young man led Mary through nearly as many backstreets and alleys as he did thoroughfares. It was tricky at times to keep him in sight without getting spotted herself, but she'd honed her skills against Imperial Japanese soldiers. At least, this youngster wasn't likely to start shooting at her. She watched him negotiate a fence by spreading two boards apart and glimpsed him hurrying between two buildings. Slipping through the fence herself, she cautiously made her way down the alley and smiled when she saw the docks just beyond the buildings.

Checking her watch, Mary smiled. She couldn't have asked for a better guide if she'd tried! They'd arrived at the docks far quicker than going by the main roads. The boy had turned to the right, but she paused before stepping out anyway, just to be sure he wasn't waiting around the corner. She heard voices and moved closer, still staying just in the mouth of the alley.

"Well?"

"I'm sorry, *monsieur*, but one minute she was there, the

next minute, she had vanished into thin air."

There was the sound of bodies scuffling and someone being slammed into a wall. "You little jackanapes always have some excuse. I told you to watch for her and follow her. She could be anywhere in Cayenne now. I don't need her bolloxing up the works."

"But, *monsieur*, she is just one woman. What can she possibly do?"

"Just one woman? Listen, you little street rat, that woman works for the United States government. The boys back home say she's been asking a bunch of nosy questions and now she conveniently turns up here? We've got a good thing going. We don't need it screwed up because someone got lovesick and called the Feds."

"I don't understand what you're saying, but I can tell you're scared of her."

There was the distinct sound of a slap and a small whimper from the boy. "Toby Bigelow ain't scared of no frails . . . or snot-nosed punks like you either. Now come on. We need to tell the boss what happened. He'll decide what to do with you."

Mary glanced around the corner and watched a large man walking with the boy, his hand clamped around the youth's shoulder, which she could see rise in protest as the man's fingers dug into his muscles. She followed, carefully maintaining her distance. She wasn't worried about Bigelow per se, but she didn't want to get into an altercation before the ship arrived.

They entered a large warehouse a few hundred feet from the main docks. She moved where she could see inside the open doors, but outside of the bustle of workers and trucks backing in and out with loads. *It looks like any other warehouse anywhere else in the world,* she mused, waiting until there was a crowd moving past her, and blending in with them to approach the warehouse from the side and discreetly survey her surroundings.

The initial report was not good. There were high windows lining the walls and she could hear the hum of large fans on the roof, but there was no way she could reach either of them without a ladder—which might be a tad conspicuous. Her mood brightened when she spotted a stairwell in the back leading to the second floor. There were only a few people in the area, and most were too busy hauling boxes and barrels to bother looking at the stairs.

Moving as quickly and quietly as she could, Mary entered the stairwell and climbed to the second floor. She listened at the door but heard only the faint sounds of the workers on the main floor below. To her surprise, the door was unlocked. Happy to catch one break, Mary eased it open and slipped inside. There was a wide catwalk going around the upper floor with random crates and barrels stacked about, and to her right there was an office. Light poured out of a large window facing the work floor below. Inside, Mary could hear raised voices and moved closer to listen.

A displeased voice came through the wall. Even without seeing the body attached to it, Mary got the impression of a large man. To her surprise, he was speaking English. "So, Miss Roche just happens to appear in Cayenne a couple of days before the shipment? Toby, there's a rat out there somewhere. Someone must be tipping the Feds off."

"Maybe. Anderson's cable implied someone rifled through his office. Could it have been Roche?"

The first voice rose in volume as something crashed against something hard. "How the blazes would I know? Do I look clairvoyant to you?"

"Clair-what?"

Mary grinned at the puzzlement in Toby's voice, but the next sentence wiped it away. "Never mind, peabrain. Look, you shouldn't have brought the kid along. He's fine for penny-ante stuff, but now he knows too much. Stuff him in a barrel. We'll find a good resting place for him later tonight."

She heard running feet inside the room and then a sickening thud. After a few seconds, the door opened and she scrunched back into the shadows. When no one appeared, she inched forward again and saw Toby and a huge man, standing almost six and a half feet tall with a shaved head and bulging muscles. The pair stuffed the apparently unconscious boy into a thick wooden barrel and nailed the lid shut. The hammer slipped and the man let out a string of curses in multiple languages—English, French, German, and Italian. He stepped away, waving his right hand. His thumb was visibly swollen from the hammer blow.

Toby finished up the job and motioned to the large man. "That looks pretty bad, Emil. You should probably have the doc take a look to make sure it's not broken."

Emil started to argue, then pain apparently shot through his hand and arm. "All right, Toby. After all, Phillipe isn't going anywhere—at least not yet."

The two men went down the stairs and Mary could hear them talking to one of the workers. She moved closer to the edge and saw them exit through the open doors. Once certain the main floor of the warehouse had resumed normal operations, she found a crowbar in Emil's cache of tools and came back to the barrel containing Philippe. Fighting against her instincts that this was taking too long and she should scram before she was spotted, Mary pried the nails as quietly as she could.

When the last nail gave way, she eased the lid off the barrel. Phillipe was still unconscious, so she tipped the barrel over and pulled him out. *You're lucky you don't weigh much,* Mary thought, hooking him over her shoulders in a fireman's carry and inching toward the back door as inconspicuously as she could. She opened it slowly and peered outside. No one seemed to be in the alleys between the warehouses, so precariously balancing herself and the boy, she made her way down the stairs. Still wary of being spotted, she slipped into the shadows of a nearby warehouse to administer first aid. After a few minutes, Phillipe stirred.

She saw the wild look in the boy's eyes as he awoke and covered his mouth with her hand before he could yell and draw attention. "Don't be afraid. I'm not going to hurt you," she said, removing her hand at his nod.

He sat up, resting his back against the wall, but his hands

were positioned to shove himself upright at a moment's notice. "You . . . you are the lady I was following."

"Yes, I am. I'm also the lady who saved your life. I think you owe me a few answers, Phillipe."

His eyes darted around, looking for a route of escape until he heard his name. Then he relaxed his arms, and one hand came up and rubbed a spot on the back of his head. "They said I was supposed to follow you. If you came to the docks, I was to take you to their warehouse. They seemed *very* worried you were in town, why I don't know. I speak more English than they think I do, so I heard them say something about you working for the United States? At least I think they said that. It was right before they hit me. They are very worried about you."

Mary gave him her most disarming smile. "So you mentioned. I do work for the United States government. That much is correct. I am looking for someone who's missing. I believe the men you work for may know something about his disappearance."

Phillipe spit on the ground. "Used to work for. Those pigs. They say they'll pay well if we do things for them, but it's never very much and they're quick with slaps and kicks. Oh, if I were only a little bit bigger, I'd get them both."

"Well, if you want to get back at them, you could help me out. I could use an assistant who knows Cayenne like the back of his hand and that sounds like you."

The boy's demeanor changed, and his shoulders straightened. "None better, *mademoiselle*. There is nowhere in this city I cannot go and no place I cannot find."

Mary grabbed a small notebook out of her purse and wrote a note. "Give this to the desk clerk at my hotel. They will let you into my room. Order a meal for yourself. We can talk when I get there. Make sure you are not seen. When those men return and see you have escaped, they will be looking for both of us. Are there others watching the hotel?"

Phillipe thought for a moment. "Maybe a couple but they do not know all the ways into the hotel like I do. I will be like a shadow at night—there but unseen."

"I'm counting on you, Phillipe. Now, hurry on. I'm waiting for a ship to arrive."

"The S. S. *Bakersfield*?"

Mary started involuntarily. "That's right. How did you know?"

"I have heard Emil and Toby talking. They get special cargos from the United States. They store them in the warehouse, then have them shipped farther inland to Saint-Georges. Once in Saint-Georges, they are flown or caravaned somewhere else. Where? I cannot say."

He noticed Mary's skeptical look and continued quickly, "*Mademoiselle*, remember, they don't think I know English. If they weren't tasking me, they ignored me like I was another box to be shipped. In fact, they paid more attention to the boxes than us."

"Very well, Phillipe, we will discuss what else you overheard later. Now, if you're all right, you need to hurry."

"I go like the wind. Be careful, *mademoiselle*. These are very bad men."

Phillipe picked himself up off the ground and shook himself to be sure everything was intact before moving almost silently through the shadows of the warehouses. Once he was safely out of sight, she slipped off in a different direction to keep her rendezvous with the mystery freighter.

About an hour later, the *Bakersfield* entered Cayenne Harbor and was nestled into place by the accompanying tugs. The deckhands hustled out and secured the old Liberty ship's mooring lines and began preparing to unload the cargo. After Phillipe left, Mary had found a spot near the dock where she could observe the ship in relative obscurity. She took several pictures of the ship, trying to spot any officers, but apparently, they were still below decks.

Surprisingly, she saw lines being run to the ship to take on fresh water and fuel. It looked like the ship was preparing to sail almost immediately, which was highly unusual. Even during the war, cargo ships would spend a day or so in port to reprovision and give the crew some rest before sailing out again. A turnaround this fast in peacetime was highly suspicious. Mary wondered if Emil or Toby had contacted the *Bakersfield*'s captain about her presence. Although, if he was carrying the supplies declared on its manifest before it departed the States, she couldn't imagine why the captain would be worried about an inspection by French customs.

Speaking of, it was equally surprising no customs agents had arrived. Ships were normally inspected before being allowed to discharge either cargo or crew. There was no official sign anyone had even noticed the ship's arrival once the harbor pilots had been paid and their tugs departed. It looked like the ship had been there for days for all the attention it was drawing. If Mary wasn't already suspicious of the *Bakersfield* and Cauldron Enterprises, this definitely would warrant a closer look.

As curious as she was, Mary looked at the guards both on the docks and the ship itself and decided there was no way to board the ship during daylight hours, especially not in the business suit she'd been wearing in her guise as shipping agent. A nighttime visit by her alter ego might be on tap, depending on what she learned from Phillipe.

After another ten minutes, Mary was about to leave when a battered pickup truck rattled up to the dock. The gangplank was run down from the ship, and she spotted Emil making his way up to the deck. A man in an officer's uniform appeared to warmly welcome him aboard. Mary got a couple of shots of the two of them together, but after that it settled back into the boring assignment it had been since the ship had arrived.

Convinced there was nothing further to be gained, Mary left the docks and made her way into downtown Cayenne. Checking every so often to ensure she hadn't picked up another young tail, she went to the American consulate. She conferred with some of the staff officers, and had her film processed and the pictures wired to a friend at the Federal Bureau of Investigations. If there was something about Emil or the *Bakersfield*, her contact should be able to get her up to speed in a hurry.

Returning to her hotel, she immediately felt the difference in the cool air indoors compared to the sweltering heat she'd just left. Walking across the marble floor, she approached the front desk, where the clerk let her know Phillipe had arrived; there were also a couple of messages that had been left for her. She glanced at them and saw both were from Tom Robinson, her boss back at the Veterans Bureau. She tucked them into her purse and took the elevator up to her room.

Phillipe was finishing off what once might have been a pile of sandwiches. He looked up at her before popping the last piece into his mouth. "Ah, *mademoiselle*, Phillipe has not eaten like that in many months. My stomach and I both offer you our thanks."

Mary sat down at a nearby table and took out her notebook. "Well, now it's time for Phillipe and his stomach to earn all that food. How long have you been working for Emil?"

"*Monsieur* Mueller? Only for a few months. One of his men went through the streets looking for young men around my age who knew the city and knew enough not to ask too many questions. People who ask questions seem to disappear permanently in Cayenne, *mademoiselle*. That is a piece of advice I offer you freely as I would not want anything to happen to you. That is how you came to their attention. I believe *Monsieur* Bigelow said you asked too many questions. Again, I apologize if I cannot repeat everything he said in proper English. It is a fine line one walks trying to listen to people without seeming to listen to them."

"Would it be easier to converse like this?" Mary asked him in French, but he shook his head.

"It's not a language issue as much as it is a hearing issue . . . sometimes I could not hear over the noise in the warehouse, or I was too far away to hear clearly. Also, you must understand, I was getting paid to carry packages and to watch people. I was not getting paid to snoop on what was going on *in* the warehouse.

These were just scraps of conversations I overheard; you understand. However, the longer I worked for them, the more their real natures came through, and I started paying attention to protect myself . . . or so I thought, anyway." He glanced away ruefully. "Apparently, I did not protect myself well enough."

"Do you know what Mueller and Bigelow are doing in Cayenne? You mentioned shipping stuff to Saint-Georges. What are they shipping inland?"

Phillipe shrugged. "I do not know for sure. They work for some people who are building something near the border with Brazil. The *Bakersfield* arrives once a month and its cargo is transferred to smaller ships that can sail up the Oyapock River to Saint-Georges. Some things move farther downriver on pirogues—shallow draft boats. The rest goes overland in trucks to the base they're building."

That piqued Mary's interest. "What kind of base are they building?"

"Unfortunately, I cannot say. I only heard the base mentioned when *Monsieur* Mueller was called up to his office to receive a radio message. No one was allowed upstairs except for *Monsieur* Bigelow or *Monsieur* LaFleur when these messages came in."

Mary looked up from her notes. "Who is this LaFleur?"

"He is from the base. He arrives by air to confer with Messieurs Muller and Bigelow. In fact, they expect him to arrive this evening. He is not a good man, *mademoiselle*. I heard he escaped from Camp de la Relégation during the war, but it may only be a rumor. Many people claim things happened during the war that cannot be proven, both good and bad. However, with him, I can believe it. His face reminds me of a hawk preparing to strike."

"Thank you, Phillipe, you've given me a lot of information to work with. Are you full or do you have room for dessert?"

Phillipe patted his stomach and smiled. "Perhaps there is a little more room in here. Phillipe's stomach doesn't believe it's filled quite yet."

After a round of dessert, Mary sent Phillipe to the bedroom

to take a nap. Once he was asleep, she pulled the two messages out of her purse and sat down to read them. Both were encrypted and it took her a few minutes to decrypt them. Neither one was a huge surprise, but it still made interesting reading.

The first message was short and to the point. Tom had learned from Lieutenant Mathewson that the gunman who'd taken the shots at Sheila had been found in a swamp south of town. He'd been shot several times before his body had been dumped, but there were no clues leading back to the killer yet.

The second let her know there were more missing ex-service members. Some had been missing almost six months now, and the reports were coming in from all over the United States. Some were even reported missing in Canada, so she was to take every precaution. It was not officially a criminal investigation yet, but the FBI had taken an interest in the case and would be reaching out to her soon.

She carefully burned the messages and scattered the ashes out the window. She was more determined than ever to look that ship over after nightfall. Pulling her binoculars out of her purse, she scanned the harbor. The *Bakersfield* showed no signs of activity. No cargo was being loaded or unloaded and the gangplank had been removed.

Glancing at the rest of the harbor, she noted a smaller freighter being towed into the berth next to the *Bakersfield.* She frowned and trained her glasses on the incoming ship. It was the *Porto de Oro*, flying a Brazilian flag.

That's odd. There are nine or ten open berths. Why are they bringing her in right next to the Bakersfield*?*

She trained her glasses on the scene and saw the dock activity pick up. A mobile crane rumbled forward between the two berths, and dockworkers were swarming around like ants whose hill had been disturbed.

I wondered why they weren't unloading the ship—was it scheduled all along or are they being careful because they discovered Phillipe's absence? Either way, there won't be any point in visiting the Bakersfield *right now. Better check on Phillipe and then head back to the docks to see if I can get the scoop on the* Porto de Oro.

Going down her list of tasks, Mary stuck her head into the bedroom to check on Phillipe, then closed the door quietly behind her and headed to the lobby. She left a note with the desk clerk to send dinner up to her room if she hadn't returned by six p.m. Stepping into the sweltering heat, she adjusted her hat to cover more of her face and moved quickly northward toward the docks. She had her Black Venus costume in a hidden compartment at the bottom of her oversized bag, but she was hoping she wouldn't need it. The longer she could keep her alter ego's presence in French Guiana a secret, the better.

She was about halfway to the docks when she realized she wasn't alone. This time, instead of a young boy, there were two large men dogging her trail about half a block behind her. She paused at a store and checked out their reflections. They seemed like they'd be more at home in the alleys of New York or Los Angeles than Cayenne, but that wasn't the worst of it. In the reflection, she saw one of them signaling ahead and a glance told her there were two more men on the street corner a block ahead with a running car.

Definitely New York. So, Mary, if you don't want to go for a nice ride into the Guianan jungle, how're you getting out of this one?

Remembering how she'd ducked Phillipe, Mary decided it was worth a shot. Moving down the street as if she hadn't noticed anything, she ducked into a restaurant. Before the waiter could say anything, she pushed by him and into the kitchen. A barrage of unhappy French followed but she didn't stop and explain. Five steps later, she was through the back door and heading south along the alley. She only went a few steps before she heard more yelling from the restaurant and knew the men who'd been trailing her hadn't been as patient as Phillipe. She chose the first unlocked door she came to and went inside, finding herself in a storage room filled with boxes.

Before Mary could get her bearings, a young woman entered from the front of the store and spotted her. She started to scream, but Mary held up a finger to her lips and then pointed over her shoulder. Before the wide-eyed woman could say anything, Mary ducked behind a couple of boxes and shifted them around to better conceal her.

Seconds later, the door banged open, and Mary heard two loud, unfriendly voices. "All right, sister, where'd she go?"

The young woman's voice quaked as she responded. "The woman in the big hat? She pushed past me and went into the store. I do not know if she's still there or has left."

"Come on, Carlos, we might still be able to catch her."

There was the sound of hurried movement and then silence. Mary remained where she was until the unmistakable sound of high heels approached her hiding spot.

"I believe they have gone, *mademoiselle*, but it's possible they may return. Who were they?"

"I'm not sure, but I know they're not with the police, if that's what you're worried about," Mary replied as softly as she could.

The other woman gave a small sniff of disdain. "I could tell that in an instant. Give me a minute to return to the store or the manager may wonder what's taking me so long."

The heels clicked away, but once the young woman was out of sight, Mary slipped out of her hiding place and opened the back door slightly before finding a different hiding spot. She had barely settled in when she heard footsteps coming into the back room. Mary peeked from her new hiding spot and saw one of the men who'd been following her checking where she had been hiding. The other man held a gun to the back of the store clerk and there was a red mark on the side of her face.

"I thought you said she was hiding here."

"*Monsieur*, she was there when I left this room. I do not know what happened."

The man holding her raised a hand as if to strike the clerk again when the first pointed. "Jean, check this out. The back door's ajar. I think she slipped out after we came through here."

"The boss ain't gonna be happy, but we don't have time to

check the entire town for her. Come on, Carlos, let's head back to the ship. It's leaving at dark, and it'll be a long walk back to the base if we're not on it."

"What do we do with this one?"

"She doesn't matter. Even if she does go to the cops, we'll be long gone. But to be sure . . ." There was a sudden movement and the sickening sound of metal striking bone as the thug brought his pistol barrel down on the back of the girl's neck. She collapsed in a heap, and the two men let themselves out the back door. Mary heard running feet and then silence. Moving to the door she peeked out but the men were out of sight. She hurried to the unconscious clerk and started working to bring her around.

After a bit, the woman began to stir and Mary helped her sit up. "Oh, *mon dieu,* he did not have to hit me so hard. Oh, it is you. But, how? You were not where I left you and they were very angry."

"Yes, I know. I was afraid they might come back so I hid over in that corner. I'm glad they took the hint of the open door instead of searching further. What gave me away?"

"My fool manager. She told them no one had come out of the back room, so the men knew I was lying. They grabbed me as soon as I came out, but I managed to stall as long as I could. Vivette! What did they do to her?" The young woman tried to bolt to her feet, and it was all Mary could do to keep her from falling over.

As she calmed the young clerk down, Mary learned her name was Celeste and Vivette was the store manager. When Mary was certain Celeste wouldn't fall over again, she helped her to her feet. In the store, they found the manager sprawled on her face behind the counter. It took several minutes to bring her around, so Mary had Celeste call an ambulance. While they were waiting, they agreed on what they would and wouldn't mention when the police arrived.

Thirty minutes later, the ambulance arrived with a police car in tow. A crowd had gathered around the shop and Celeste had already chased them all outside twice. The attendants rushed in and one of the policemen followed while the other pushed the crowd back.

Celeste told the police what she could, describing the two men. Mary corroborated her story and added a few additional details. Vivette was taken out on a stretcher while protesting she felt well enough. As they were shutting the ambulance doors, she was still telling Celeste to get the store back in order and to not close too early. The policeman gave both Celeste and Mary a look that said he didn't believe a word of their story, but he dutifully copied it all down and said he'd be back to have Celeste sign the report.

Mary kept checking her watch, fretting about how much time this was taking. She felt the policeman's frustration, but she could not be trapped into staying in Cayenne for an extended investigation. That would accomplish the thugs' mission as well as if they'd captured her themselves. Still, as a guest of the French Guianese government, she felt awkward withholding information from them. She knew the police would interview the staff of the restaurant next door eventually. Once they learned of her scamper through the kitchen, they'd probably have more questions, but like the men she was pursuing, she was counting on being gone before that happened.

When things started to settle down, Mary excused herself and grabbed a taxi to the docks. She hurried to the Port Authority's office, checking over her shoulder to see if she was being watched. To her relief, no one was paying attention, officially or otherwise.

Once she arrived at her destination, it took several knocks on the counter to get someone's attention. A sleepy-looking clerk finally wandered out from an interior room and made his way to the desk.

"It is too hot for such a racket, *mademoiselle*. We're normally closed between one and three."

"I'm sorry to disturb you, but your door was unlocked."

"And why shouldn't it be? Most of Cayenne closes during the heat of the day. Ah, but I can tell by your dress, you are a visitor. Very well, how may I help you?"

Mary presented him with her credentials, which stated she was a representative of the Acme Shipping Company, New York. The man pulled out a well-worn pair of glasses that perched precariously on his nose and scanned the document thoroughly. After a few seconds, he refolded the papers and handed them back to Mary.

"I'm expecting some cargo from France. It's arriving on the *L'île Noire* and it should be arriving any day now. I was wondering if you could give me the status or location of that ship."

"As you wish," the clerk said and bowed his head sleepily in her direction. He shuffled off to a large board on the wall and pulled down a pointer. He ran the pointer down a list of ships and then cross-referenced it against a map of the Western Atlantic and Caribbean. He tapped the board a couple of times and then went back to the list to double-check his findings, before returning to the counter. Mary tried to hide her impatience. Getting on the clerk's bad side wouldn't help move the process faster.

"The *L'île Noire*'s last reported position was two hundred miles northeast of Trinadad. We anticipate it will arrive here four days from today. There are no reported storms in the area, so we foresee no reasons for delay. Will that be all?"

"I think that covers . . . oh, wait. That ship in the harbor there, the *Porto de Oro* . . . has it recently arrived?"

The clerk glanced out the window at the ship before turning his attention back to Mary. "Indeed it has. It is a local trader. It carries cargos from here to Saint-Georges about every two weeks. Generally, it delivers agricultural goods here and picks up machinery and other equipment for plantations and other works deeper in the country's interior. Is the lady interested in enquiring about booking her shipment on her?"

"No, I noticed she is already taking on a new cargo. I suspect she will be leaving before my ship arrives."

"Yes, that is true. The *Porto de Oro* never stays overnight. Her captain is a hard man, *mademoiselle*. Some might even call him a slave driver. It is said he hates Cayenne and refuses to allow any of his men off the ship for fear they will desert him. Some people say the only way off his ship is to retire due to old age or injury, or . . ."

"Or?"

The clerk didn't say anything, but he held his hand out level and then dipped one end of it while he made a whistling sound. In any language, Mary knew what that meant—burial at sea. "Surely he cannot force men to sail for him?"

"While his ship is at sea, his word is law, *mademoiselle*. When it is not, well, there are few ways out of Saint-Georges other than by sailing and the captains there fear Captain LeBeou. They'll not take one of his sailors aboard as crew or passenger. No, once you sign on with the *Porto*, you sail for life. Such is the way of the sea. Now, should you decide to use him, I cannot rate him highly enough. He's never lost a cargo to pirates or to a storm. He has several warehouses here on the docks where he stores cargo between runs. Would you care to see?"

Nodding, Mary stepped behind the counter and followed him over to a row of windows overlooking the warehouses. "Their office is over there," he said, pointing to a familiar one. "Along with shipping, they also own several warehouses here on the docks where they store goods destined for the interior. Would you like me to call ahead and let them know you are coming?"

Keeping the expression on her face steady, Mary shook her head. "Perhaps another time, *monsieur*. Although now that my ship is nearing port, I do need to arrange for warehousing my cargo."

"But, so late? *Mon dieu,* this is not your New York or Miami. Cayenne has only so many warehouses. *Mademoiselle,* it is my duty to find you appropriate warehouse space and quickly, lest your cargo be simply piled on the docks for thieves and the elements to ravage."

Mary allowed herself to be led over to a chair where she helped the clerk fill out a warehouse request for her imaginary cargo. She hated wasting his time but didn't know if Emil Muller had an agent or two of his own in the Port Authority offices. He already seemed to know more about her than was healthy, and she didn't want to draw any *more* attention.

Chatting with the clerk, she found the *Porto de Oro* was due to sail at seven o'clock that evening. When the last form was filled out, Mary thanked him profusely and left, catching a cab for downtown Cayenne.

Stopping several blocks short of the American consulate, Mary meandered through a couple of stores to ensure no one was following. When she decided she was clear, she hurried to her destination.

Mary reported to the front desk and told them why she was here. After a short wait in the lobby, three large men came down a stairway off to the side and approached the desk. The secretary pointed her out and the men came over. Mary wasn't quite sure what was going on, but she could tell by the way two of them were positioned that they were making sure she couldn't make a break for it.

"Miss Roche?" said the one in the middle.

"Yes, that's right." She smiled at him as if she was completely oblivious to what was going on.

The first man looked uncomfortable, but he pushed on. "If you'll please accompany me?"

"If you'll please give me a reason to do so . . ." Mary replied, trying to feel out the situation.

He tugged at his collar and continued. "I'd love to, but a public lobby isn't the place. Let's say it has something to do with the pictures you dropped off earlier today."

Ah. Feeling marginally better, Mary extended a hand, and the gentleman assisted her to her feet. He led her to the side stairwell and up two flights of stairs. They went down the hall and paused while one man went ahead and worked a combination lock on a door several feet ahead of them. Once he'd unlocked the door and turned off the alarm, he motioned for them. Mary was led into a spartan room, with five desks and as many filing cabinets. She was directed to one of the chairs and the man who'd spoken to her took his seat at the desk across from her. One of the other men shut the door and secured the lock. The last one turned on the air conditioner. It fought against the heat of the day, but eventually there was a faint cool breeze coming from it.

"Miss Roche, I'm Special Agent Solomon Barton with the FBI. Here are my credentials." He handed her a leather wallet, and she examined his ID card and badge before handing them back. "These are Agents Scott Fielder and Tim Hershey, my assistants here in Cayenne. Your pictures stirred up a hornet's nest back in Washington. We'd like to ask what your interest is in the S.S. *Bakersfield* and anyone associated with that ship."

Mary explained what had brought her to French Guiana, to include all the information she'd "received" from Black Venus about Cauldron Enterprises. She also produced the documents from the Veterans Bureau authorizing her to follow up on her suspicions and her authorization for being out of the country. Hershey and Fielder were taking copious notes while Barton just watched her while she spoke.

When she finished, Barton asked Fielder to place a call to have some refreshments sent up. Once that was done, Barton went to a three-drawer safe in the corner of the room and after unlocking it, grabbed a couple of folders out and put them on the table in front of Mary. One of them was a folder on Emil Mueller.

The other was a folder on her.

Solomon leaned back in his chair. "So, before we go much further, should I call you Miss Roche or should I call you Black Venus?"

"You may call me whatever you wish, Special Agent Barton, but Mary is my real name and it's much easier to say."

He smiled at her. "Gotcha. I'm Solly. And, no offense, but anyone still flying a fully functional and armed P-38 . . . well, let's say you've drawn the Bureau's attention."

"Completely understandable, Solly. I'd be more concerned if I hadn't."

"Appreciate you being so understanding. Anyway, I'll let you take a look at that file on Mueller. But here's the shorthand notes—he's a former S.S. officer who got out of Germany one step ahead of the Soviets tanks in 1945. He was not only a brilliant infantry commander, but a chemical scientist before the war. And if that's not bad enough, he was also well placed in other areas, to include the Black Wolf Society. However, no one could officially tie him to any atrocities in Europe. He's been relatively well behaved here, so the Bureau decided it's easier to keep an eye on him in Cayenne than chasing him around the world should we need to put our hands on him."

"And you're concerned that my presence here might scare your bird into flying the coop?"

A knock on the door halted Solly's response. Fielder went to the door and spoke into the intercom. Once he had the answer he wanted, he unlocked the door and was handed a tray of glasses, a bottle of water and an ice bucket. He served everyone and took the tray over to his desk. Once Mary had enjoyed the cool water, she relaxed a bit as Solly started speaking again.

"That is a concern, but our office back in Washington spoke to one of your friends, a Lieutenant Mathewson. He speaks very highly of you—both of you to be exact—so we decided this could work out to our mutual benefit."

"You know, I *really* am just trying to find out what's going on with a bunch of our vets who've turned up missing."

Solly nodded. "Trust me, Mary, we're interested in what's going on too. But we also don't want to move in on Emil Muller's operations too soon. *If*—and I repeat, if—something is going on in the jungles of French Guiana, then we absolutely want to bring thing to a halt, but we must do it in conjunction with the French government. DeGaulle is having enough troubles trying to get everything pulled together over in France proper. French Guiana, while still technically part of France, has been left on its own for a while along with the rest of the French Caribbean islands. Several ex-Vichy and criminal syndicates have taken advantage of the situation, so we're going to need proof—solid enough to stand up in the face of any doubt proof—before we can go to the prefect and have him commit either police or soldiers to the interior."

"So, there *is* something going on in the interior. I overheard them speaking of a 'base' earlier today."

"Yes, Mueller filed several claims for gold mines in the interior. Heck, if not for the gold strikes in the region, Saint-Georges wouldn't even exist. It was an old penal colony back in the 1800s but now it's booming . . . well, as booming as things get around here. It's overrun with prospectors, mining companies trying to get started, flimflam artists trying to make a buck when the miners return—think of a place like Tombstone or Dawson during the gold rush days. Still, whether he's struck gold or something else, he's doing something out there and he's taking a lot of machinery out there to work on it—machinery and men."

"The missing veterans?"

"Again, until we had talked to you today, we hadn't heard of any missing veterans. But if Cauldron Enterprises is tied to Mueller, then I'd say there's a darn good possibility that's where they are. Still won't be an easy nut to crack, though. Once you get south of Saint-Georges, you're pretty much on your own. It's mostly tribal lands with a few plantations here and there. Actually, it's more rainforest than anything else. Not an easy place to get in and out of, much less undetected."

"That wouldn't be a problem if the State Department hadn't objected to me flying my own plane down here.

"Well, that's an issue we're going to need to address when you return to the States. A number of agencies have concerns about your P-38. The biggest issue I have with it is not the fact that it's still armed and operational, but that it's *obviously* armed and operational. We need to find a better way to disguise your weaponry, so it doesn't become a target for any air pirates. No matter how well you think you have it secured . . . it's never secured enough.

"I have been very careful using it. In fact, I've only used it against criminals who have their own access to war surplus weaponry."

"I know and I'm grateful for your discretion. However, the idea of a plane armed with fully functional heavy machineguns and a cannon flying overhead, especially in the hand of a civilian makes a lot of people nervous. In fact, if Wild Bill Donovan and several others hadn't personally vouched for you, we'd have confiscated it long before now. I hope you understand our position on this.

"Point noted and taken. But let's get back to this. What do you want me to do that won't interfere with what's already going on?"

"I'm going to ask you to stay away from Mueller's warehouse while you're here in Cayenne. In fact, I think it's time for Mary Roche to depart from Cayenne. They've already tried to kidnap you once. I don't think they're likely to stop."

Before Mary could protest, he got up and went back to the safe but opened a different drawer. He rummaged around in it and came out with a passport he handed to Mary. "Tanya Ross, photographer and reporter for National Geographic, on assignment to French Guiana. It's not a hundred percent match but you look close enough to the picture to pass. We'll fly you over to Brazil and have you take the ferry to Saint-Georges. You'll wander around, take pictures, interview the natives, make arrangements for a trip into the rainforest, and be there when the *Porto de Oro* arrives in four days. See what you can find out about where and when her cargo is moving."

Mary shook her head. "If you fly me down there, that means I don't have access to a plane. Even if I don't have access to my P-38, it doesn't mean I can't rent a commercial plane and fly it there. Sort of goes with the whole globe-hopping reporter you're setting me up with here. At least with my own plane, I could possibly trail them from the air whenever they depart Saint-Georges to wherever their base is.

Solly shook his head back at her before grinning. "A civilian plane landing *at* a town like Saint Georges might be as well be a P-38 Lightning. It's going to draw a lot of unwanted attention. Again, I can't officially stop you from flying there, but I'd highly recommend against it. Besides, if you think security stinks around here, it's damn near Fort Knox compared to the airport at Saint Georges."

Mary started to object again, but she realized Solly was right. After all, he'd been working down here a lot longer than she had been. "All right, Solly. As much as I hate to admit it, you make a lot of sense. Still, it seems wrong not to have it available. We've been through a lot together."

Solly smiled. "I completely understand. I didn't log all those hours over Italy and Germany in my own P-38 just to forget the feeling you get up in the air. Don't worry, I have a feeling you'll get to do whatever it is a Black Venus does before this is all over."

"We'll swap war stories after I get back."

The town of Saint-Georges was exactly as Solly had described it. The local French authorities were using the old penal colonies' decrepit buildings as a makeshift seat of government. Houses were going up haphazardly. Most were just shacks with thatched roofs to keep the daily rains out. One thing Mary noted was almost everyone was armed. A couple of buildings were selling surplus weapons and ammunition. It seemed like everyone carried machetes and knives . . . and most looked well used.

She sat in an open-air café where she could observe the docks. From what she'd heard, the *Porto de Oro* would tie up just downriver from the town and unload its cargo. From where she was sitting, she had a good view of the dock, and her camera was hidden in a box she'd sat on the table facing that direction All she had to do was press a corner of the box to trip the shutter. As long as the crowd wasn't too thick, she'd be able to get some good shots.

"Another caffe, *mademoiselle*?" the waitress asked.

"No thank you, Lunette. I am just resting a bit before I take more photographs. It's been a very busy day."

The waitress did a deft spin around yet another amorous prospector and then rested her tray edge down on Mary's table. "Pardon me for saying this, but I do not understand you

Americans. What is there to take pictures of here in Saint-Georges? Mud and waddle huts? Prospectors who haven't bathed since the end of the war? Perhaps the latest knife fight over twenty centimes of gold dust?" She gave Mary a conspiratorial look. "If I were you, I'd be taking pictures in Paris or Marseilles, or even the Riviera, not some godforsaken pigsty like this."

Mary laughed. "Oh, Lunette, if only you were my editor. Unfortunately, if I want to keep my job, I go where he says and take pictures and write stories he wants for the magazine. Oh, if only I'd gone into fashion photography instead of nature. Although to tell you the truth, I think there are more wolves in fashion than in the wild." Mary gave her a knowing wink and Lunette nodded sagely.

"I think you made a bad choice then because it appears all the wolves in the world have descended on Saint-Georges. Ah, and speaking of wolves, I'd better tell Marcel to put some more beer in the ice chest. I can hear the *Porto de Oro*. She's about two turns of the river away. There'll be a flood of thirsty sailors in a few hours."

"I heard the *Porto* was making runs here even before the first gold strike."

Lunette glanced around but no one seemed to be paying attention. "It is best not to ask questions about that ship, but yes. The crew converted one of the old cell blocks into their personal keep. This is as far down the Oyanock River she can sail. It gets much shallower upriver. There are a few steamboats that can get all the way down to Camopi, but after that, you can only get a pirogue farther into the wilderness. I have no idea why anyone would ever want to go that far. Camopi makes this place seem like a metropolis and beyond . . . nothing but tribes of natives and the Amazon jungle. No, I am content to sell wine and beer here and save my money to get back to Cayenne or even farther someday."

"I admit, I never expected to find such a philosopher in Saint-Georges."

"Philosophy is for wealthy people. I call it common sense,"

Lunette said before waving her hand and heading over to another table to take an order. Her hearing was certainly good though. Just as Lunette left, Mary could see the freighter slowly making its way upriver against the current.

Captain LeBeou might be a harsh master, but there was no question he knew this section of the river intimately. Even to Mary's untrained eyes, he eased the ship into its berth like he was parking a car. As soon as the ship was even with the dock, men on shore seemed to spring out of nowhere to catch the lines being heaved over the side. Almost like magic, the ship was snugged into place and an old crane wheezed out of the jungle and ran its arm out above the deck. Between the crane mounted on the ship and the dockside one, and the dockworkers, the crates and metal boxes were soon piled in neat stacks on dull green flatbed trucks to be hauled away.

Mary snapped a series of shots of the ship, the crew, and the various trucks that came out of the jungle only to return as soon as they were loaded. She wished she could have used a better telephoto lens or been able to focus on specific sections of the ship, but as Solly said, in this case discretion wasn't only the better part of valor, it was also the best way to stay alive.

As the ship finished unloading, a crowd of people pushed into the café—older men, women, children. Mary assumed they were friends and family members of the crew. A buzz ran through the club and Mary chose that opportunity to discreetly move to a small table in the corner. She was hoping the crew would be in good spirits after reaching their home port, and maybe someone would let something slip.

That hope was dashed a few minutes later when a large car pulled up and the crowd got quiet. People started moving back as five men wearing ship uniforms and packing pistols exited. After they had taken their positions, a sixth man stepped out of the car. From the way he carried himself, there was no question in Mary's mind, this was Captain LeBeou.

He eyed the crowd and then spoke in a loud, but surprisingly pleasant voice. "Good evening, everyone. I'm pleased to see such a large group of family and loved ones. Unfortunately, a few crewmen have come down with a strange illness. For your safety, we're quarantining the crew for a while to ensure this illness does not spread. There are doctors flying in from Cayenne, so you may see some unfamiliar airplanes over the next few days. There is nothing to worry about. Simply a precaution. We'll give these men shore leave as soon as it's safe to do so. Thank you for your patience and know your husbands, fathers, and lovers are thinking of you. That is all. Men, gather our supplies. We'll head back to the compound."

Like someone sticking a pin into a balloon, Mary felt the expectations of the crowd deflate with every word the captain spoke. Most stood stunned and then a few people on the fringes broke away and left the café. Eventually, only a few die-hard onlookers and the regular customers were left. Mary glanced over at Lunette and there was a mixture of fear and concern on her face. As one of the guards came through the café with a case of beer, Lunette intercepted him.

"Please, can you tell me . . . is Rayan affected? I must know if he is safe or not."

The man paused, glancing to see whether the captain was in sight before speaking softly. "Do not ask questions, Lunette. The captain has told you all you need to know."

"But he is my little brother. I must—"

The man brusquely pushed past her. She turned to follow, but Captain LeBeou appeared as if by magic next to her. "Lunette, I am sorry, but I cannot make exceptions. You will learn of Rayan's condition when the rest of the townspeople do. It would be unfair to tell you he was fine if he is not. It would also be unfair to tell you something and not tell the rest of the town. No, we will wait until the doctors can examine everyone and tell us what we are dealing with, and when the crew will be allowed to come home. You must be strong . . . for Rayan's sake."

Lunette started to say something else, but a stern look grew on LeBeou's face, and she swallowed whatever she was about to say and made a slight curtsey before retreating. He glanced around the café to see who else might challenge his decree.

When his gaze fell on Mary, his eyes narrowed and his mouth set in a straight line. He turned quickly on one heel and walked back to his car with the rolling gait of a man who's spent most of his life at sea. He motioned to one of the guards, who blew a whistle. The rest of the guards hustled to the car and loaded their goods into the trunk before piling in after the captain.

The way LeBeou looked at her made Mary uncomfortable. She wasn't sure why, but it was clear she was at best an unknown quantity, and at worst someone he'd been warned about. From the way everyone kowtowed to him, he was used to his authority extending over the town as well as his ship. She had tried to get a few pictures of him for Solly, but with the crowd milling about, there was no guarantee any would turn out.

She waited for the final stragglers to clear out before approaching Lunette. "I'm sorry, but if someone is really sick, it's probably better to keep them isolated for the moment."

"That's what worries me. The captain has always insisted on his own ship's surgeon to treat any illnesses. There must be something seriously wrong if they're flying in doctors from the capital."

Mary filed that under things to investigate before she left Saint-Georges. However, she also needed to investigate the compound to determine where those trucks might be heading. From her two days in town, she'd determined the base was nowhere near Saint-Georges—not enough unexplained people to warrant the townsfolk's curiosity considering the way they'd been visiting with her for news from the capital and the world.

She had been quite a hit with some of the older women who wanted to talk about Paris and other places in France. Her alias's profession as a photographer gave Mary a way to explain her presence to the more curious. She was certain a few of the people who'd hung around her the first days were informants, although for Mueller, LeBeou, or both, she wasn't sure.

She talked with Lunette a bit longer until she felt she could take her leave without drawing attention. She returned to her lodgings, such as they were, and turned down her bed as if she was getting ready to call it a night. She left all her regular photography equipment out so if her room was searched, they'd find lots of rolls of film about locals, natives, and animals. The important rolls of film were secured in the leg of her table. It hadn't taken her long to hollow out a section big enough to hide a few rolls of film.

When she was satisfied no one was snooping around, she slipped into her black catsuit and boots, adjusted her hood and mask, and ensured she had her small bag of tools and the camera with infrared film and bulbs. If LeBeou was already suspicious of her, she couldn't wait too long to find out what was really going on.

She slipped out the window and made her way silently through the jungle surrounding Saint-Georges. Glancing into the town, she spotted a number of armed men wandering about, apparently on patrol—but on whose authority? Mary shook her head. Boomtowns hadn't changed all that much since Sutter's Mill.

The moon was starting to rise when she reached the old prison camp. From what she'd read in Solly's reports, this area had been deserted for almost sixty years, and the prison compound showed it. Nature had wasted no time reclaiming its own. Some of the buildings had collapsed; others had trees growing through the roofs. The prison's walls had started crumbling under the weight of the vegetation eating into their surfaces.

Still, it was clear where humanity's return was going on. A large area had recently been burnt and cleared, the dark ground still visible between the few trees and plants that had been spared. She could see some buildings had been converted into warehouses and another into a garage to house and repair the fleet of trucks that supported the *Porto de Oro*. Across the open field, she saw the flickering lights of the dormitories.

Wait a minute. There are too many lights spread too far apart in those buildings. That ship can't have that *big a crew. Even allowing for port staff, they should all fit in one of those buildings. There's no logical reason for lights in three of those old jail blocks.*

She glided among the shadows using her suit's natural

camouflage to let her slip up to the buildings. As she maneuvered around, she spotted patrols of two moving around the compound. From the way they held their weapons, she was certain they were carrying submachine guns, which caused her to raise her eyebrows in surprise. *That seems like overkill for simply guarding machinery for a gold-mining operation.*

A smaller building occupied the central position on the compound and from the lights and traffic in and out, she decided it would be her first stop. She waited until she thought she had the guard's routine mapped out in her head and then flitted from shadow to shadow until she reached her target. The building had been repaired, but it still had some rough spots on the outside from nature's assault, which made perfect climbing holds for her. She eased up the side of the building until she reached the roof. Flattening her body against the roof, Black Venus inched her way across it, trying not to alert the occupants.

Finally, she reached a small open skylight and peered inside. The captain was arguing with someone in a shadowed part of the room. She shifted a bit to hear what was going on.

LeBeou's voice was a mixture of anger and concern. "I don't like it. Things are happening that shouldn't be."

The other voice sounded familiar, but Mary couldn't quite place it. "Look, LeBeou, you knew when we started there was always a chance something could go wrong. Anytime you start something this complicated, mistakes are inevitable. What's kept the Triumverate one step ahead so far is correcting them quickly. This is not some fly-by-night operation. Some of us have been preparing for this for almost thirty years."

"Yeah, and your last project didn't work too well, now did it?"

The voice in the shadows sounded only a little aggravated at the captain's sarcasm. "The only way to ultimately succeed is having multiple projects going. Not putting all the eggs in one basket, right? So one failed a few years ago. It was not a complete loss. While everyone had their eyes on it, several other projects, including this one, took advantage of the distraction and made great progress. In fact, one more shipment should make us self-sustaining. After that, you might only carry cargo for us once or twice a year."

"No offense, but that suits me fine. I've been dodging or paying off customs agents in two countries to ensure I'm not boarded. It'd be a pleasant change to get back to hauling standard cargoes."

A chuckle came from the corner. "Yes, I'm sure you'd sleep better at night."

LeBeou paled and waved his hands in front of his body. "Now, wait a minute. Don't think I'm backing out on my side of the bargain. Your money spends just as well as the next person's and I'm firmly behind the cause. It's that I've been bucking the odds for the last eight months running these cargoes. Sooner or later, I'm going to get inspected and it would be nice to know there's nothing for them to find."

"I told you . . . one more trip and we'll be done. The airfield should be done in the next couple of months, depending on the rain. Once it's capable of taking heavy transports, we'll be able to ship directly from multiple locations. It'll make it harder to find our base until it's too late to do anything about it."

There was a rustling sound and the other speaker, Oliver Anderson, stepped from the shadows to spread a map out on the table and point to a particular location. Mary eased her camera out and slipped an infrared bulb into the flash. She focused on the map but couldn't get a clear picture. She shifted positions a couple of times but either they were in the way, or the light wasn't good.

She shifted one more time—and the weathered roof gave way. She fell into the room in a cascade of wood and tin. Before she was able to pick herself up, two men came rushing in with MP-40 machine pistols pointed at her, but Anderson raised a hand to keep them from firing.

"Captain LeBeou, it appears we have a stowaway all the way from America." He chuckled turning back to Mary, "So glad you could drop in on us, Black Venus. I'm sure you have many questions . . ."

His eyes narrowed. "And so do we."

The next few days passed in a painful blur. After her inglorious entrance, she had been tossed into a small room and questioned repeatedly by Anderson and LeBeou. She had managed not to answer any of their questions so far, but the guards assigned her had proven equally unresponsive to her attempts to make them drop their guard so she could escape.

Several hours later, they'd shown up with her personal belongings from her room, but she noted they hadn't found the film she'd hidden in the table leg. She hung her hopes on Solly finding it since he was the one who'd arranged for her to stay there. They'd brought in a hatchet-faced native matron to search her and her outfit. After Mary had changed into her civilian clothes, the matron left her Black Venus outfit behind with a contemptuous sniff. Mary folded it carefully and slipped it into the hidden compartment in her suitcase.

Never know when it might come in handy. This is a bad spot, but I'm not done for yet. Since they haven't killed me, that means they want something. It's just a matter of not giving it to them until they slip up. I've been in tough spots before, just have to keep my head and pay attention.

Three days later, after little sleep, less food, and lots of questions, she was given a shot and woke up hours later stuffed into a wooden crate. From the movement, she could tell she was in an airplane. She remembered Philippe had mentioned they transported equipment from Saint-Georges to "the Cauldron" by air or truck. After a few hours, she felt the plane descending and after circling a few times, it came to a bumpy landing. Eventually, she heard the sound of crowbars biting into wood and then the lid rose, and two sets of hands roughly dragged her out of the crate.

Once her eyes adjusted to the light, she noticed she was at a rough-cut runway in the middle of a rain forest. While two guards watched her, the rest fell in and started unloading supplies off the plane. In the distance, she heard truck motors, and a small jeep came out of the underbrush and pulled up between the shacks. Mary was still shaking out the cobwebs, but she recognized one of the men. He was the gunman who'd shown up at her apartment—Sid.

He glanced around in appreciation. "Glad to see you made it. Any complications?"

Anderson smiled and poked a thumb over his shoulder toward Mary. "Nothing we couldn't handle. Some might say good fortune dropped in on us."

"Oh, ha, ha," Mary said, mirthlessly.

Sid glanced at her and squinted his eyes. "I don't believe I've met your passenger before, boss."

"Oh, but you have, Sid, but she was wearing a more identity concealing garment then."

A thin smile formed on Sid's lips, and he took two steps toward Mary before a couple of the crewmen stopped him. "You! I owe you big time for that footstool in the face. I've been stuck down here ever since because of you."

Mary knew she was taking a chance, but she couldn't resist needling him. "Why, Sid, I think the tropical sun has done wonders for you. You've lost that jailbird pallor."

He lunged at her again, but Anderson stepped between the two of them. "Now, Sid, you shouldn't let her bait you like that. After all, she's going to be our guest for a long time. You two will just have to learn to get along." He turned back toward Mary, "And you, my dear, should learn your place. I'll not have you riling up my men like that."

Before Mary could react, his beefy fist slammed into the side of her head, rocking her back. Her knees went wobbly, but she managed to hang onto one of her guards until her head cleared. As she got her balance back, she slowly straightened up and wiped the trickle of blood away from the corner of her mouth. "That's your one free one, Oliver. Make the next one count."

She saw a momentary flicker of fear in his eyes before the muscles in his neck and shoulders bulged. He motioned to his crew, and they marched her over to the jeep, unceremoniously tossing her into the back before climbing in on either side of her. A few minutes later, Sid and Anderson climbed into the front and the jeep roared off into the surrounding jungle.

The darkness of the jungle closed in around them as they traveled away from the river. After about an hour, light began to spear through the overhead foliage here and there. When they emerged, Mary let out a startled gasp in spite of herself.

In front of her was a large valley completely cleared of any signs of the jungle. At its heart lay a military camp with rows of barracks surrounded by a ten-foot-tall wall of razor wire, and guard towers every forty feet. An aerodrome was being established at the far end, with large balloons at either end—no, not balloons . . . zeppelins. Another section of the valley was under cultivation, with men dragging plows while other men tried to steer them. Another section seemed to have a series of large buildings under construction.

"Welcome to the Cauldron," Anderson chortled. "As I told your friend, I was hiring men for work in France. After all, French Guiana *is* a department of France, not a colony. So, is it *my* fault those ex-servicemen didn't read the fine print?"

He laughed again, but this time it was more venomous. "Not that I care, because, just like you, none of them are ever leaving here. Speaking of which, we probably should introduce you to your new home. When you get there, make yourself comfortable. You're going to be here for a *long* time.

Sid snickered. "Yeah, think of it as a retirement home for washed-up heroes."

Chuckle all you want, smart guy. You'll be laughing out the other side of your mouth when I get out of here.

She let a wry look settle on her face before continuing that thought . . . *if I get out of here.*

The jeep moved down the ridge. Just beyond the compound was a smaller group of buildings apparently designed for the camp staff, and the jeep pulled up in front of one. Anderson motioned for her to get out. She followed him inside as Sid and the two guards waited outside.

"This will be your temporary home," Anderson said,

waving his arms around in a slow circle. "Oh, you'll move inside the wire, but not quite yet . . . after all, we haven't had time to make proper preparations since you just 'dropped in' on us."

"I think I'll survive."

He gave Mary a nasty look. "Let's hope so. Since your unexpected arrival, I've had time to make other plans for you. It'd be a damn shame if something happened before then."

He led her back to the jeep, and they drove away from the staff area to the main compound. After a quick conversation with the guards, the first set of barbed-wire gates was pulled back and they drove inside. There was a fifteen-foot dead zone between the two sets of fences and the guards on the inside waited until the outer gates were secured before opening theirs. Mary couldn't help noticing the towers were all manned and sported nasty-looking MG-42 machine guns. Anyone caught in that no-man's-land wouldn't last more than a few seconds before the guards finished them off. She also noted glass insulators mounted along the top of the razor-wire. *Armed guards and electrified fences—Anderson isn't taking any chances.*

Anderson spoke as if he'd been reading her mind. "I see you're taking everything in. I hope you realize the futility of trying to escape from inside the compound."

"You've certainly adapted the best of the stalag techniques."

"Don't flatter yourself. A prison camp is a prison camp the world over. After all, the prisoners in Stalag Luft III were treated more humanely than those in your own Andersonville."

"That was over eighty years ago. How do you explain Dachau or Auschwitz?"

"Not my department. Not my responsibility."

Convenient, Mary thought, but she bit back the retort and set her features to show nothing as they drove deeper into the compound. The barracks were well built and more modern than she'd anticipated. Sid pointed to another set of barbed wire–surrounded barracks. "That's where the suckers sleep. One set of guards stay in these other buildings. They rotate every week or so with another group outside the compound.

So's even if these ex-GIs got it in their head to riot, they'd have to not only defeat all the guards in here, but a second set out there. It helps convince them to play nice. Most have the good sense to do just that."

"And the ones who don't?" Mary asked, not really wanting to know the answer.

"Well, the lucky ones wind up in the cooler. The unlucky ones . . ." He smiled, drawing a finger across his neck.

"That'll be enough, Sid. Black Venus is our guest and will be treated accordingly. Keep your ghoulish comments to yourself." Anderson glanced over his shoulder at Mary and shook his head. "You can take the boy out of the Bronx and all that."

"I don't understand something, Anderson. I can tell you're a native of Germany, despite your manners and accent, but Sid? What's in this for you?"

The thin man didn't bother looking back, but she could imagine the look in his eyes. "It's simple, chickie. Cash. Lots and lots of cash. Being American didn't do squat for me. Growing up on the wrong side of the city, I got kicked around a lot. So, I decided the way not to get kicked was to have enough money to kick back. And believe me, this is funding a whole lot of future kicking."

If you live long enough to collect, Sid. Mary thought wryly. *Anderson doesn't seem the type to leave loose ends lying around.*

Anderson pulled up in front of a one-story building. "You'll be staying here. There will be men outside the main doors, so please try to limit your urges for nocturnal strolls. Also, Sophie and Melanie will assist you in getting settled. *Please* do not assault them or try to turn them to your side. They're both wanted criminals back in France as collaborationists. They agreed they'd rather take their chances here than hang. In fact, I think you and Melanie will get along famously."

Sid snickered as Mary let herself be hustled out of the jeep and into the house without a fuss. Still puzzling over Anderson's comments, she stepped inside and noted a living room that wouldn't have been out of place in Paris or New York. A tall, blond woman came in through a door leading farther into the building. "Ah, it's you," she said to Anderson before pausing and doing a double take at Mary. The hard look snapped back onto her face before she spoke again. "I see you have someone new. Is she going to be joining us?"

"Temporarily. I'd introduce her to you, but I don't know her real name. She used the name Mary Roche when I knew her back in the States, but it's probably an alias. During the war, she was known as Black Venus. Supposed to have been quite the terror to our Japanese allies." He turned to Mary and waved his hand toward the other woman. "This is Sophie."

Sophie's gaze took Mary in and then she sniffed and flopped into a chair, affecting a bored air. "She doesn't look all that terrifying to me. Perhaps they just spook easier."

Anderson chuckled. "Don't let looks fool you, *chéri*. She's more dangerous than she looks. Where's Melanie?"

"Changing. Those Americans may not enjoy working for you, but they enjoy our shows. That helps keep them calmed down. The rest of the gals are down at the cabaret getting ready for tonight's performance."

Anderson chuckled again. "You see, my dear Black Venus, we're not complete barbarians here. And it wouldn't be a trip to France—or in this case, French Guiana—without a floor show in a cabaret." The door opened behind them and one of the workers tossed her bags inside before shutting the door again. "Your bags have arrived. I'm sure Sophie can show you to a place to clean up and rest. Your room will be ready in a few hours. Who knows, perhaps you'd enjoy performing for your countrymen some evening?"

With that, he turned and walked out the door, chuckling to a private joke. Once the door shut and the jeep started up again, Sophie's bored expression fell away, and righteous anger replaced it. "That *pig*. One of these days I'm going to find him alone and he'll be wearing his intestines on the outside."

Mary took a step back at the vehemence of Sophie's reaction. She decided to take a chance speaking in French to the upset woman. "He said you'd come willingly. I take it he may have stretched the truth just a bit?"

Sophie stopped, eyeing Mary with new suspicion. "You have a Parisian accent. You are not American?"

"I am, but I lived in Paris for five years. I was a dancer at a club in Montparnasse until the German occupation. I managed to get to Spain and from there to the United States one step ahead of the Gestapo."

Sophie sniffed at her in derision. "And what interest would the Gestapo have for an American dancer . . . even for one as beautiful as yourself?"

Mary smiled at Sophie before continuing. "They were trying to collect me as a favor to a certain Japanese officer who had an unhealthy interest in me. I'm happy to say he died most horribly for his emperor during the war."

Sophie relaxed just a bit and then rose from her chair. "So, you worked in the fancy joints. I too was a dancer, but in Montmartre. When the occupation happened, one could continue dancing, or one could starve. I do not look good as a skeleton, but certain of my countrymen did not see it the same way. Melanie arranged a way for us to flee the country, but as you can see, we didn't flee too far. Oh well, if you're joining us, you might as well have a drink." She moved to the other side of the room and opened a cabinet, pulling out a bottle of wine, uncorked it and poured three glasses. Before Mary could ask, she tipped her head in the direction of the door she'd come through. "Melanie will want one too, although she does not share my opinion of Anderson. She and he were quite chummy before and during the war."

Almost as if on cue, the door Sophie had indicated swung open, and Melanie came through. Mary had to stop her jaw from falling open. Now she understood Sophie's surprise because looking at Melanie was almost like looking in a mirror down to their hairstyle.

After a few seconds, Melanie found her voice first. "*Mon dieu,* am I seeing a ghost?"

Mary replied, "I was about to ask the same question."

"Sophie, who is this person?"

"An American who'll be staying with us for a while. She's called the Black—"

"The Black Venus." A light of recognition flashed in Melanie's eyes. "Of course, I saw your act in Paris before the war. Your face is a little older, but then again, we all are." Melanie laughed harshly before continuing. "Now it all makes sense. I was wondering why Oliver was insisting on my flying lessons. Oh, this will be a grand joke on the Americans."

Alarm bells were going off in Mary's head at that comment. "You're learning to fly?"

"Yes, I have flying lessons every afternoon. It's rather comical; it's such an old-fashioned plane. I'd rather learn how to fly one of those new jets, but Oliver insists this is important. Plus, learning to fire the weapons is boring. Who wants to shoot up a bunch of trees and such?"

Who indeed?

Sophie motioned for Mary to follow. "I guess I should show you to a room you can use. I'll be back a bit, Melanie. Don't drink all the wine before I get back."

"I have to leave in a bit for my lessons. I'll have my share of the wine after I get back," Melanie called as the two women stepped through the door into a narrow hall leading back into the interior of the building.

"I swear, she gets worse every day. Anderson has her wrapped around his fingers with his promises of fine furs and jewelry." She stopped and spun around, pointing in all directions as she turned. "As if it would do us any good. Where could we show them off here in the middle of nowhere?"

"Where exactly are we?"

"Somewhere near the border with Brazil. From what I've heard, Oliver has contacts in Venezuela and Brazil who're seeking additional sites for cauldrons."

"Someone's got some serious money to spend it on carving airfields out of the jungle."

Sophie shrugged. "I eat, I sleep, and I dance. I stay out of politics—that's what got me stuck in the jungle in the first place. Someday I hope to get out of here and go somewhere like America, but it's not going to happen anytime soon, so I keep a *very* low profile. If *you* want to stay healthy, I'd do the same."

Sophie stopped in front of a door and motioned for Mary to proceed. "I don't know why you're here, but I don't think Oliver intends for you to ever leave. Still, I hope you find a way to escape, and I hope it hurts him a *lot* when you do."

Around dark, the jeep pulled up in front of the house and Sid walked in. "Yo, Black Venus, time to go."

She noticed he didn't bother picking up her suitcases, so she grabbed them and trudged outside. The sight of the two guards with their submachine guns convinced her not to smack Sid with one of them and he placed them in the back of the jeep. The two guards climbed in, and Sid drove out of the compound back to the staff area. She noticed the windows to her cottage were all sporting brand-new steel bars. Sid paused the jeep just long enough for the guards and Mary to pile out and grab her bags before he roared off. The guards took up positions on either side of her door and locked it behind her after she entered.

She gave the cottage the once-over, but they had done a good job converting it into a very comfortable jail. She walked into the bedroom and pulled the shades back to look at the sliver of the waxing moon rising over the jungle canopy. She felt something on her arm and brushed it off without thinking. To her surprise, she spotted a faint dusting of sawdust on the ground. Glancing upward, she noticed more sawdust falling from the ceiling and realized the shade had hidden the work of ants chewing at the wood above the window.

She went through the effort to unpack her bags and made the general noises of someone getting ready for bed. After a couple of hours, she crept to one of the windows and noticed only one guard there and he was sitting in a chair leaned back against the wall. She slipped back into the bedroom and worked one of the slats out of her bed. Taking one edge, she dug at the wall where the sawdust had come from. As she had hoped, the ants had chewed through a large portion of the wall right above the window. Pausing every so often to ensure no one was coming to investigate the sound of her exertions, she carved a deep groove around the window. After a while, she started seeing the ends of the bolts holding this window's bars in place and stopped. She carefully swept up the debris and disposed of it and arranged the shade to cover her handiwork.

As she slid into bed, a plan began forming in her head and a smile settled on her face.

The next day, she sent word to Anderson requesting permission to take a walk with her guard escorting her. To her surprise, he not only agreed, but a few hours later showed up at her door volunteering to escort her himself.

"Ah, it is so nice to have someone new to show the camp. Most new arrivals never see this side of the fence . . . not that they have any business here outside of visiting the interrogation station."

They made small talk as they walked around the camp and Mary silently noted what had to be the radio shack as well as the armory. She also noticed one building toward the center that had guards stationed by the front door. Mary did her best to ensure Anderson's attention was focused on her, which to her surprise she found an easy task.

"I noticed Melanie and I share a marked resemblance."

Anderson nodded absently. "I noticed it back in the States when you first visited the office. It was all I could do not to mention it, but then again, I thought I'd never see you after we hustled you out."

"Yes, I believe Sid's job was to see to that."

He chuckled nervously. "Well, I've had time to reconsider, I'm glad he failed. Still, I'm certain it was quite a shock when you saw her."

"And to her too. Still, she seems rather fond of you."

"She's been a good companion, and she has a major part coming up to ensure our future success."

Mary decided to take advantage of the opening. "This is an awfully large project. Just what exactly do you have going on here?"

"Oh, no, my dear, you'll not catch me monologuing. Let's just say this is only one part of the plan. A major part, but simply one part."

"Can't blame a girl for trying."

"True, however, the Triumvirate takes a very dim view of sharing secrets, even if you know the recipient is not long for this world."

Mary gave him a coy look and lowered her voice to a slightly lower register. "Perhaps I could be more useful to you than Melanie."

He stumbled and then took her by the arm. "Perhaps we have walked enough. I think you should return to your quarters. Tomorrow, I'll have someone else assigned to your walk."

"As you wish, Oliver."

He turned beet red and picked up his pace. Mary mentally smiled at cracking his resolve and the fact that at least she had a name for Anderson's bosses, although who or what the Triumvirate was still needed to be discovered.

After her dinner dishes had been collected, she made a big show of turning in early and put out the lights. Once her guard had settled in for another night's snooze by her door, she retrieved her Black Venus costume and slipped it on, then went back to work on her bedroom window, carefully exposing the bolts and worked the bottom and side ones out. Leaving the top ones to hold the bars, she pushed hard and managed to get the bars to slide away at the bottom of the window just enough to slip through. She put the bolts back in their holes to make it look secure and then slipped into the darkness.

Her first stop was the main building in the middle. While the guards were still on duty, there was no sign of anyone in the building. She found a drainpipe and was pleasantly surprised it was securely attached to the building. She eased up to the second floor and worked a window open. Slipping through, she immediately wished she had her flashlight. Still, there was only one thing she was looking for, and it would likely be on a wall.

She slipped into the hall and began searching room after room until she found what appeared to be an operations room. The faint moonlight filtering into the room gave her just enough light to see the large map on one wall. She managed to work it loose and carried it over near the window. Squinting against the dim moonlight, she finally found the Cauldron marked on the map along with notes for additional ones to be established in the near future. She jotted down as much information as she could and then replaced the map.

Working her way back down the drainpipe, she noticed the activity in the camp had picked up a bit. Mary crept close to a couple of guards to see what was going on. She heard jeeps approaching and barely moved into the shadows before the headlights shone on the spot where she was. She watched a squad of men jump out of the jeeps and rush up to the entrance.

One of the guards saluted as the squad rushed past. "What's the situation?"

The squad leader stopped and snapped at the two guards. "The silent alarm went off inside the building you're supposed to be guarding. Has anyone come near this building?"

The two guards looked at each other and then back to the leader. "No one has come by this building since we came on duty. Nothing could have gotten past us."

The squad leader ran a hand down his face and then rushed past them to go inside.

Mary headed toward the radio shack. *I was going to wait and to send a message tomorrow night, but with this commotion, I might not get another chance. Here goes nothing.*

There was a guard by the door of the shack, but she found a window he couldn't keep an eye on. Pulling a small piece of flexible metal out of the heel of her boot, she used it to unlock the window, then carefully eased it up. There was just enough light to keep from tripping over anything, and she soon found the radio transmitter. She turned it on and waited impatiently while the tubes warmed up, then set the frequency to one she'd gotten from Solly.

Trying to tap out the message as quietly as she could, she sent the coordinates of the Cauldron and a brief message instructing Solly what she had planned three times, praying to anyone who wanted to listen that Solly or someone at the embassy was monitoring the frequency, then turned the set off and reset the frequency to the original setting.

She hurried back to her quarters and eased inside, switching from her uniform to her nightclothes when just moments later there was a pounding at her door. She made her way through the darkened house to the door. "Who's there?"

"Oliver. Just checking if you're safe."

"Good heavens, is something going on? Is the guard missing? Why wouldn't I be safe?"

There was a quick discussion in German outside her door as Oliver questioned the guard about his and her activities for the night. Seemingly satisfied with the guard's response, Oliver switched back to English. "There was a false alarm in the camp. Nothing to worry about."

"As you wish, Oliver. After all, my safety is in your hands," she said in her most coquettish voice.

She couldn't see him, but his strangled response told her he was blushing to his roots. "Ah, yes, very well. We'll speak to you at a more reasonable time of the day. Have a good night, Mary."

It was all she could do not to laugh as she returned to her bedroom. She went through her bag and sacrificed one of her outfits to push enough cloth into the grooves she'd dug to help hold the bolts in place. She knew it'd never survive a real inspection, but all it needed to do was not fall out for one more day.

One way or the other, this will be resolved tomorrow. All I can do is hope Solly got my message or it's going to be a very long day.

Around noon, Mary sent word to Oliver that she'd like to go visit Melanie and Sophie. It took some cajoling, but after a bit, Oliver relented. Mary noted he almost seemed relieved to see her go into the compound. Sophie answered the knock on the door.

"Didn't expect to see you back so soon."

"I thought since you're the only two other women I know at this base, we might as well hang out together. By the way, where's Melanie?"

Sophie pointed over her shoulder toward the bedrooms. "Her highness? Still sleeping in. Seems Oliver and she had a fight last night. She took several sleeping pills to calm down. Honestly, I'm not sure she's going to make her flight training today."

"Really?"

"Uh-oh, I recognize that look. Do you know what's going on?"

Mary took a deep breath and answered. "I'm thinking Oliver has a wandering eye. The fact I look like Melanie is why he hasn't had me killed yet. But if they're fighting, I'm afraid I'm the one who's going to get caught in the middle."

"Yeah, let's just say Melanie is a sore loser. There was this one native girl that Oliver was attentive toward. They found parts of her in the jungle. The official word is a wild animal killed her. I tend to agree," she said, pointing toward the bedrooms again.

Mary nodded. "Look, Sophie, were you serious about wanting to go to the States?"

Sophie's head shot up and her eyes narrowed. "Why would you ask me such an impossible question?"

"Just answer—were you serious?"

"Sure, for all the good it'll do us. We'll never leave this camp. Melanie might, if she doesn't ruin things between Oliver and her, but we're stuck here for the rest of our lives."

"Isn't Melanie's flight lesson coming up soon?"

"Yeah . . ."

"How are you at makeup?"

"*Cherie*, I've been in the theater since I was old enough to go on stage. What do you have in mind?"

"What if "Melanie' makes her lesson?"

Sophie's eyes grew wide. "*You* want to take her place? *Mon dieu*, but Melanie is a beginner and you . . . well, you are *the* Black Venus. You'll be discovered in an instant if you go up in the air, unless you can fool them into thinking you're a neophyte.

"There's only one way to find out. Can you get Melanie to take one more sleeping pill just to be certain she doesn't get up too soon?"

Sophie's sharklike grin told Mary all she needed to know.

An hour later, there was a knock on the door and then Sid's voice came through the door. "Hey, Melanie, it's time for me to take you to the airstrip. Those Americans may not be good for much, but they finally got that new flight line done last night. You can see how you like it."

"One minute!"

"Oh, God. I know how long one minute can be for you. Come on! Hauptmann Becker doesn't like to be kept waiting."

The door swung open, and Mary stepped outside dressed in her Black Venus uniform. Sid's eyes narrowed and he growled, "What's the big idea?"

"It was Oliver's idea. He wants to use me as a faux Black Venus, so I thought I'd try the uniform today. Do I look right? After all, he says you've seen her in her outfit."

A leering smile crossed Sid's lips. "Oh yeah, that outfit looks *real* good on you. You even fill it out better than the real Black Venus. No question the cameras are going to love you dressed up like that . . . especially when we film you shooting all those ex-G.I.s when we're done with them. Just think, Black Venus caught on film as a traitor. That'll cast suspicion on all those costumed freaks back in the States. Anything that helps the big bosses' plans is dope in my books."

Mary kept the same smile on her face that she'd greeted Sid with, but inside she just wanted to punch his leering face into oblivion. Not only were they planning to massacre the veterans, but they were going to frame her for it. She'd suspected they intended for Melanie to replace her for propaganda purposes, but nothing this heinous. She moved around and slipped into the seat next to Sid. She wanted to question him further but didn't know how much Melanie knew and didn't want to raise suspicions.

A few minutes later, they pulled up to a hanger next to the

newly completed airfield. Sid jumped out and headed toward the hangar doors. As Mary approached, the doors rose and sitting there was a gleaming black P-38 Lockheed Lightning. It was all she could do not to do a double take. Moving closer, she realized this was not her plane. It was too new, too pristine. Even the best mechanics can't buff out real battle damage.

A man in a Luftwaffe flight suit came out of the hanger and moved to meet them. As soon as he took off his goggles and helmet, Mary recognized him instantly. He was Joe Baker, the medic she'd met at Sheila's hit-and-run. Suddenly, the pieces fell completely into place.

Sid spoke up. "Hey, *Hauptmann* Becker. Here's Melanie, ready for her lessons."

"Sehr gut." He turned to Mary. "Interesting choice of costume."

"Oliver said I should get used to flying in it."

Becker gaze roved over the tight-fitting leather suit and nodded in approval. "Good, you look enough like that American flyer, I wasn't sure who Sid was bringing to me. Do you remember what all we went over yesterday?"

Mary raised a hand to her head. "It was *not* a good night, last night. Could you give me a quick review? I don't want to have to try and remember if you're expecting me to concentrate once we get into the air."

The German captain and Sid exchanged looks and then Becker gave her a recap of the lessons. Mary was relieved to see Melanie was soloing now, so she wouldn't have to dumb down her flying skills like she would with a trainer in the cockpit with her. After he had gone on a while, Mary held up her hand. "That's enough. I remember now. What are we going to do today, and please don't say just shooting at trees again. Isn't there something more exciting to do in the air?"

Becker's expression changed to a nasty-looking smile. "Might as well see if the princess here has the guts for what Anderson has planned. Get a few volunteers and take them to the clearing in a half hour." He then turned and barked orders at the other men in the hanger to load Melanie's plane with a full load of ammo and some bombs. Mary followed him into the hangar and began giving the plane a visual inspection. She wouldn't know how it handled until she had it airborne, but it felt familiar enough.

Becker came over and gave her a puzzled look. "You do not seem happy to see me today, Melanie. Another fight with Oliver?"

"A beastly one. I think that new girl is going to have to have a little accident one of these days. Oliver is getting too enamored with her."

Becker moved closer and dropped his voice so the mechanic loading the 20mm shells into the P-38 couldn't hear them. "I thought you wanted him to let you go on his own accord so we could be together? Have your feelings for me changed?"

"It has to feel like it was his idea. I can't make it too obvious. He's a jealous beast and I'm afraid what he might do to you if he suspects."

Becker smiled warmly at her. "Beauty and brains. I never had a chance against you."

Mary swallowed some bile and smiled back at him. "Never. And you never will. Now, let's get this lesson started before some of Oliver's toadies get ideas."

Becker nodded and climbed into his Messerschmitt Bf 109. Mary waited until her mechanic gave her the thumbs-up and then climbed into the cockpit. She went through her own mental checklist to ensure everything was working and then hit the ignition. First one engine and then the other turned over and she could feel the plane trying to inch forward as if as anxious to rise into the blue sky as Mary was. She adjusted her goggles and followed her mechanic's signals as she taxied out of the hanger and into place behind *Hauptmann* Becker's plane.

"Now remember, follow my lead and try to do everything I do."

"Roger."

There was a short pause and then Mary noticed a curious change in Becker's tone of voice. *"Are you feeling all right today, Melanie?"*

"Just trying to get into character. The Americans at the base seem fond of that phrase. If someone were to overhear my radio signals, I want to sound as American as possible."

There was a chuckle over the radio. *"As I said, 'brains* and *beauty.' All right, follow me and we'll do some slow warm-ups before we try anything new."*

Mary congratulated herself for getting out of that and decided to keep all radio communications to a bare minimum until her own plan was ready. She concentrated on getting her craft into the air and doing only what Becker did or advised her to do over the radio while she got the feel of the airplane. She noted it wasn't balanced quite the same as hers, but it was easy enough to compensate for.

After a few minutes of doing drills and slow loops and circles, Becker's voice came over the radio. *"That's enough warm-up. We'll practice climbs and dives today. We'll go up high enough to not have to worry about the canopy below. Stay on my tail and try to do everything I do."*

"I'll do my best."

"I'm sure you'll do fine. Here we go."

Initially, Becker took her through some basic maneuvers, but as the lesson went along, Mary noticed he was starting to do more advanced techniques. She did her best to look like she was trying to follow along but made sure to make mistakes here and there. She was certain the *hauptmann* was questioning her flying technique and was testing to see what was going on. Not for the first time did she wish she knew just how much Melanie knew or didn't know about flying.

"You're doing well. We'll review some of your mistakes when we land. I received the signal from Sid. Your more interesting *targets have been set up for you. We'll go to the target range now."*

Mary fell in behind Becker's plane again as he sped off to the north. She spotted a clearing several miles from the camp and noticed Becker was waggling his wings. She sped up to draw near to his plane.

"You'll take the lead. We're going to fly low, just barely above the treetops. As you reach the clearing ahead, find your targets in your sights and open up with your machine guns. On the second pass, we'll test out your cannon, and if there's anything left, we'll

drop those bombs you're carrying. There's no one around here for miles, so there's no way we'll expose ourselves."

Mary waved a hand in acknowledgment and Becker dropped into a trail position. Mary wasn't sure what they had set up, but some of the excitement she'd always felt getting ready for combat came back—the tightness in her stomach, the slightly shorter breaths. It was almost as if she and the airplane were becoming one.

She swept down to treetop level and mentally started counting down until her plane cleared the green foliage beneath her. Becker stayed right on her tail as she rushed toward the clearing. Her fingers were tightening on the trigger when she finally saw the target—twenty men tied to stakes in the middle of the field. She pulled her nose up slightly and fired, her rounds skimming harmlessly over their heads. She banked quickly to the left as a series of tracers forced her to turn back to the right. Becker's mocking voice came over her radio as she avoided the fire from the plane that seemed glued to her tail.

"No, no, Melanie. Those are your targets. We weren't sure you could shoot unarmed men, but Oliver convinced me you were the woman for the job. So, you're going to learn how to get your hands dirty now. So, either you swing back around and actually aim at your targets or I'm going to regretfully blow you out of the sky."

Mary decided it was time to end the charade. "Sorry, Joe, but I think you'll find shooting me out of the sky harder than shoving an innocent woman in front of a car."

Before Becker could process what she'd just said, she kicked her rudder and did a quick roll to the left, breaking away from the trailing Messerschmitt. She jerked the nose of the P-38 hard to get some air to maneuver in. However, she quickly realized *Hauptmann* Becker hadn't gotten his rank from a box of Cracker Jacks. A neat line of bullet holes appeared in one of her wings, narrowly missing her right engine.

The two planes roared over the clearing and Mary glanced down to see people moving up to shoot the tied-up men. Momentarily ignoring the bullets flying around her plane, she nosed down into a dive. Leveling off near the clearing, she lined up the would-be assassins and opened up with the four .50-caliber machine guns in her plane's nose. A few tried to return fire, but they disappeared in a cloud of dust as the bullets ripped through their midst. The survivors piled into a jeep and tore off into the thick jungle as she lined up for a second pass. She snapped off a shot at the retreating vehicle and some of her rounds ripped into one of the trucks at the edge of the field, hitting the gas tank. The truck exploded as she passed over it, buffeting her plane just enough to keep Becker's next burst from finding it.

I'd better deal with him first, or there won't be anyone left to help those men.

She whipped her P-38 through a series of maneuvers, and while Becker couldn't get a clear shot at her, he hung onto her tail like a bulldog with a hambone. The only advantage she had was unfamiliarity. He knew how Melanie flew, not her. She had to hope that he'd expect her to react like he'd trained Melanie. Unlike the Japanese pilots she'd faced, she doubted rumors of Black Venus's flying skills had made it back to Europe.

After narrowly dodging another burst from his machine guns, Mary did a loop into a dive that she knew a rookie wouldn't make. However, Becker seemed to take the bait and followed her down toward the deck. She could feel him lining himself up for the kill when she slammed her flaps up, which brought her nose up sharply and cut her airspeed almost to stalling speed. Before Becker could react, he'd shot past and she leveled off and fired a full five-second burst into his tail section. Pieces of his plane flew off as her rounds chewed into it.

He tried to juke away, but Mary knew she had to take advantage of this momentary opportunity. She lined up her shot and opened up with both the machine guns and her nose cannon. Becker's plane seemed to halt in midair for a split second before bursting into flames. She watched as the Messerschmitt tried to right itself, but it dove into the jungle canopy and exploded when it hit a tree at high speed.

She swung back around to the clearing and landed near the bound men. Climbing down off the wing, she rushed over to the first one and cut his hands free.

"Black Venus? What are you doing here?"

"Right now, I'd say I'm getting ready to make a whole bunch of faux-Nazis very unhappy. Are you all right?"

"I didn't think we were going to be when you popped over that tree line. Thank goodness you missed us. But you've got one thing wrong. Those aren't pretenders. They're the real thing—leftovers from the war. Some guy named Mueller is the big boss, but that Anderson guy and that French radical, LaFleur, handle the day-to-day stuff. I heard a few of the guards talking about it when they didn't think I was listening. There's something big coming down the pike. I mean, you don't just build a place like this without some serious cash and influence."

"You have a point there. Can you free the rest of your men here?"

"Sure, but what good's it going to do? We're outside the fence but we have no clue where we are."

"One of those trucks looks like it's still drivable. You're about a half hour's drive north of the camp. Head that direction and wait in the woods nearby. I think there's about to be some changes in ownership. No time to explain further. They're going to notice I'm overdue if I don't get airborne soon."

The fact she would be returning alone would probably set off enough alarms, but there was no sense in worrying the captives about it. She hadn't heard Becker calling back to the base, so at least no one *should* be immediately suspicious.

She climbed back into her cockpit and took a close look at the clearing. It was going to be tight getting out of here, she'd taken off on shorter runways before. Once a few more of the prisoners had been freed, they helped her maneuver her plane to one end of the clearing and then backed away as she revved her engines as high as she could. The plane shot across the bumpy clearing and climbed into the Guianan sky like an overladen duck. The wall of trees at the other end was closing fast, but she did everything but climb out of the plane and push it higher into the sky. Still, her undercarriage and landing gear sheared off a few feet of branches as she skimmed over the trees and fought her way into the sky.

Whew. I hope I don't have to make a hard landing when this is all over. I'm not going to be comfortable until I get this thing on solid ground again. A feral feeling like a big cat getting ready to pounce on its prey settled in over her. It was a feeling she hadn't had since she had returned from the Pacific. *I don't know who Anderson is really, and I don't know anything about the Triumvirate other than its name, but I'm going to do my best to turn that camp into sawdust. I hope the Triumvirate took out a good insurance policy on it, because they're about to collect.*

The P-38 screamed its way south, hugging the treetops. Mary kept checking her watch and tuned her cockpit radio to Solly's frequency, wondering if the message she'd sent out the other night had been received. She knew she could do a lot of damage, but it was an awfully big camp, and this was only one airplane. What worried her the most was knowing there had to be air defenses there too. Still, no point in worrying about it now. She'd done everything she could. All that was left was to play out the hand.

Approaching the base, she slowed down slightly to not arouse more suspicion than necessary. She lined up on the rows of hangars and then at the last second hit the bomb release. The explosive eggs she released found their homes among the hangars. A savage grin spread on her face as she saw the secondary explosions going off after her bombs hit. People scrambled away from the buildings, heading toward hidden gun emplacements, and she came in low, spreading machine-gun fire at the weapons before the men could reach them. She didn't know how many she'd hit but she knew she'd set off some of their ammo.

Tracers reached out from other parts of the base like angry hornets. She did a hard left turn and spotted what might be an ammo dump. She rolled to avoid fire coming from one of the zeppelins and dropped her last two bombs. She didn't know for certain what she'd hit, but her plane bucked beneath her as the shock wave went out in all directions. Fighting the controls to get her plane level, she found she'd drifted almost to the edge of the camp. Pointing her nose north, she shoved her stick forward and dove toward the staff camp just beyond. Black puffs began rising out of the jungle around the camp and she could feel the reverberation from the flak going off near her plane. Luckily, most of it had been set for higher altitudes, but it wouldn't take them long to adjust it.

She spotted the radio shack and the antenna and feathered the trigger for her 20mm cannon. The plane shook from the recoil, but the large rounds slammed into the shack and the tower. Two passes later, the tower gave up the fight and with a shriek of metal collapsed into the middle of the small village. Men were running around firing a variety of small arms into the air, but it was the antiaircraft positions that worried her the most.

A burst from some flak shook her plane hard and it began to sluggishly respond to the controls. She managed to get it back under control and headed back toward the camp. Now, the guard towers were firing at her along with the antiaircraft guns. She swept down toward the two nearest the main gates and let loose with all her weapons. Several men slid down the ladders to the ground below, but she wasn't worried about them. One of the zeppelins had slipped its mooring and moved toward the center of the base, its weapons trying to bracket her.

Her craft shuddered from hits and black smoke erupted from her left engine. She double-checked her parachute and then did a sweeping turn back toward the main gates. She climbed to bare minimum altitude to jump and then lined her crippled bird up on the gates. Sliding the canopy back, Mary inched out onto the wing before launching herself into space. The doomed ship traveled like an arrow, slamming into the fences at over three hundred miles an hour, before exploding in a cataclysm of fire and molten metal.

The white canopy barely had time to catch air and slow her descent before the ground reached up to meet her. It wasn't her most graceful landing, but besides an assortment of bruises and bumps, she was still alive and mobile. A burst of machine-gun fire ripped up the ground near her, and she knew she had to get moving if she wanted to stay that way.

She rolled to the side and then rushed toward the center of the camp. She was hoping to lose herself among the chaos. An explosion from the ammo dump knocked her to the ground, but she recovered quickly. Spotting Melanie and Sophie's quarters, she remembered her own civilian clothes were there. The quicker she got out of her black flying suit, the harder it'd be to identify her as the one who'd bombed the base.

She burst through the door to find Sophie hiding behind a couch, her eyes wide with fright. "What is going on out there?"

"There may have been a small accident at the ammo dump. Something about a bomb going off there. Quick, I need to change clothes."

Sophie just pointed toward the door and crouched down as another explosion rocked the base. Mary hurried through the house and stripped out of her flight suit and into her regular clothes. She thought about hiding the suit inside her purse, but a quick glance told her Melanie was somehow still sleeping through all the ruckus. She hid the suit underneath Melanie's bed and then joined Sophie in the living area.

"*Mon dieu*, Mary. What is going to happen?"

"I don't know for certain, Sophie. I was expecting something to happen by now myself. It appears the cavalry is late."

"Cavalry?"

"I'll explain later."

Between explosions, she heard a vehicle pull up and a few moments later, Anderson and Sid came rushing in. Sid was nursing a bandage on his side, but it seemed he'd avoided the worst of Mary's strafing run.

Sophie rose from behind the couch. "What is going on, Oliver?"

"Where is Melanie?" Oliver shouted as Sid pulled a nasty-looking automatic out of a holster.

"Back in her room."

Oliver burst through the door and headed into the interior. Mary started to follow, but Sid stepped in front of her. "The boss doesn't want to be disturbed. I think it would be healthier for the two of you to grab a seat right over there."

Mary and Sophie moved in the direction he indicated with his automatic as Sid stood guard by the door. The two women could hear shouting and the sound of a body slamming against a wall. Mary knew she needed to do something but wasn't sure what she could do with Sid watching them so closely.

"That's it, I need a drink," Sophie said as the cries and shouting grew in intensity. She walked over to the liquor cabinet before Sid could say anything. Setting a bottle down in front of Mary after pouring herself a drink, she turned and glanced over Sid's shoulder. "Oh my God!"

Sid instinctively turned. Mary grabbed the bottle of wine and brought it down on top of Sid's head. She didn't know if she'd killed him or simply knocked him out, but there was no time to check. Mary rushed into Melanie's room and realized Anderson had found the flight suit and was trying to use it to strangle Melanie. Mary launched the wine bottle but only caught Anderson on the shoulder with it. He dropped the now-unconscious Melanie and turned, his face flushed with rage and his eyes almost unseeing.

"You. I knew I should have killed you as soon as you dropped into our laps. Now I see. Melanie didn't have anything to do with this. This was you . . . all you."

"So, what are you going to do about it, fatso?"

With an inarticulate scream, Anderson was on her like a man possessed. He slammed into her and drove her into the wall across the hall. Mary knew she was in for the fight of her life because no matter how hard or where she hit him, nothing seemed to have any effect. He saw everything he'd been building disappearing, and it was as if his mind had snapped. They rolled onto the floor and Mary managed to get her legs underneath him and shoved upward as hard as she could, throwing him back down the hallway.

He looked at her with hate-filled eyes, his mouth foaming in his frenzy. "That's not going to stop me. Nothing is going to stop me, do you understand? I don't care if I have to kidnap and kill thousands of your ex-soldiers. They're stupid and easy to lure down here. But you won't be around to see the new Cauldron I build from these ruins. The Triumvirate will recognize my brilliance. I cannot be stopped."

There was a sudden sharp report and Anderson's gaze dropped to the spreading red spot on his chest before falling forward on his face. Standing behind him, a pale-white Sophie stood holding Sid's gun, smoke curling from the barrel. Before Mary could move, Sophie slumped to the floor. Mary rushed over to her, but she had only fainted.

The sound of heavy engines caught Mary's attention. She rushed to the window to see a squadron of Spitfires, Airacobras, and Mustangs sweeping over the base, attacking the antiaircraft positions while the sky filled with white parachutes coming from transports passing overhead. And leading the fighters was a black P-38. Mary grabbed a mirror from Melanie's bedroom and rushed outside. After using the mirror to signal overhead, the black craft came circling down near the barracks and Mary rushed out to meet it.

"Took you long enough, Solly."

"You have no clue what it took to get this much cooperation with the French government this fast, much less talk the air jockeys into letting me lead this expedition. It took some doing but they let us coordinate with a British squadron over in Georgetown or we might not have gotten here at all. You're just lucky we caught your signal last night."

"I know. Now, you go secure that building there while I commandeer your plane. I've never gone balloon busting before, and I don't want that zeppelin to get away."

By nightfall, the last pockets of resistance had crumbled, and the French soldiers were escorting the captured soldiers from the camp and interning their former guards inside the compound. Mary, Sophie, Solly, and Colonel Allard of the French Air Force were sitting in the bullet-pocked operations building.

Colonel Allard looked at the smoking ruins of the camp,

shaking his head. "This is amazing. To think they were building a military camp on French soil, especially a camp run by former Nazis, to be used against us and no one had spotted it. How did you ever discover it?"

"I don't think you can call them 'former,' Colonel. From just a quick review of these records, many of these men escaped in the confusion right at the end of the war. Someone or some organization made sure they slipped through our fingers, but for what purpose? It's going to take some digging to discover the truth there," Solly said, shaking his head in disgust.

Mary chimed in. "Several people have mentioned something called the Triumvirate. I don't know if that means three people or three organizations, but it's something to start with."

"Oh, you'll be happy to know that Le Fleur and Bigelow were captured when we raided the warehouses in Cayenne. I understand the French Navy has taken control of the *Porto de Oro*. Captain LeBeou has a lot to answer for and apparently there are many inhabitants in Sainte-Georges who're more than happy to speak up now."

"That's great, but I didn't hear a specific name mentioned yet."

"Emil Muller? Somehow that guy managed to slip out of Cayenne seconds before we raided the place. But, don't worry, we're putting the word out with all the neighboring countries. If he raises his ugly head, I'll be there to chop it off."

Mary suspected she hadn't heard the last of Emil Muller, but the colonel spoke up just then. "It'll take a while to go through all the documents we've discovered here." He paused, waving his hand around the debris-strewn room. "Once we get the radio tower that your friend here knocked down operational"—he pointed to Mary—"we'll get word back to Cayenne and then by cable to Paris. I think there will be some very interested people."

Solly moved in front of the colonel. "And, as always, America stands by to assist France. We are certainly willing to send experts down here to assist with the cataloging and research."

"Yes, yes, I'm certain whatever is going on here is not just isolated to French Guiana. This is going to take a concerted effort to get to the bottom of this."

There was a soft noise in the hall and while Solly and the colonel danced around the diplomatic niceties, Mary excused herself and headed toward the door. Stepping into the hall, she saw a shadowy figure moving up the stairs, so she eased down the hall and went up the stairs herself. Reaching the next landing, she saw the figure standing by an open window.

Before Mary could do anything, the figure spoke to her. "It is going to take a concerted effort, but not just by governments."

"Just who the hell are you?"

"We've never met, but I think you've heard of me, just like I've heard of you, Black Venus." The figure turned a flashlight on herself, to reveal a blond masked woman wearing a red, white, and blue costume. "I'm Miss Victory. I'm recruiting a team to take on the Triumvirate." The heroine stepped forward to hand her a card. "If you're interested, when you get back to the States come to this address. We don't have much time to get organized, so I'm going to need a yes or a no."

Mary smiled. "If you need a pilot, I'm your girl."

Miss Victory smiled back before snapping off the light and a second later, Mary knew she was alone. She made her way downstairs, wondering how she was going to explain this upcoming absence to her boss back at Veterans Affairs. Then again, Tom was an understanding guy. He had to be to employ Black Venus, after all.

MISS ESPIONAGE

SHADOWS OF THE PAST

It was another busy day at the War Department. The room buzzed with the sound of muted conversations and typewriters clacking like dozens of other postwar offices in Washington, D.C. A dozen young women sat in neat rows going through stacks of papers, taking down information and transferring it to files for research later.

The sudden sound of a phone ringing broke the monotonous clicking of keys. The lady sitting closest to it rose quickly and picked up the receiver. "Petroleum Department, Miss Reed speaking."

Gabrielle DuMond brushed her brunette hair out of her eyes and glanced up to see that Lucy had answered the office phone. Her friend got a strange look on her face and then turned toward Gabrielle.

"Gabrielle? There's a phone call for you."

Gabrielle looked up from the notes and smiled at her coworker. "For me?"

The young woman smiled at her and then pointed over her shoulder at the door at the end of the room. "Don't be on too long. Mr. Harris doesn't like us taking personal calls at work."

Gabrielle winked conspiratorially and walked over to the phone. "Gabrielle DuMond. May I help you?"

"Your car has a stuck carburetor. You'll need to come to the garage so we can discuss the price."

Gabrielle recognized the code words but kept her face impassive. "That's most unfortunate. What time should I swing by?"

"The sooner, the better, I'd say, Miss. This is going to be a complicated job."

"Very well. I'll be there as soon as I can."

The line went dead, and Gabrielle hung up the phone. "Lucy, I'm afraid I'm going to have to leave. Can you please let Mr. Harris know I'll—"

"Let me know what?"

Gabrielle knew she should have glanced around first. Her boss had an annoying habit of just appearing like a ghost the moment his name was mentioned. She turned and put on her best damsel-in-distress look, knowing he saw himself as a father figure to all the young women who worked in his department. "Mr. Harris, my garage called. They need me to come down to discuss some repairs. I was just about to clock out. Obviously, I'll make up my time later."

Mr. Harris's red face reflected the expression so commonly seen on middle managers across the U.S. government. "You were just going to clock out? And why do you *need* to go down there?"

Gabrielle looked up at him, all wide-eyed innocence. "But, Mr. Harris, you've impressed on us *so much* that we *absolutely* must keep any personal calls to a bare minimum. Why, this call could have taken up to a half hour to resolve. I just didn't feel it was appropriate to tie up one of our main lines that long. Has your policy *changed*?"

Harris realized everyone was looking at him and adjusted his tie nervously before responding. "No. No, Miss DuMond, I think you made a very responsible decision. Of course, I'll approve this absence . . . just as long as you make up the time, like you said."

"Certainly, sir."

"Very well." Harris glanced around the room. "All right, ladies, back to work. Those reports aren't going to write themselves."

Harris beat a hasty retreat to his office and the young women tried to keep their giggling as soft as they could. Gabrielle grabbed her hat and purse and made a beeline for the door. A few minutes later, she exited the Munitions Building, looking out on the National Mall, and hurried over to the curb where a Yellow Cab waited.

"Miss DuMond?"

"Yes."

The cabbie didn't say anything else and opened the rear door for her. As soon as the cab began moving, dark windows rose, cutting off the view of the passenger compartment from anyone glancing in from outside. Twenty minutes later, the cab crossed the bridge going from Washington into Alexandria, Virginia, and then continued into the Virginia farmlands west of the capital. The cab pulled into a large estate and rolled up to the front door. When the shaded windows came down, the brunette office worker was gone and a red-haired woman dressed in an expensive skirt, blouse, and jacket with matching hat and purse allowed herself to be assisted from the car.

"Thanks, Tony."

The cabbie grinned. "Anytime, Miss Espionage. Big case?"

"You probably know more about it that I do."

"Pfeah," he muttered, scuffing his toe like a little kid who'd been caught in the cookie jar. "I just go and fetch people. They never let me in on the big stuff."

"Trust me, you probably sleep better. Be good and stick around. I may need you." She gave him a pat on the shoulder before going inside. She had to show her identification to guards outside, just inside, and at the top of the second-floor landing before being escorted to a door at the end of the hall. She punched in the code and with a buzz, the door opened, allowing her in. A secretary pointed to a door with frosted glass. "He'll be with you in one minute."

"This better be damn important, Diana. I spent a lot of time getting the Gabrielle persona down. What's going to happen to her?"

Diana Petermann gave her a somber look. "Tragic automobile accident. Hit by a drunk driver while on the bridge crossing the Potomac going toward Virginia. Car won't be found for several days, and you'll be declared another victim to the vice of alcohol. Body must have been taken by the current. If we need to, they'll eventually discover a woman's body many miles downriver after the crabs have found it." Diana suppressed a shiver at the thought and then shifted in her seat to face Miss Espionage better. "Were you making any headway?"

"A few hints, but I think we can take Jonathan Harris off our list as possible suspects. He's not the guy passing the info about oil reserves to the Soviets. I'm not sure where the leak is yet, but I'd say it was more likely in the research office."

"I'll pass that along. Ah, I hear them breaking up."

The glass door opened and two older men in uniform came out with a younger man in civilian attire escorting them. "We're in agreement, gentlemen. I'm going to assign my best people to investigate this. We'll keep you up to date as information comes in."

One of the older men turned to him with a fierce look on his face. "You'd better, McGurk. Harry may have decided to put Hillenkoetter in charge of the agency, but I haven't forgotten how to run missions. I've got connections all over Europe and Asia. Something big is happening and if you can't handle it, I'll take care of it."

"Don't worry, sir. If we learn anything, you'll be among the first to know."

"I'd better be." The old man paused and then his face softened before he shook the younger man's hand. "Well, good hunting, McGurk. I look forward to meeting the men you're putting on the job."

McGurk smiled broadly. "We'll schedule something soon. Thanks, General Donovan."

Miss Espionage watched as the older man maneuvered through the room like a battleship moving out to face a rival and disappeared through the door. Toby McGurk waited until he was safely gone before running a hand down his face in exasperation. "I don't know how he does it, but that man has sources I'd love to track down. I swear he knows about things before I do—and *he's* retired."

Miss Espionage smiled at Toby. "He's not known as 'Wild Bill' Donovan for nothing, Toby. We had extensive files on him back during the war. While the Office of Strategic Services was never quite as professional as the British Special Operations

Executive, the OSS was in some ways more of a threat because we never could anticipate what General Donovan might come up with. I take it his presence here has something to do with your call to me?"

"It does and if you'll follow me . . . ?"

She rose and followed Toby through his office door, giving Diana a quick wave. Toby walked through his office to the far wall and pressed a knot in the wood paneling. A section of the wall slid in and back, exposing a door with a cipher lock. Toby punched in the code and pushed the door open, revealing a large room with several people working at desks within.

They moved through this room, greeting the analysts who were preparing reports, probably for the president's daily briefing, and stepped into another office just beyond. Toby motioned her to a comfortable chair near his desk and then slumped down into his own executive chair, resting his chin on his hands.

"Wow, General Donovan must have put you through the wringer. You look like you just got back from your physical fitness test."

"General Donovan is the least of my worries currently, Klara. At least, I'm reasonably sure he's on our side."

Miss Espionage frowned. Toby had used her real name, Klara Zelle, which was never a good sign. She knew he must be good and spun up if he let that slip. As the daughter of Margaretha Zelle, better known to the world as Mata Hari, she had been raised by her German spymaster and trained since she was a small child in the arts of seduction and espionage. Only a few people in the world knew she had fled Germany after the end of the Second World War and taken up the mantle of Miss Espionage to make amends.

"Maybe if you told me what was bothering you, Toby, we could find a way to make both Wild Bill and you happy. There's no way you'd be this upset if it was just the usual Soviet moles or war profiteers we've been up against so far."

Toby took a deep breath to settle himself. "This could be the biggest case the International Counter-Spy Organization has ever faced. It's a two-pronged issue. The more straightforward issue is that Germans are disappearing underneath the noses of the occupying forces. Not just wealthy or politically connected, but everyday people—technicians, doctors, machinists, chemists, many experts in their fields."

Klara took a deep breath and stared up at a map of occupied Germany Toby had on his wall. The lines dividing her homeland into the different occupation zones resembled scars after an operation, but this wasn't the time to get homesick. "There always was a plan if defeat was inevitable to exfiltrate as many people as possible and move to new locations around the globe. Regroup, watch, and wait for the right time to establish the Fourth Reich."

"You'd think they'd have had their fill of this master-race nonsense after the pasting they took in the war."

"That's because you surround yourself with open-minded people, Toby. The National Socialist regime in Germany drew from a wide swath across the people. Not all were foaming-at-the-mouth fanatics like Hitler and Himmler. Some fanatics are quite cold-blooded and calculating. You'd never have known they were true believers until it was too late."

She paused, remembering some of the parties and meetings she had attended before pushing on. "The main reason the Allies did as well as they did was because Admiral Canaris was actively sabotaging the *Abwehr.* Trust me, there was a solid group who, while not loyal to Hitler, were quite loyal to Germany. I easily can believe there's a movement afoot to reestablish themselves somewhere—whether in South America, Africa or South Asia, I can't say—but that's where I'd start looking."

Toby reached over and picked up his pipe, tapping it against his palm before opening a drawer to pull his tobacco pouch out. Klara could see a dozen thoughts forming and being filed away as he mechanically loaded his pipe and held the match to the bowl, so she waited until he was ready to continue.

"That will be one of the questions we need you to find an answer to when you return to Europe."

Klara smiled bitterly. "Toby, you and I both know there are only about seven people in the world who know I'm still alive and even fewer who know I work for you. If word gets out, the operative phrase used in your movies would be 'Wanted—Dead or Alive . . . preferably dead.' I'd prefer the dead over being caught by the NKVD. The Soviet secret police doesn't pay attention to niceties."

Toby nodded but pointed the well-chewed end of his pipe at her. "I'm aware of the risks, but you're the only person who has the contacts to the bottom of this. We've identified over fifty people who've vanished in the past month alone, and God only knows how many managed to slip away before we knew to start looking. For all we know, they're reaching the end of their list, so we don't have time to get someone else into the country and infiltrate the organization. We need someone who will be recognized and accepted with a minimum of suspicion."

"Toby, I've been out of circulation for over two years . . ."

"And we'll help you account for this time. We have a few pet Nazis who we're keeping out of the Soviets hands who can vouch for what you've been doing and where you've been—with the right persuasion. We need you in Vienna as soon as possible. We've tracked some of the people there, but the trail goes absolutely cold after they arrive."

Klara took a quick breath before blurting out, "Vienna?"

Toby nodded, exhaling a small cloud of smoke before continuing. "I believe you have worked in that city before."

Klara let a rare smile cross her lips. "I grew up there. My handlers wanted to expose me to a wider world, so I lived there before going to college at Oxford and doing my master's degree at Vassar."

"Vassar?"

"It's good to see you can still be surprised. Vassar, Class of '37. I graduated with my master's at twenty-one, even though my papers said I was twenty-three. I was also working for the *Abwehr* while I was in college. German Intelligence had quite the dossier on the graduating classes at West Point from '36 and '39."

Toby shook his head. "I'll pass on some notes to my counterpart at the Point. He might want to update his personal security plans to include cute coeds."

"I guarantee some of the young ladies dating your cadets speak perfectly good English when they're not speaking Russian during their debriefings."

"I swear, if it's not one headache it's six new ones." Toby paused a beat, then shook his head." That's a problem for another day. We need to insert you into Vienna so you can make contact with some of your former coworkers. However, that brings us to the second problem . . . the one thing that makes me hesitate to send you."

Klara's internal alarm started ringing and her eyes narrowed. "And that would be . . . ?"

"You've heard of *Fraulein* Doctor?"

Klara felt the tension leave her body. "Annabelle? Of course I've heard of her. She was one of the greatest German spies in the Great War and a good friend of my mother's. I started my training under her, but she retired from fieldwork before the war. The high command put her in charge of the best analytic team we had and on occasion she still trains elite spies, if they catch her eye. We worked together many times."

"Yes, your initial debriefs mentioned your relationship. We believe she's one of the major players in Vienna. There's a good chance she's the reason we've failed to get any other agents into position. Still, we don't think she's detected our preparations to get you into Vienna so far."

"Don't be too sure. Not much gets past her. Although Annabelle was never a member of the Nazi Party, once she left fieldwork it was more the excitement of outwitting someone that kept her in the game. If she's involved, there's a good chance I will be able to connect with the pipeline and find out who's running it and why."

Klara noticed Toby was staring at her as if he was going to say something more, then his features shifted back into those of the no-nonsense boss she was more familiar with. "Klara, I can't order you to do this because you're not officially part of the ICSO. Hell, officially, you don't even exist. I've run a dozen plans through my head since I heard about this fiasco, and this is the only one I can imagine succeeding. Besides, you heard Wild Bill. Word's starting to get out and if I can't fix it, he's going to round up his old gang and have a go at it. I don't *even* want to have to deal with the possible diplomatic fallout from that."

Klara could only imagine the hullabaloo if the press got a whiff of that. "That bad, eh?"

"The worst. And there's no use denying, it's a bad deal all the way around. The second you get off the plane in Europe, you're on your own. ICSO cannot risk tipping *anyone* you're on our side. It's a crappy job, but you're the only person who could pull it off."

She stood next to the map, staring at a spot somewhere over Toby's head before finally coming to a decision. "All right, Toby, when you put it that way, I can't really say no. Besides," she said, the hint of a smile forming on her lips, "if I pull this off, it'll be the greatest coup of my entire career."

"I also have a small surprise for you. The kids in the lab have been working on something I think you'll find rather interesting."

"Now, I'm officially worried."

As she disappeared down the hall, Diane walked to the door and stuck her head in. "Did you tell her *everything*?"

Toby picked up his pipe and glared at the cold bowl as if he'd been betrayed. "No. I didn't have the heart. This is going to be a tough enough assignment as is. If she knew the whole truth about *Fraulein* Doctor, I was afraid she'd lose her focus. On this assignment, she can't afford any mistakes. With luck, she'll never need to know."

"And if she finds out?"

Toby stared at the ceiling. "If she survives, you may need to arrange my funeral . . . and I won't blame her a bit."

The airliner taxied to a stop at Tulln Airport near the terminal. Miss Espionage waited patiently as people jostled each other to retrieve their luggage and make their way forward as soon as the stewardess had opened the cabin door. She let a young man help her out of her seat and unsteadily made her way forward with her small case clutched in her hands. The stewardess smiled at her and assisted her onto the stairway that had been rolled up to the plane. One of the Air France workers helped her down the stairs and escorted her to the terminal doors.

"You are certain you'll be all right, Madame Bissonette?"

"My young man, one does not get to be seventy-two and survive two wars by being fragile. I appreciate your assistance, but I can make it from here."

The young man smiled to humor her obvious frailness. "As you wish, Madame. If you need anything, Air France stands by to attend your every need."

"*Merci.* However, there is something you could help me with. Could you have my luggage brought to the St. Mark's hotel in Vienna. I'm afraid I'll have trouble enough getting there without dealing with it."

The young man pulled out a pad of paper and copied down her information and a description of her luggage. She smiled and slipped him a small bundle of francs for his troubles. He tried gallantly to refuse it but quickly slipped it into his pocket. After making her way through the Customs area and having her visa stamped by both the French and the Soviet inspectors, she made her way to the cab stand out front.

It didn't take her long to notice the Soviets agents busily examining the incoming passengers against a photo sheet. Those weren't the ones who worried her. It was the ones she couldn't spot immediately that concerned her. Tulln Airport was deep in the Soviet Occupation Zone and if something went wrong, no one would *ever* know what happened to her.

After a short wait, one of the cabbies came over to her. "Where would you like to go, ma'am?"

She noted his British accent and smiled up at him. In halting English, she gave him the address of the St. Mark's and the driver held the door while she climbed in. They left the airport and took a long, circuitous route before they reached Vienna. The driver tried to make small talk, but Miss Espionage only said a few things in French and kept her eyes focused on the scenery and he eventually gave up. She had moved to where she could glance at his side mirrors and didn't spot anyone following them, which was a good sign. After almost a half hour, they finally reached the outskirts of Vienna and another ten minutes of dodging traffic brought her to the steps of the St. Mark's.

The cabbie hopped out and got the door for her. After settling the bill, he started toward the driver's side but stopped and doubled back. "I don't know what's going on, ma'am, but do be careful and always have your papers on you here in Vienna. The occupation forces are supposed to be cooperating with each other, but the Russians . . . well, they've been a lot thicker over here in the British sector than usual. They're not supposed to be walking around without one of our blokes with them, but that ain't never stopped them before. I don't think there'll be any trouble but be sure to have your papers. Even your age isn't a guarantee there won't be trouble."

"Why, thank you, young man. I appreciate your concern, but why do you think to tell me that? I'm just visiting my son. I can't imagine anyone noticing me."

The cabbie shrugged his shoulders. "Honestly, I'm not sure why I brought it up. Might be because there were so many Russian cops at the airport. Something's got them stirred up. Me? I just drive a cab and try to stay out of trouble. Well, enjoy your visit."

Miss Espionage watched him drive off and made a mental note to change hotels as soon as her baggage arrived. The cabbie could have been one of Toby's men or it could have been a simple coincidence. In her business, though, coincidences almost never happen. She checked in and left word with the concierge her baggage would be arriving shortly and went to her room.

After securing her door and ensuring no one could see through the windows, she turned her attention to her small carry-on bag. Setting everything inside on her bed, she removed her wristwatch and popped the back off, revealing a small key. The key fit into a concealed hole in the corner of her bag and with a twist, the false bottom came free. She eased out her Walther PPK and checked it over. Once certain it was fully functional, she strapped a holster to her upper thigh and fixed it into place before slipping in the small automatic.

She examined herself in the mirror and made sure it was well hidden in the folds of her dress. There was a small slit held in place by a string allowing easy access to the gun in case of emergency. She also slipped a pearl bracelet on her wrist and examined it closely. Without a microscope, it was impossible to spot the seams in the two biggest pearls, where an explosive had been inserted. Toby swore this new formula contained enough power to open most locked doors but was quiet enough to not be heard more than ten feet away. She hadn't tried them yet, but the boys in the lab were known for making interesting toys.

Klara had just put everything away when a knock at her door announced the arrival of her luggage. She tipped the porter generously and began setting up her gear. It was obvious the customs personnel had given her bags a thorough search, even though everything was still neatly folded. She ensured she hadn't acquired any listening or tracking devices before she pulled out her watch key again and opened the false sides on her steamer trunk.

On one side were other items that she might find useful while she was in Vienna. The other side contained the most ridiculous outfit she'd ever seen. Toby and she had argued for several hours after he showed it to her, but he kept referring to other mystery men and women who'd been active in the United States, Europe, and the Pacific theater of the war.

"Toby, you have got to be kidding," she'd said. *"It's a swimsuit with boots, a half cape, a beret, and a mask. How is that not going to bring attention to me?"*

"And that's the whole point, Klara. They're going to be staring at the outfit, not your face. They're going to wonder who the new mystery woman is. Then when you show up in civilian clothing, no one's going to pay attention to you. Unless you really want to spend the rest of your life wearing makeup and false wigs. Face it, it's tough to keep coming up with new looks for you just here in the D.C. area."

"But, Toby, espionage means not *being noticed. I can't wear this and not be noticed. Besides, I'd freeze to death."*

"The outfit is made with the latest in ballistic cloth, so it'll protect you against most small-arms fire. There's a leather pouch you wear on the waist to carry any equipment you might need when you're on assignment, and it makes it easier for you to get to your weapons. Think of it as a modern version of your mother's gear."

"No offense, Toby, but my mother was an exotic dancer in Paris. She wore normal clothing around town."

"And did anyone recognize her as the fabulous Mata Hari when she was in mufti?"

"I was fifteen months old when she was executed, but I guess you have a point there. All right, for this mission I'll go along with this insanity, but if it doesn't work, I'm never getting in it again."

"Deal."

Klara held up the one-piece outfit and modeled it in the mirror, staring at it in disbelief. *Deal? I should have my head examined to agree with this.* Muttering softly, she consolidated the important items into her small bag and the other clothing from the secret compartment into her suitcase. Everything else was shoved into the steamer trunk, which was then secured with a lock.

After dinner, once darkness had settled over Vienna, she set to work with her makeup kit. The gray-haired grandmother who'd checked into the hotel was now a middle-aged woman with black hair. Once she'd repacked everything, she eased out of the window onto the fire escape, then cautiously lowered her baggage down to the back alley with a rope. Reaching the ground, she maneuvered through several alleys until she came out onto a major thoroughfare and walked over to the nearest cabstand.

A short ride brought her to the Hotel Sacher, which was on the other side of the British zone. Inside, she identified herself as Mrs. Anthony Mabry of New York City and that she had a reservation. The clerk called over one of the British MPs, who reviewed her papers before escorting her past several offices commandeered by the British Occupation Forces to the elevators. He informed her that she had full run of the lobby and bar area and her floor, but the first five floors were off-limits.

She went to her room to secure her luggage and then returned downstairs to visit the bar, where she had a martini and made small talk with the bartender. Having established herself as a lonely widow who'd decided to get away from her deceased husband's greedy relatives, she got some change and went to the lobby phones, where she placed two phone calls and then returned to her room, to get the first good rest she'd had since Toby had called her four days earlier.

She was enjoying her breakfast and the morning newspaper when the phone in her room rang. She picked it up carefully. "Mrs. Mabry, speaking."

A voice with a hint of a German accent spoke. "Oh, I am so sorry. I was looking for Lorelei. They must have patched me through to the wrong room."

"Don't worry about it. I'm sure it happens all the time."

"More than it used to. Sorry to bother you. Good-bye."

There was a click as her caller hung up and then a softer click. So, someone at the switchboard was listening in, but for which side? Klara set the phone back on the receiver and glanced at the clock. Lorelei was one of her former code names when she was working in the *Abwehr.* The second line contained ten words, so that meant she was to be on the street at

10 a.m. She wasn't sure how they'd contact her, but she knew they would.

At 9:50, the elevator deposited her in the lobby, and she walked across the marble floors until she spotted a redheaded soldier with an MP band on his arm. She put on her most innocent smile. "Excuse me, but could you tell me how to get to the Vienna Opera House?"

"Excuse me, ma'am?"

She could tell he was from somewhere in Scotland and that she'd completely flustered him with her question. "The Opera House. Surely even soldiers get to go out once and a while?"

"Ma'am, I don't know if you've noticed or not, but this is an occupied town in a former war zone. We've been a *bit* busy trying to keep law and order in this area. So, you'll pardon me if I make a lousy tour guide."

"But Officer—"

"Sergeant. Sergeant Ian MacDougall, ma'am."

"Excuse me, Sergeant. I'm not asking you to take me. Can you just point me in the right direction? After all, I've walked around Manhattan enough times, I'm certain Vienna can't be much worse."

"Coo, what lasses are they sending us these days? Ma'am, you don't seem to understand. Vienna is divided into different occupation zones. It's tough enough getting around when you know where you're going. Please, if you insist on touring the city, take a cab."

She let out a long sigh as if exasperated by the sergeant's behavior. "Very well, but I'm perfectly capable of taking care of myself."

"Save me from Americans," he said, escorting her to the entrance to the hotel. "Please use the cabs, ma'am. They can use the business, and I won't have to bail you out from some other sector's jail."

"I appreciate your sentiment, Sergeant MacDougall, even if I disagree with your methods. Very well. I shall use the cabs."

Satisfied that if anyone asked, she was safely on her way to the Opera House, a place she'd spent enough time in to describe it blindfolded, she left the hotel at ten on the dot and walked down to the cabstand. She passed the first couple of cabbies who offered her a ride, enjoying the cloudless day and the warmth of the sun reflecting off the buildings.

Another cabbie approached her. “Ride, miss? We do a special tour along the Danube.”

“Why yes. That sounds wonderful.”

The cabbie held the door for her and then jumped into his seat. As the cab lurched forward, he turned the mirror so he could see her clearly. Once he had gotten into traffic, he began speaking in German. “You are taking quite a chance coming out this openly, Lorelei.”

She kept her facial expression neutral and answered in German. “I am taking *no* chances. However, I do not answer to the messenger boy. When we arrive, then we will talk to the one who sent for me.”

“Yes. Yes, you will.”

The threat hung over the cab for the rest of the ride. After the cabbie had satisfied himself they were not being followed, he pulled up at the front of a warehouse and honked. The large doors rumbled open, and he pulled forward into the darkness. When they reached the middle of the room, a bright light turned on overhead, revealing the warehouse was empty except for the car. Klara glanced out the window and saw figures moving around on the catwalks above. Her hand rested lightly on her PPK, but she was there to talk, not get into a gunfight.

The cabbie exited and opened the door for her. She stepped out and was directed to the side where a set of stairs led upward. When she reached the first landing, a voice came from above telling her to stop. She waited as a figure moved to the top of the stairs and the others moved to where they had a clear line of sight. The cabbie remained at the bottom of the stairs, effectively boxing her in.

“So, you are Lorelei.”

“So *you* say. I don’t know you.”

Mirthless laughter rang down from above and the figure

moved closer to her but stopped well short of where she stood. "Good. You don't trust me. I don't trust you, so we're even. Where have you been the past eighteen months?"

"Geneva, New York, Honolulu, and Paris," she answered truthfully.

The figure paused before responding. "Geneva, I can understand, but why America?"

"Can you think of a better place to hide than right under their noses? They were tearing up Europe looking for me. So, the best option was not to be here."

"But you are here now."

"I received word people with my 'talents' could be useful again. Only now, it's a more lucrative profession. After all, a girl must eat."

"Some say it's a more *dangerous* profession these days. Some of our former friends turn up in the river from time to time. When they turn up at all."

"So do some of our former enemies. But enough of this. You contacted me. If you don't believe me, why did you respond to my call last night? You could have ignored me, and I would have left in a day or so to my next stop. Instead, you reached out to me."

"Because I am not stupid. If you are Lorelei, then you *could* be a great asset to us. If you are not, then we need to convince your superiors they are playing the game poorly."

Klara stared up at the shadowy figure. There was something in his accent and his shape that seemed familiar. "I can prove who I am, but I will not do it here in front of a bunch of stooges, Otto Piske. So, do we go somewhere and sit down like professionals, or do we keep playing cloak and dagger for the assembled audience?"

The shadowy figure applauded as he moved to her landing. Otto Piske, a tall, blond man who looked like he stepped out of a German Army recruiting poster, smiled broadly as he stepped out of the shadows. "I should have never doubted it was you, Lorelei. When was the last time we saw each other?"

"Amsterdam, January 1945. You had just eliminated that

Dutch double agent, and I was moving toward Paris with the refugees to infiltrate U.S. High Command. I heard you were dead."

"I heard the same thing about you. Seems you just can't believe anything you hear these days. Come, we will go to my office."

He took her by the elbow and guided her to the car after motioning to the assembled shadows above to leave. The cabbie climbed into his seat and once Otto and she were comfortable, he drove out of the warehouse toward the center of town.

"As you can see, Vienna was spared the damage most German cities suffered. It should be back on its feet in no time. As a matter of fact, Vienna's become quite a hub for importing and exporting things from both sides of the Occupation Zones. Seems the Russians have gotten a taste for decadent Western goods. Since they can't officially buy them, well . . . let's just say, there's good money in becoming a procurer of these things."

"And the Americans, British, and French just *let* you do this?"

"Of course not. They get their cuts too. That's why prices are so high these days." He inched closer to her. "But we're not here to talk about my business."

"Actually, I think we are," she said, scooting toward the far side and staring at him as if daring him to move closer. He shook his head sadly and inched back to his side of the cab before she continued. "I believe you when you say you're importing and exporting things, but I don't *quite* believe you're only supplying the Russians with luxury items. Let me take that back. I believe that's what you're doing overtly. I'm more interested in what you're *covertly* exporting these days."

He made a small choking noise. "Lorelei, I think you have me all wrong."

"*Do* I? Then you can let me out at the next corner. Otherwise, quit talking nonsense. I have my reasons for asking."

Otto motioned toward the driver, who was pointedly acting like he wasn't listening. "Let's say I don't discuss business details in automobiles or on the sidewalk. It'll have to wait until I get to the office."

She settled back to wait. She'd met Otto a few times in the early days of the war. He'd been a firebrand then, fully devoted to the Party and the *Führer*. He never was much of an operative, but he was a whiz at getting equipment to people and recovering gear after it had been used. The ICSO had traced him to Vienna and if anyone was smuggling anything, Otto would be the first person they'd contact.

When they pulled up in front of a moving and storage company, she wasn't surprised at all. Otto beamed as he pointed to the building. "See, I can be as legitimate as I want to be. I just don't want to be very often. Markus, stay with the car. After we finish our business, you'll need to take Mrs. Mabry back to her hotel."

Entering the building, they went into his inner office and Otto flipped on the lights. After checking around—no doubt to ensure nothing had been touched while he was out—he pushed a button on his desk and a section of the desktop slid back, revealing a thin map with lines etched on it in different colors.

"You were asking about *covert* cargoes, Lorelei. It's very simple. I help people get out of Germany, especially those whom other people would like to stay there. I don't handle finding them or getting them to the rendezvous, that's a different section's responsibilities. What I do is get them out of Germany, process them, prepare them for travel, and then get them en route to the next location. Once they arrive, money appears in my bank account, and we secure the area for the next shipment. We leave nothing behind to tip anyone off, even the next set of cargo. That way, if anyone is ever caught, all they can do is name a barn or a warehouse where they were brought to or taken out of at night. It's quite simple and efficient."

"I thought you'd be doing this for the future Reich," she said, glancing at the map.

"Oh, I am. I am. But, until it's established, I have a business to run, employees to pay, police to bribe, taxes to file . . . It's not easy to get the finer things of life in an occupation zone. With the right amount of money, anything is negotiable. Although, with your looks and skill, I doubt you've known a hungry day in your life."

Miss Espionage spun around and speared him with a look. "My personal life is none of your concern, *Herr* Piske. Ther's no question you've done very well for yourself and the cause. I see these routes all wind up in Istanbul, and that we're still taking advantage of Turkey's fondness for Germany, but I never considered using it as a base for a comeback."

"Istanbul is just one part of the trip. I don't know where they go from there, but Turkey isn't as friendly a place as it was six years ago. The *verdamnt* Soviets have been putting pressure on Turkey and driving it right into the hands of the Americans. They're as ham-handed as ever, so we must be circumspect to avoid drawing the American military's attention, not to mention the French in Syria or the British in Iraq. But never fear, I have faith in my other companions who are responsible for the other stages."

"You were always the best procurer."

Otto preened at the compliment. "Yes, I was . . . and still am. That's why I'm here. Trust me, getting people through the occupied zones in Germany and Austria and slipping them down the Danube right under the Russians' noses is not a job for an amateur."

There was a frantic knocking at the office door, and Markus called out, "Otto, something's going on. Two jeeps full of Soviet MPs pulled up just outside and they're heading this way."

"Don't those Bolsheviks ever give up? Are there Americans?"

"I didn't see any. We have to go. *Now.*"

Otto pointed to a door in the back of his office. "Go. I'll be right behind you."

Miss Espionage moved to the door and eased it open, exposing a small alley leading to a gate at the far end. A glance over her shoulder revealed Otto closing the desktop and then pushing the pen and pencil in the set level with the desktop. As he ran to the escape route, she heard the front door crash open and the sound of submachine guns. Otto slammed the door shut behind him and rushed toward the other end of the alley.

"What about Markus?"

"What about him? Now run or you can find out what happened to him yourself."

When they opened the gate, two things happened almost simultaneously: the door behind them flew open, and a huge explosion shot a fireball into the air. They dove into the rustic garden as flames danced behind them.

"What in the hell was all that?" Klara asked once the ringing in her ears subsided.

Otto got off the ground, brushing the dust and ash off himself. To her amazement, he sounded blasé about the entire incident. "Occupational hazard, I'm afraid. Let's just say I occasionally have unsatisfied customers. Seems that group discovered those nylons I sold them were cheap imitations. Luckily, that was only one of my offices. I move every so often to avoid little incidents like that."

"No, I mean that explosion!" she clarified in exasperation.

"Ah, Soviet plastic explosives. I trade them stuff, they trade me stuff. The Soviets aren't subtle like the British. They *like* big explosions. Still, it gets the job done. I have all my offices set up to destroy all evidence if discovered. It's just good business practice."

He led her through the garden and into an abandoned office building. She heard fire trucks' sirens rushing toward the scene of the explosion, but he placed a hand on her arm and nonchalantly walked out the front door and down the street. He opened the door to a car and ushered her inside.

"You've seen what I'm up to, Lorelei. This shows my good faith. Now, we're going to go talk to some other people who've also taken an interest in why you've come to Vienna. I certainly hope you prove your good faith to them. They're much less trusting than I am, even with an old compatriot."

Klara heard footsteps moving closer to her as she sat in the darkness. Otto had made a phone call and then taken her to a farmhouse a few miles outside Vienna. Once there, he tied her to a chair and placed a hood over her head. That had been over three hours ago, and her arms and legs were numb from sitting unmoving for so long. She'd heard people coming and going, but no one had spoken or approached her since she'd arrived.

Suddenly, there was movement behind her and the hood was snatched roughly off. Before she could react, a bright light flashed into her eyes. She instinctively tried to raise her hands to block the light before remembering they were still securely tied to the chair. Squinting, she was able to make out two dark shapes, one on either side of the light. She smelled strong cigarette smoke and knew whoever was across from her was smoking a European brand.

After a minute, the large figure to the right spoke and she recognized his Bavarian accent as soon as he spoke. "Ah, Lorelei. The years have been good to you. The last time I saw you was in 1940."

She thought hard for a moment and finally placed the voice. "Baron Emil von Kruger. I hate to disagree with you," she said, "but it was April 1942 in Berlin when we last saw each other. You'd just returned from Vilnius."

A soft chuckle escaped von Kruger. "Your memory is as good as I remember. There are many who wondered what happened to you after the war. Your departure was rather . . . sudden."

"Just because few knew what I looked like did not mean no one did. In my position, I felt it was best to remove myself from harm's way."

She heard the rustling of paper beyond the burning light. "Yet, you are here now?"

"I still have contacts in Europe. I've heard a snippet here, a careless word there, and thought my talents might be useful. Same thing I told Otto when I met him. Nothing has changed in the past four hours."

The other figure rose and moved to the left, out of Klara's sight. That person worried her more than von Kruger, but secured as she was, there was little she could do about it. The room remained silent except for the faint sound of footsteps behind her, almost as if both von Kruger and she were waiting for the other to make the next sound. She tried to pick out any details of the room, but the lights were too bright.

Finally, von Kruger let out a deep sigh. "We don't know what your sources have told you, but our sources say very little about you. You vanished in early 1945 and now you just turn up here in the middle of a project we've gone to great lengths not to advertise."

He paused and clucked his tongue against the inside of his cheek. "Tsk, I hope you can appreciate why some suggested we eliminate you immediately. Others suggested we do so after we dig your secrets out of you." He shook his head sadly. "Obviously those people never met you before. A small but influential faction, of which I am one, suggests we take advantage of this windfall. Luckily for you."

She'd heard more believable used-car salesmen back in the States, but if it kept her alive, she wasn't going to complain. "What about your silent partner here? Which side do they fall on?"

There was a sudden movement, and she felt the unmistakable chill of Prussian steel honed to a razor's sharpness pressed against her throat. A husky feminine voice whispered in her ear, "I was part of the 'kill you right here and now' faction, but Emil feels you offer us something not easily replaced. However, do not worry. Should you prove to be untrustworthy, I will never be too far away." There was a hint of pressure, and she felt the faint trickle of blood on her neck.

She saw the shadowy figure to her front move in and then the pressure on her neck lessened. "Baroness, you're getting ahead of yourself. The council agreed you could eliminate her *if* she proves unfaithful, but not yet."

"You've all gone soft. If I were in charge—"

"But you're not, Baroness. You were granted a position of authority due to your reputation as one of the Reich's greatest warriors. Do not disappoint the council."

The two figures moved out of Klara's vision, but she could still feel the memory of the knife against her flesh. It finally occurred to her who the other person in the room was. Baroness Katarina Blud, code named Baroness Blood, the famous aviatrix who'd tangled with her British counterpart, the Black Angel, on numerous occasions. From the reports she'd read about the baroness, her jealousy was well-known as was her hatred of any woman she felt more attractive than her. That might be something she could use against the baroness later but being tied to a chair and unable to defend herself called for finesse if she hoped to escape unscathed. Besides, she needed to find out more about this council Emil had referred to earlier.

"She has a point, Emil," Klara said.

The heated discussion stopped mid-word and she heard footsteps coming closer. "And just *what* do you mean by that?" the baroness said, her voice almost as sharp as her blade.

"If I had known the baroness was associated with this project, I would never have approached Otto. It's obvious you don't need my assistance. I should have investigated further before offering my assistance. Perhaps another section could use me more effectively."

"Don't think you can flatter your way out of this, Lorelei," the baroness snapped, but Klara noted the woman's voice had mellowed slightly. "And, where else do you think you could be useful?"

"With all due respect, Baroness, I was a master spy. I could either aid you by securing personnel in the occupied territories or I could assist them in getting through Istanbul to their next destination. After all, von Kruger knows I was in Istanbul in '43 and '44 hunting British agents. My old network may be in disarray, but there are many who still owe me favors."

She could almost hear the palpable relief in von Kruger's voice. "An excellent point, my dear Lorelei. However, as you said yourself, going to Germany might not be the best use of your talents. No matter how good an actress, there's always a chance someone could recognize you there. The allies' counterintelligence dogs are thick in the Fatherland. Besides, I understand there's still quite a price on your head."

He paused for a moment before starting again with a conspiratorial tone in his voice. "But there are a few issues here and in Istanbul that require attention. Having an agent on the ground working for me who is not well-known within the organization could be quite useful."

Aha! Slipped up a bit, didn't you, Emil? "You mean working for the council, Emil?"

Even as a silhouette, she could see him give a nervous glance toward the baroness. "Of course. After all, my goals are mere echoes of the council's goals." He laughed nervously and changed the subject as he approached and began loosening her bonds. "It's time you returned to the city. Otto knows how to reach you when we're ready to speak to you again."

Klara walked into the hotel lobby and noticed it was unusually quiet. As she approached the elevators, Sergeant MacDougall stepped out of the shadows and rapidly approached her. "Good evening, Mrs. Mabry. Did you have a lovely time at the Opera House?"

"I took a detour before going there. The cabbie recommended a lovely boat tour of Vienna. I think you might enjoy it when you have some time off, Sergeant."

"Might I now? Ma'am, if you'd please accompany me, there are a couple of gentlemen who've been waiting most of the day to speak to you."

"A couple of gentlemen? To see me? God, please tell me it's not my stupid nephew's lawyers again?"

"You're safe there, ma'am. To be honest, I'd really appreciate it if you'd come along quietly without a fuss. I'd rather not have to carry you there across my shoulders, but these gentlemen aren't going to take no for an answer."

Miss Espionage glanced around and noticed the three British guards who'd taken up positions by the main entrance and two others guarding the stairwell. She was certain the back door and the one in the kitchen were suitably guarded also. Sighing mentally, she slipped her arm through Sergeant MacDougall's and smiled up at the blushing Scotsman. "By all means, Sergeant, let's not keep those men waiting any longer."

He led her into the area marked off for the Commander, British Occupation Zone and into a well-lit room. If she was going to be interrogated yet again, at least this time it wasn't theatrically lit and dingy. She glanced at Sergeant MacDougall but he shook his head and shut the door behind him, leaving her in the room by herself. She tried to relax in an overstuffed chair, but only a minute or so passed before the door opened again.

A familiar voice caught her off guard. "I have to admit; I didn't expect to see you again."

The hint of a smile curled her lips as she saw an old nemesis standing in the doorway. "Life has a funny way of changing our plans, Major Smithson."

The tall, dark-haired American officer smiled back at her. "Lieutenant Colonel Smithson these days. I'm glad you remember me, though you look a bit different than last time."

"You've barely changed at all. Come to settle some old scores?"

"Maybe pay back some old debts."

She started to say something else but paused, seeing the older British officer standing just behind Smithson trying to resist the urge to interrupt. She hated feeling off-balance and Smithson had managed to do it to her once again. The American officer must have realized what was bothering her and quickly motioned for both to sit down as he took a seat on the edge of the desk and began speaking again.

"Mrs. Mabry, this is Colonel Whitby-Smith, the senior intelligence officer in the British Occupation Zone. Colonel, this Mrs. Mabry, but she is better known as the infamous Miss Espionage, formerly with German intelligence, with an emphasis on *formerly*." With the introductions made, he turned back to Klara. "While I'm certain the colonel has *many* questions for you, I have only one: Where did you go after von Bruno tried to kill you?"

"Is this 'off-the-record,' Lieutenant Colonel, or for a military tribunal? After all, the war's been over for several years."

"This is strictly for the colonel's and my edification."

She turned to the colonel and addressed him directly. "After then-Major Smithson foiled my attempt to gather names of Germans cooperating with the occupation forces, my handler, von Bruno, who I trusted implicitly, tried to eliminate me. Major Smithson showed up in the nick of time."

She thought for a moment, remembering that day, before continuing. "I realized the von Bruno I had known was a carefully constructed lie and I never meant *anything* to him. I was not the daughter he'd led me to believe, just his puppet."

She paused to settle her breathing before continuing, "So, I took advantage of Major Smithson's inattention—real or feigned, I didn't care—and flew to Geneva in the plane von Bruno had intended to escape in. After several months of thinking, I decided to see what this American dream was for myself. I made my way to the United States and have been there until two days ago when I arrived in Vienna." She turned and frowned at Smithson. "Does that satisfy the lieutenant colonel's curiosity?"

Smithson wordlessly reached into his jacket and produced a dark leather case from which he pulled a piece of paper and handed it to her. She glanced down at the writing and then up at him. "You're—"

"We have the same boss, yes." He turned to the colonel. "I can vouch for her actions since she arrived in the States. I arranged for people from my organization to approach her and she's been working for us ever since. She may yet have to answer for her actions before and during the war, but she has proven to be dedicated and resourceful, sir."

She handed him back the paper and he slipped it back into the leather case. "How did you know I would even go to America? And how did you know I had arrived? I entered in disguise and with an actual American passport."

"Let's just say the theft from the American embassy in Geneva didn't go unnoticed, but that's because I suspected you'd attempt it. Whoever arrived in the States with that *particular* passport, man or woman, would be immediately put under observation. Either they'd be you or they'd lead us to you. Believe me, you've more than proven your worth to us."

She stared up at her benefactor. "Just who exactly are you, *Lieutenant Colonel*?"

"I'm whomever I need to be. For now, Lieutenant Colonel Smithson works fine for my work in Europe. Not unlike your Gabrielle DuMond?"

"Touché." Klara paused for a second. "Wait a minute, our *boss* explicitly stated that I was on my own and no one was to know who I was. And now you're just exposing me in this public way? What in the hell is going on?"

"Our *boss* didn't send me. In fact, I'm not officially here. I happened to be in Vienna for another matter and took the chance in case you needed assistance."

"Who said I needed assistance?"

"Don't you?"

Colonel Whitby-Smith discreetly harrumphed to gain their attention. They glanced from him to each other and then both turned toward him, faces burning red. "This is all very interesting, Colonel, but it does *not* begin to answer my questions. Now, Mrs. Mabry—if you'll allow me to use that pseudonym for now—it's the nature of your business in Vienna that concerns me. While your knight errant insists you can be trusted, you have been spotted with several individuals we've been keeping a close eye on. While we initially believed them to be common criminals, your presence makes me believe there's much more to it."

"Colonel, I will be happy to fill you in on everything I can once my mission is complete, but you, of all people, should know I cannot discuss this with any unauthorized personnel, regardless of rank or status. In fact, publicly hauling me in here has jeopardized what I've accomplished up to now. Whether or not I can succeed will depend on how you and your men at the hotel treat me. If I am seen as nothing more than the wealthy American widow I'm supposed to be, I may yet survive. Any deviation might as well tie a noose around my neck or worse."

"Dash it all, woman, you're putting me in a very awkward spot."

"Colonel, I'm in a life-threatening spot. If you cannot make that guarantee, then I must abort my mission right now and I'll be certain to inform my superiors why."

The colonel's face flushed, and he stood up from his desk. "Young woman, you have no grounds to try and threaten me. Why, if Lieutenant Colonel Smithson weren't here, you'd be on your way to the stockade or worse. After all, you're still a wanted criminal."

"And that brings up the question, why are you here?" she asked Smithson, ignoring the colonel's blustering.

"Coincidence. Strictly coincidence. You have your investigation, I have mine. I just happened to be talking to the colonel when the sergeant reported your cabbie was a known underworld figure. When you never showed up at the Opera House, he was suspicious and started asking a lot of questions. I suspected it might be you and was afraid a full-blown investigation would compromise you." He held up his hands to hold off her angry retort. "I only told him you needed to be free to continue to work unhindered in Vienna."

The colonel tried to reinsert himself into the conversation. "By the way, young woman, would you happen to know anything about an explosion earlier this afternoon?"

"Yes."

"And?"

"Someone's nylons were in a twist." With that, she walked out of the office, leaving the colonel turning a brighter shade of red and Smithson to try and calm him down.

Klara's eyes flew open as she heard her room window sliding upward. She checked and found her Walther PPK still tucked securely under her pillow. Keeping her breathing as even as possible, she feigned being asleep, waiting for her nocturnal visitor to make their intentions known.

She waited until the figure was halfway through the window before springing from the bed and pressing her pistol into the small of their back. "Stay very still and answer my questions."

The figure stiffened but the chuckle caught her off guard. "Rather spry for an American widow, Lorelei."

She moved back but kept the gun pointed at the figure. "Otto, you idiot. You were one inch from being a very dead intruder."

He turned toward her and motioned with one hand. "May I come in?"

She pointed toward a chair and then shut the blackout curtains. "What in the world made you think sneaking into my hotel room was a good idea?"

"The fact that walking in the front door past the British military police was a worse idea. Speaking of which, why were you called in to speak to the police when you returned?"

"Because your boy Markus was known to be a black marketer. The sergeant who escorted me to the cab station recognized him. I had to go over my entire day's itinerary with the officer-in-charge and then got a twenty-minute lecture on avoiding the black market because of that slipup. That means we'll have to move up our timetable."

"What do you mean?"

"For the next several days, I'm certain I'm going to have a tail on me to see if the lesson stuck. While *I* could easily shake it, Mrs. Mabry would only arouse more suspicion if she somehow managed to avoid these Scotland Yard imitators. Unless you think Emil and the baroness are willing to wait a week or more to get started, we must move quickly. To be blunt, if they want my help, it's got to be tomorrow."

"That's impossible."

She walked over to her closet and began tossing clothing on the bed. "You three have two options: you can take me to Istanbul so I can aid the council, or you can catch up with me in Istanbul after you make up your minds. I'm *not* going to sit around waiting for your amateur crew to screw something else up. Seriously, Otto, I thought better of you, but you're already compromised with the British and Soviet authorities. Seems your interest in making money is more important than the cause. I don't think the baroness would be too pleased to find that out."

Otto's eyes grew wide. "Now, let's not be hasty. I'm certain something can be worked out. Go ahead and pack. I'll be back in a few hours and let you know what the answer is."

She motioned him toward the window and waited until he was several flights down the fire escape. Taking a deep breath and trying to force her embarrassment back, Klara slipped her costume out of its hiding place and donned it, ensuring the blond wig was secure on her head before following Otto. It felt almost as if she was putting on a second skin. Before Miss Espionage wasn't a pseudonym, it was just who she was. Now, it felt as if she were two separate individuals. Taking a deep breath to focus, she hurried down the fire escape to catch up with Otto. She wasn't certain where he was going, but if there was a chance to find out the identities of "the council," it would be worth the risk.

Klara stuck to the shadows, partly to avoid Otto spotting her and partly to avoid being seen by anyone else. Thinking of a thousand different ways to take revenge on Toby once she got back to Virginia, she almost missed Otto slipping down an alleyway ahead of her. She hurried to catch up but paused before turning the corner in case Otto had just ducked in to see if he was being followed. Peering around the corner, she spotted him in front of a doorway about halfway down. Once Otto entered, she rushed to the doorway. It was locked, but the lock was cheap and only took her a few seconds to tumble it.

Creeping inside, she heard a door shut down the hall. She pulled a small flashlight out and examined the hallway. There was a fan pattern in the dust showing her which door Otto had gone through and again, a quick twist with the lockpicks allowed her egress. A flight of stairs descended into the building's basement. Before she followed, she carefully examined the stairs ahead of her and found a small hump in the runner.

She eased past it and discovered a small pressure switch that probably led to an alarm. It took her a bit longer to traverse the stairs, but she didn't find any other alarms.

The basement was large and barren, but a careful exam found faint traces in the dust along one wall. Looking around, Miss Espionage spotted what might have been a worn spot on one of the nearby bricks. She pushed until she heard a click and a section of the wall swung out. She caught it before it opened completely and listened at the gap.

"I don't care who she is, it's impossible," an angry voice in German was saying. "We're risking everything we've been working for on a phantom."

Another voice spoke in a calming fashion. "She was one of the Reich's greatest assets. The fact she's avoided capture this long right under their noses says she has the nerve for this mission."

A voice she recognized as Baroness Blud's spoke then. "All we have is her word she avoided capture. For all we know, she's working for them now. It's not like she was a real soldier. Lying comes naturally to her."

To her surprise, Otto spoke sharply in her defense. "Watch your tongue, Baroness. A good spy or assassin can accomplish more than a squadron of bombers. We *all* served the Reich in our own way."

There was an inarticulate shriek and the sound of bodies scuffling. Miss Espionage took advantage of the distraction to slip through the false wall and into the shadows of the room. The only light came from a bare bulb hanging over a table and figures were returning to their chairs after the altercation. She recognized some of the faces at the table, while others were new to her.

Once everyone had settled down, a figure standing in the shadows away from the table spoke up. "If you children are done squabbling, we need to come to a decision. Lorelei *could* be valuable for Operation Rheingold, but she could be bait for a trap. My recommendation is to transport her to Istanbul, but have a team keep an eye on her there. If there's the slightest hint of a problem, then eliminate her without mercy. No second chances, no let's see what happens. It must be done and done efficiently. If her aid proves useful in Istanbul, we can bring her to the oasis for full indoctrination. The Triumvirate does not throw away valuable tools."

The Triumvirate? And, what or where is the oasis?

"I still do not like it. It's like spotting a transport flying with no escort. It's never that easy," the baroness said, still sulking over her earlier rebuke.

A woman spoke from a different spot in the basement and Klara's eyes widened when she heard the voice—one she hadn't heard in a long time. "Baroness, you do not know Lorelei. Otto knows her, but he does not *know* her like I do. After all, I am the one who trained her before von Bruno completely bungled the job. I need to meet with her. If she is Lorelei, I will know. If she is not, she will never leave the meeting spot alive. No matter how well briefed she is, I know things no one else could possibly know."

One of the other shadowy figures spoke up as soon as the woman ceased. "But *Fraulein Doktor*, the risk . . . your presence in Vienna is our greatest asset. We cannot possibly risk it if she is a plant."

"Risk? You were still in diapers when I was operating in England and Belgium in the First War. If you want to speak of risk, *you* cannot risk taking her to Istanbul without being one hundred percent certain who she is. Do not think you can make a mistake of this magnitude and survive. The Triumvirate has a long memory and a longer reach."

The first shadowy figure nodded slowly and then turned to face Piske. "Your concerns are duly noted. Otto. You will be responsible for ensuring Lorelei gets to Istanbul safely once *Fraulein Doktor* vouches for her. She will not be leaving tomorrow. We will make the arrangements ahead of time. However, since you have recommended her to us, you are also responsible for keeping her under observation and eliminating her should the need arise. If she escapes, she will not be the only *ex*-spy in our organization."

Otto swallowed heavily and then straightened his back before replying. "Understood."

The leader looked at the assembled group and then nodded in satisfaction. "If there is nothing else to discuss, we are finished here. We'll meet again at our usual time and place. Baroness, remain behind. I would like to speak to you privately."

Klara hated letting the council just disappear, but something told her the upcoming conversation would take some of the sting out of the loss. She made a careful note of everyone she knew and tried to get a good enough look at those she didn't for her report. Before she left Vienna, she'd get a message to Smithson to pick up as much of the council as they could.

Once the room was emptied, the shadowy figure moved into the light. Like Miss Espionage, he wore a mask over his face to hide his features. There was something familiar about him, though, but she couldn't quite place him.

"What is it you wished to speak about, Herr Snow?"

"I do not trust Otto's judgment here. Lorelei may be a true patriot, but Otto has gotten soft with his affluence. I'm not certain he's able to make the hard calls any longer. I'm assigning you to Istanbul also. Your job will be to watch Otto. If Lorelei proves unfaithful and Otto wavers, you will eliminate both. Rheingold is too important to allow personal feelings to get in our way. Do not disappoint me, Baroness."

The baroness saluted and left the room. Herr Snow examined the area to ensure nothing had been left behind and Klara decided to take that opportunity to leave. As she moved toward the hidden door, her foot caught something small and sent it skittering across the floor. She froze immediately, but the damage was done.

Snow fixed his gaze in Klara's direction. "Ah, my little *flittermaus*, you might as well come out of the shadows. You may have entered unobserved, but since you are here, I'd like to know who decided to eavesdrop on our meeting and why."

"What purpose would that serve?"

"It's simple—either you're here to prove how useful you

can be to me, or you're an enemy. If the former, then I'll want to test you to ensure you're useful to the cause. If you're an enemy, then you're about to die."

"It is good to be confident."

"Confidence comes from accomplishments. I have killed many men with my bare hands. I'm certainly not concerned about a wisp of a girl such as you."

Klara edged toward the door as Snow moved into the center of the room. "While being tested by you might be amusing, I'm afraid I don't have the time. So, if that makes me your enemy, so be it, Herr Snow—or, should I say, Baron Teufel. Yes, you can hide your face, but you can't hide your voice from me."

She could imagine the smile crossing the baron's face from the way his body relaxed into a fighting position. "So, you know who I am. Then you know what I can do. This will be even more enjoyable than I anticipated. Who may I say I have the honor of killing?"

"A bit premature, but you may call me Miss Espionage."

"Miss Espionage?" he said with a sneer. "You Americans are so fond of your outrageous code names. Well, I can see we're going to have to do this the hard way."

Klara knew it would be impossible to talk her way out of this situation, and that the baron would catch her before she could reach the door, so she stepped into the circle of light. He glanced up and down, taking in her costume, and his body relaxed. Apparently, he no longer took her as a serious opponent and Klara vowed to make him pay for the indignity of his gaze.

Teufel circled to the right, trying to get a measure of her fighting style. Klara watched how he rose on the balls of his feet to move, how he shifted his body to keep his weight centered. Not for the first time was she thankful for all the training she'd received from the Japanese Ambassador's aide during the war.

Baron Teufel feinted a few times to draw her closer before making a grab for her arm. She stepped back and snapped a kick, catching him just below the kneecap. He grunted in pain and swung at her head with a meaty fist. Twisting at the waist, she caught his hand as it slid past and tugged, then shoved her hip into his and used his momentum to toss him over her shoulder into some of the nearby tables.

He let out a yowl and rolled up to his feet. Before Klara could close in, he lunged at her, slamming a shoulder into her waist. She grabbed his coat's lapels as they fell. As they hit the ground, she let herself roll backward and shoved her feet upward, breaking the baron's grip on her and sending him flying into the darkness across the room.

She retreated out of the light in the other direction and waited for her eyes to adjust to dim light. She could see him moving across the room but couldn't quite make out what he was doing. Deciding there was nothing to gain engaging him physically, she reached down and unhooked the flap on her holster. She watched as the baron moved closer and then she heard the whistle of a whip moving through the air. She dove to one side as the black leather snaked out toward her, cracking just a few inches over her back.

She could hear the hate and embarrassment in his snarl. "Yes, run, you little mouse. Run."

Clawing her Walther out of its holster, she rolled on the ground to avoid a second strike. Before the baron could move out of the light, she had it in her right hand and snapped off two shots. One of them struck the baron in the shoulder, spinning him backward. She took quick aim, and her third shot shattered the single bulb illuminating the room. She rolled to the left and froze, straining to hear anything. The darkness was impenetrable, and she held her breath, trying not to give her position away.

Now it was a matter of whose nerves would give way first. When they found each other, they were likely to be right on top of one another, rendering her pistol useless, so she inched it back into its holster and drew a thin knife out of her boot. Squatting as low as she could, she slowly turned her head, trying to figure out where the baron had gone.

The seconds stretched out in the Stygian blackness, and it felt like an eternity between each heartbeat. She reached out with her left hand, and it brushed against an overturned chair. Carefully rising, she hooked her hand around the metal folding chair and then tossed it to her left. The chair clattered across the floor, and she heard the crack from a whip striking near where the chair had fallen.

The baron must have realized he'd given his position away as she heard his footsteps retreating toward the far wall. She moved forward just in time to hear masonry shifting. There was a small flash of light, revealing the baron slipping through a false panel on the other side of the room. She raced across as the panel closed, only to stumble over another chair in the sudden darkness that sent her and her knife tumbling in different directions. Cursing a couple of bruised shins in four languages, Klara picked herself up and recovered her knife after some searching.

Round one had gone to the baron, but the game was still young.

When Otto did not call the next day, Klara began wondering if she had overplayed her hand the other night. If the council panicked, they would scatter like dandelion seeds before Smithson could hunt them down. She was counting on Teufel's pride not permitting him to admit he had discovered an infiltrator and then let her get away. In fact, she suspected the baron was covering up all evidence she'd ever been there. He had to find and eliminate her quickly and quietly because if "Miss Espionage" exposed his failure, his life would be measured in hours. After all, at his own admission, this "Triumvirate" had long arms and an even longer memory.

As evening fell, there was a knock on her door. She grabbed her pistol and positioned herself just out of the line of fire before responding. "Who's there?"

"Sergeant MacDougall, ma'am."

She quickly hid her pistol and opened the door. "Why, Sergeant, I'm surprised to see you. What brings you here?"

"Pardon the bother, ma'am, but I noticed you hadn't come down for dinner. I'd like to invite you to join me . . ." He paused before blushing slightly. "I'd like to make up for the unseemly way I behaved yesterday."

"You were only doing your duty."

"No, ma'am. I'd like to redeem myself for my beastly behavior, if you'll give me the chance."

Klara saw the blush spreading and decided to tease him a bit. "Why, Sergeant, are you certain this is an *official* invitation?"

Before the Scotsman hyperventilated, she stepped forward and placed her hand on his arm. "I'm sorry. I'd be delighted to accept. Give me a moment to get changed and I'll be right down."

Sergeant MacDougall took a deep breath and put on a brave face. "I'll have the staff keep the kitchen open a bit longer."

She watched with amusement as he nearly ran back to the elevator and shut the door behind him—in time to see her window curtain blowing in the evening breeze. She froze and glanced around the room, then with a swift movement pulled the door to her washroom open, her pistol at the ready.

"Good evening, Lorelei."

Klara's weapon didn't waver, but she felt the tension leave her face. "Good evening, *Fraulein Doktor*."

The older woman stepped into the room, ignoring the gun trained on her, and sat down at the makeup table. "Please, this is a social call. Call me Annabelle."

Klara set her pistol down and sat down on the bed, facing her former mentor. "I'm pleased to see that you haven't lost your touch."

Annabelle laughed softly. "Please. It was easy. The poor sergeant had no eyes for anyone but you. The whole hotel could have disappeared in a cloud of smoke, and he wouldn't have noticed. I am surprised *you* didn't catch the window raising, but the sergeant certainly made a good distraction. I'm glad to see you haven't lost your touch at flustering your opponents. You are your mother's daughter, without a doubt."

A wry smile made its way to Klara's face. Getting any praise out of Annabelle was an accomplishment, but for her to mention Klara's mother, Mata Hari, was high praise indeed. They had been contemporaries and friendly rivals in the First World War, so to be compared to her mother meant Annabelle saw her as a colleague rather than a bumbling student.

"You have been waiting for a call, yes?"

Klara tensed slightly, wondering if the baron had spoken to her or not. "I was, but I'm guessing Otto ran into some difficulties."

"Oh, no difficulties. But regardless of your apprehensions, you will not be going to Istanbul. At least not yet."

"But if I do not go soon, I'm not sure if I'll be able to go at all without raising more suspicions. Otto's incompetence already put me at risk. The British *seem* to have bought my story, but I cannot be certain."

"Do not worry. I am the reason you're not going to Istanbul quite yet."

"You?"

"My dear, you seem like Lorelei. You sound like her . . ." Annabelle paused as she walked around the room, glancing up and down at Klara. Klara noticed she never quite got close enough to put herself in danger and had no doubt Annabelle was armed in some way that she'd never see until the last moment. "You look like her . . . even move like her. However, one cursory examination is insufficient to prove the truth."

Klara felt like a bug under a microscope and needed a break from those staring eyes. "I'm honored to draw your interest. I'm assuming that since you are here, you're part of the council that Otto mentioned?"

"Otto says many things he probably shouldn't. He fancies himself to be a modern-day soldier of fortune, but he's easy to read. Someday, his need to be the center of attention will mean he'll be the center of a bull's-eye."

And there's the Fraulein Doktor *who frightened the hell out of me when I was younger.*

"Anyway, this is neither the time nor place to discover the truth of the matter. In two days, a car will come for you. I have a small place outside of Innsbruck. You're going to be contacted by one of your New York relatives, who wants to meet to discuss your disputed inheritance. We will settle things then."

Annabelle walked to the window and ensured no one else was on the fire escape before she slid the window up. "Now, hurry along. We don't want to keep the poor sergeant waiting. If you stand him up, he might just keel right over."

Later that evening, Klara shut the door to her room behind her after thanking the sergeant for escorting her to dinner. Her eyes narrowed as she noted a small card laying on her pillow and she did a quick check of the room once she was certain she was alone. Nothing seemed out of place and her luggage appeared to be untouched, but she found herself staying out of direct sight of the windows just in case.

I swear, the way people come and go from this hotel room, I might as well be sleeping in Grand Central Station. She glanced out the window, but only the night scene of Vienna was visible. *So much for being circumspect. It seems like everyone in Vienna already knows who I am and where I'm staying. To be honest, I'm getting a little tired of people using my room more than I am.*

She picked up the card and turned it over in her hands. To her surprise, it was blank. She thought for a moment and then a smile crossed her face. She walked over to the lamp and removed the shade. Holding the card close to the light bulb, the card slowly revealed brown letters. Someone had used lemon juice to send a hidden message.

Come downstairs to Room 828.

She slipped her Walther into her clutch and then walked down the hall to the elevator. A short ride later, she approached room 828 and knocked. The door opened a crack before swinging open to allow her in. She stepped in to find Smithson standing there, smiling at her.

"I hope you had a pleasant visit."

A note of exasperation escaped when she replied. "Why are

you *still* interfering in my mission?"

"I am doing my best *not* to interfere. However, it *was* hard to miss a middle-aged woman spryly making her way up the fire escape right past my window. And before you ask, yes, I did take this room once I knew you were here so I could keep an eye on things."

"And you weren't concerned that might be a bit suspicious?"

"Not when everyone is keeping their eyes on you. I'm virtually a ghost in Vienna thanks to your presence." He motioned her toward one of the chairs in his room before sitting on his bed and opening a leather briefcase. "We have people gathering information on the report you submitted. When do you leave for Istanbul?"

"I don't."

Klara took no small satisfaction out of the dumbfounded look on Phillip's face. Before he could recover, she continued. "As you noted, I had a visitor. That was Annabelle, or *Fraulein* Doctor, a name you're probably familiar with. She has *reservations* about me, so she wants me to come to Innsbruck. If my memory is correct, she owns a small villa there. Her cousin married into Austrian nobility before the First War."

"Innsbruck is in the French Sector and about as far from Vienna as you can get."

"I think she intends to test me without interference from the other members of the council. I do not believe she knows about my encounter with Baron Teufel, but I wouldn't put it past her. She sees more than she admits and saves the information for maximum effect."

"You think she has plans beyond just ensuring you are who you are?"

"Of course. If all she needed to do was verify my credentials, she certainly could do so in Vienna, with or without the baron's influence. No, I think she has her own plans for both Operation Rheingold and me. Perhaps she wants another loyal set of eyes."

Klara rose and paced around the room before turning to Smithson. "It wouldn't surprise me if she answers to someone on this *Triumvirate* outside of normal channels. Having your own internal intelligence and security network to ensure the loyalty of your underlings is a very German thing to do, after all."

"If you're right, this could be the break we're looking for."

"Unfortunately, there's no time to get permission from Toby, so I'm making a command decision here, Phillip. I'm turning the Rheingold investigation over to you. You keep saying you're not involved in my investigation, but you also pointed out everyone's eyes are on me. It's the perfect time to switch things up. Let them worry about me while you work your magic. If it turns out this is merely Annabelle testing my loyalty, we'll have two different vectors into Rheingold. However, if I can move closer to this mysterious leadership, I think that takes precedence over smuggling people. Who knows, if you follow one trail and I follow the other, we may wind up at the same spot and have the entire organization."

Phillip leaned back on the bed, staring up at the ceiling. After a bit, he sat back upright and looked at Klara. "I don't like the fact you're going to be completely exposed like this, but I also know you're best when you're calling your own shots. All right. I'll wait a few days before contacting Toby and then pick up the threads here. You've given us enough to get started."

She nodded and headed toward the door before Phillip spoke up again. "And for the record, I wasn't sent here to keep an eye on you. I really was working on a different issue in Garmisch when a little bird told me you were going to be in Vienna. Toby didn't even know until I contacted him right after Colonel Whitby-Smith decided to question you. The colonel already knew me, so I thought having someone vouch for you would make things go smoother."

"So, if you weren't assigned to this mission, why *did* you come?"

"Same reason I let you *escape* the first time we met."

Klara felt her cheeks getting warm and grabbed the door handle. "We'll have this conversation another day, Phillip. You know how impossible that is right now."

"Here's to another day."

She turned and lifted an imaginary toast back to him. "Another day."

As she walked down the hall to the elevator, her smile turned grim. *Another day. In our line of work, there are no guarantees we'll even see the sun rise tomorrow. We can worry about fairy tales and happy endings when we both retire. If either of us lives that long.*

Several days later, Klara watched as Innsbruck station came into view. The middle-aged American widow had been left behind in a washroom in the Vienna station and a vivacious, young, raven-haired woman stepped off the train. Speaking fluent French, she shamelessly flirted with the baggage handler and arranged for her luggage to be delivered to her hotel. Ensuring her hat was securely fastened, she picked up her hand luggage and strolled through the station and out to the taxi stand.

"*Mademoiselle* le Clerc?"

"*Oui.*"

A large gentleman in a driver's uniform approached her and extended his hand for her bag. "There is a car waiting for you outside."

"Oh, you are too kind. The hotel did not need to go to all this trouble."

"I'm afraid you're operating under an erroneous assumption, *Mademoiselle*. I am here to take you to the villa, per your earlier arrangements."

Klara smiled innocently at the driver. "Oh, what a surprise. I wasn't expecting to go to the villa for a few days. I had so hoped to get to explore Innsbruck."

The driver frowned and motioned for the bag again. "We all have a few hopes that occasionally get dashed. Your new employer thought it best to get you settled at the villa first. Once you're comfortable, then you will have time to explore the rest of the countryside."

"Yes, I suppose that is best. Very well, please lead on."

Klara followed him into the low-slung touring car, then waited as he secured her luggage from the baggage handler and placed her bags into the trunk. He held the rear door open for her and she slid in behind the passenger seat. He moved with military efficiency around to the driver's side and quickly had the car moving into the morning traffic.

After a few minutes, Klara's curiosity got the better of her and she spoke to her silent partner. "I am surprised you were waiting at the station for me. Is my host that anxious to see me?"

"We have an efficient way to deal with our guests. If you are who you claim to be, then it's best the Allies do not spot you here in town and begin nosing around. If you are not *who* you claim to be, well . . ." He paused for a moment for emphasis before continuing. "It's best that few people in town see you. They can't miss what they didn't know was there."

"Comforting."

"*Efficient*. You may as well sit back and relax. It's going to be a while before we reach our destination."

Klara glanced at the rearview mirror. She could tell from the set of the driver's mouth he was done talking, so she sat back and enjoyed the scenery of the Austrian Alps. She had spent time in Innsbruck before the war, taking skiing lessons during the day and dancing lessons at night. *Fraulein Doktor* believed her protégés should be well-rounded individuals. It made it easier to fit into any circumstance at a moment's notice.

Klara remembered the impromptu quizzes her mentor would spring on her, ranging from obscure Baroque composers to the effective range of a Browning Hi-Power with a silencer attached. Woe to the person who failed these tests. If you were lucky, you spent a night in the villa's library studying a list of topics as punishment. If you failed repeatedly, then you could be disciplined—or worst case, expelled from the program. However, if you were far enough along, where expulsion could threaten the organization . . . well, one learned not to ask questions when there was an empty spot at the dining table the next day.

Klara noted the driver was taking a roundabout way to reach the villa. Whether he was trying to see if he was being tailed, or if he had the hope of confusing Klara was unclear. She allowed herself a small smile at that thought. There would be no tail—she'd made certain of that before leaving Vienna, and even though it had been ten years since she'd been here, she knew this area well, thanks to her mentor's training regimen.

Eventually, the touring car pulled into an unfamiliar driveway and stopped before a fence. The driver pushed a button on the pillar next to the gate and spoke into a radio embedded into the concrete pillar. With a ponderous motion, the gate slowly swung inward and the car continued. Once through, the driver pressed a button on a pillar on the other side and waited to ensure the gate swung back into place and locked securely. He then steered the vehicle up a long, tree-lined driveway to stop in front of a large villa that showed signs of being recently renovated.

"Welcome to Ansitz Steyrer. Her other villa was damaged during the war, so she acquired this one while repairs are being made. It suits her purposes well."

"I remember this place. Wasn't this originally a children's mental hospital?"

"I can't speak for its original purpose, but yes, it was a hospital, but it's been abandoned for years. We've modified it to be *Fraulein Doktor*'s new school. The building's reputation discourages the curious, which is advantageous for us."

"Charming, I'm certain."

He finished parking the car just outside a large, detached garage and looked over his shoulder at Klara. "If you'll come with me, I'll show you to your room. You'll have ten minutes to store your things, at which time I'll take you to see the *doktor*. Any questions?"

"Short, sweet, and to the point. I only have one question."

"Which is . . . ?"

"Who do I have the pleasure of addressing?"

"You may call me Johann. You need not introduce yourself. I and the rest of the staff have been thoroughly briefed."

Klara nodded and waited until Johann opened the door. After a short visit to her room and a quick walk through the villa, she was ushered into a sitting room where Annabelle was waiting with a small cart holding assorted pastries and a silver teapot.

Annabelle lowered her cup to the cart when she spotted Klara. "Ah, Lorelei, please won't you be seated. It's not often that I get to host one of my graduates."

Klara did not allow herself to be fooled by Annabelle's relaxed attitude. While there was a broad smile on her face, that smile did not reach her mentor's eyes. Klara felt like a mongoose entering a cobra's lair. Exuding a casualness she did not feel, she sat down in the proffered chair and waited until Annabelle glanced at the teapot. Klara carefully refilled her mentor's cup before pouring one for herself.

Fraulein Doktor smiled broadly and gave Klara an approving nod. "Ah, you have remembered the proprieties. This is good. So many young people have let their manners slip since the war. After all, manners separate beasts from men and peasants from the nobility. They may have stripped our titles, but they cannot remove the nobility of our blood and our spirits."

"I'm afraid I only can claim the nobility of the spirit. As you well know, my lineage is about as far from noble as you can get. However, you didn't send for me to review my etiquette."

"No child, I didn't but humor an old woman. When one approaches her mid-sixties, one is allowed to take their time and occasionally reminisce. Your presence stirred up a hornet's nest in Vienna, my dear. I do not know what you did to poor Katarina, but the girl was positively foaming at the mouth for a chance to go one-on-one with you, especially when she discovered you were a trained pilot."

"Katarina?"

"Katarina Blud. You probably know her better by her code name 'Baroness Blood.' Really, couldn't the former Reich come up with a better name? And worse, they had to design such a ridiculous costume? Obviously from a man's drawing board."

"Ah, yes. I had the opportunity to make the baroness's

acquaintance back in Vienna. However, we never crossed paths during the war."

"Probably just as well. She did a passable job against the average Allied aviator, but she couldn't keep her focus on the mission. Always getting distracted by a pair of pretty eyes and a good physique. But she's good at what she does and suits Rheingold's purposes. Which brings us back to the question at hand: Do *you* suit Rheingold's purposes?"

"While I would like to flatter myself and say yes again, I must point out that while I made the initial attempt, it was your organization's choice to contact me. If you don't want to take advantage of my talents, that's your decision. However, I think you'd be making a mistake if you turn me away."

"Or eliminate you."

"If you believe you can."

A real smile crossed Annabelle's face. "Oh ho! I was wondering when poor Klara Zelle would bare her teeth and become Lorelei. You do the passive bystander very well, child, but you're not fooling me. Even now, you're mentally cataloging everything around you, examining and discarding courses of action from killing me outright to the best escape route from the villa. I would not and do not expect less from you. Your very stillness betrays your thoughts to me."

"I also would expect nothing less from *Fraulein Doktor.* Your lessons were taken well to heart."

"The desire of a protégé to surpass their mentor is a tradition stretching back to Socrates and Plato and even further. The question is, how far is the protégé willing to go to achieve this goal and what sacrifices are they willing to make?"

Klara knew this was no idle banter. It was no longer a question if she had been accepted as Lorelei. Still, there would be a cost. What was her mentor conjuring up behind that dragon's smile?

"Do you believe I came back to Europe to usurp your place in the organization?"

"What I believe is immaterial, Lorelei. What *is* important is what I discover over the next few days. Take a little time. Get to know the grounds. Your tests begin tomorrow."

With that, Annabelle picked up her teacup and rose from her chair, moving to the piano across the room with steps so precise and silent, it almost seemed she was gliding just above the floor. Klara knew it was a technique her mentor had perfected to make her target uncomfortable. Luckily, she'd seen it so often, it would have been more concerning if Annabelle didn't move like that. She allowed a slight triumphant smile to settle on her lips for a split second before fixing her face in an inscrutable look. Annabelle's playing echoed through the silent villa as Klara retraced her steps to her room.

She glanced over at the luggage she had brought, knowing it had been thoroughly gone through while she was at her initial interview. Standard procedure for a situation like this. She thought about the costume in the hidden compartment in the bottom of her suitcase and knew there was no point in donning it anytime soon. While the shocking lack of material might distract her male opponents and the garish sight would distract any females, Annabelle would see through the disguise in seconds. Having been trained to observe and report since she was a teenager, the fifty intervening years had only sharpened her mentor's skills. No, it was going to take old-fashioned espionage work to ferret out the secrets of this villa and get her mission back on track.

I talked a good game with Phillip, but even if I can convince Annabelle I am who I am . . . which shouldn't be hard since it is the truth . . . there's no guarantee she's going to recruit me to work on Rheingold. There's every chance she's running her own operations and will assign me to that. It's a golden opportunity, but I hate deviating from my main mission when I was so close to getting into the pipeline.

Unsurprisingly, her windows were barred. Given the history of this building, it made sense the new occupants hadn't changed that. However, she would need to find ways to come and go without drawing attention to herself. Continuing her examination of her room, she searched for listening devices or cameras, but either they were so well hidden she couldn't find them or there were none. She resolved to assume the former just to be sure. A thorough exam of her wash closet showed no signs of bugs either, which made her feel a little more comfortable.

Since Annabelle had told her to familiarize herself with the grounds, she decided to take advantage of the opportunity and prowl around. Learning the layout of the villa and the grounds was probably the first test and she wanted to get off on the right foot with her mentor. The last thing she needed was remedial training.

The top floor of the villa was filled with rooms closely resembling hers, but only a few had new furniture and fixings. Some stood empty while others were filled with boxes and crates of unknown materials. While it was tempting to discover what lay hidden behind those slats, she forced herself to continue with her journey.

Moving to the main floor, she found the kitchen and dining room, although a dining hall would have been a better description. It was obvious from the size of the two rooms that the old hospital had held thirty or forty patients at any one time. The other rooms on the first floor contained offices, probably used by the original hospital staff, now used by Annabelle's personnel. A cursory search turned up nothing suspicious and Klara suspected this was the part of the villa open to any visitors. No, the true nature of the villa was elsewhere. She discovered Annabelle's living area just off the hall where the sitting room was located, but a quick glance at the guards at the hallway entrance told her that "explore the grounds" did not apply to this area. She passed by without slowing, resolving to make time to return when she might have the advantage.

A large oaken door opened to concrete steps descending into darkness. Finding the light switch, the naked bulbs hanging by wires from the ceiling cast a feeble light against the blackness waiting at the foot of the stairs. Klara felt the hair rising on the back of her neck and a wave of horror rushed over her as she eased onto the first step. She knew she was letting her imagination get the better of her, but if haunted houses were real, this was one.

At the bottom of the stairs, she found another light switch and flipped it on. There were several doors along one wall and two examination rooms on the other side. The examination rooms seemed normal enough, although what types of examinations were anyone's guess. The rooms across were little more than three-meter-by-three-meter squares, consisting of a metal bed fixed against the wall, a small toilet, and a wooden table bolted to the floor. She noted each door could only be opened from the outside and they had large sliding bolts as well as keyed locks. A single light illuminated each room, shining down from a recessed light behind thick glass. The switch for the lights was out in the hallway too. She could barely imagine being stuck in one of these rooms, completely at the mercy of whomever was on the outside.

A soft sound caught her attention and every nerve in her body screamed at her to head back upstairs into the sunlight, but she forced herself to act as if she hadn't heard a thing and continued her examination. At the far end of the basement, she discovered a metal door. To her surprise, despite its rusted and unkept appearance, the door swung open soundlessly. Just beyond was a large room with a table and several chairs. A large rolltop desk stood against one wall with a modern radio set resting on the desktop.

The sense of being observed grew stronger and as tempting as the new room was, she couldn't see any exits other than the door she stood in. Not wanting to be trapped, Klara went back to one of the examination rooms and grabbed a heavy notebook off one of the desks. Returning to the metal door, she opened it wide and wedged the notebook under the door, holding it open. Satisfied no one could just nudge it out of place, she stepped into the radio room and moved quickly to one side, freezing in place.

She heard and sensed nothing as she waited and was almost convinced her imagination was getting the better of her when she heard the distinct sound of footsteps approaching. She tensed and her patience was rewarded when a hand reached toward the notebook. She pounced like a wildcat, grabbing the hand in a pressure lock and twisting.

"I don't know who you are, but if you want to keep this hand, move carefully out where I can see you."

There was a moment of hesitation, so she applied more pressure, and she felt the arm go slack in defeat. Without releasing her grip, she moved out into the main room and was unsurprised when she discovered Johann on the other side of the door.

"Would you care to explain yourself?" she demanded.

"Would you?"

Klara fixed him with a pitying look. "I have express permission from *Fraulein Doktor* to examine the house and the grounds today. Do you have permission to interfere with my task? What could you possibly hope to gain by following me around?"

Johann let out a self-depreciating laugh. "You've obviously been outside the Fatherland too long. I watch you, someone else watches me, and everyone eventually reports back to *Fraulein Doktor.* That is the way of things. Even the *doktor* is watched by someone else. No one *ever* just wanders around unobserved."

Klara felt a shock at this revelation but tried to keep her face calm. "And who watches the *doktor*?"

Johann sniffed at the audacity of the question. "Above my pay grade. Now, would you mind turning loose of my hand? I'm losing all feeling in my fingers."

"One more question before I do: what did you hope to gain by locking me in a room with a radio set?"

"It was a test. Of course, the set is rigged only to communicate with the offices upstairs. There were questions about who you would try to contact if you believed you were captured."

"You're assuming there is a standby waiting to come rescue me?" she said with a laugh. Tightening her grip, she made sure he was looking directly at her before continuing. "Dear Johann, you did not pay attention when you were briefed on me. I don't work with a partner. I may have a contact to pass information to, but no one tells me how to do my job or checks over my shoulder to see if I'm doing things right. I'd be more likely to disassemble the radio to create a means to escape. And if the good *doktor* suggested this futile effort, then she's not the mentor I remember."

"No, this was my own personal test. One can never be too careful."

"But one can be stupid. If you wish to follow me around the rest of the estate, you're welcome to walk along with me, unless you're trying to improve your tracking skills. I think you'll find the walk rather boring. I will probably spend the hours until dinner getting intimately familiar with the outside, the garage, and at least one more trip through the villa proper. You may watch, but if you try to interfere again, I suspect *Fraulein Doktor* will have to put out a help-wanted ad, because she's going to need a new driver."

Johann shot her a look of pure hate once she released his hand and muttered something just below her hearing range before retreating up the stairs. Klara secured the notebook and slipped it into her handbag just to be certain it didn't disappear before her next visit and left the radio room without another glance. She was certain Johann wasn't the noise she'd heard earlier, his footsteps were too heavy, but there was no point in letting her other tail know she'd been made. If she exposed this one, they'd only assign another person, and she'd have to spot them all over again.

The villa's grounds were rather unremarkable except for the large stone wall surmounted with iron spikes. The walls angled inward slightly to make climbing them more difficult. After all, no one expected people to break *into* a mental hospital. Klara found a spot under a tree and sat down, trying to spot her tail. When staying in one spot didn't draw her shadow into the open, Klara found a tree with low limbs and climbed up high enough to see over the wall, but still low enough to keep an eye on the grounds surrounding her. She settled onto a large limb with her back against the trunk, trying to present an image of someone admiring the Alps beyond.

As she had hoped, her tail shifted position to get a better

look at what she was doing. Klara only caught a quick look at her face and noted the dark men's clothing she was wearing and a shock of platinum-blond hair before her tail disappeared into a nearby cluster of bushes. Satisfied she'd be able to identify her tail among the villa's staff, she climbed back down and did a thorough inventory of the villa's grounds. In the garage, she discovered four cars and a motorcycle, all in perfect condition. Above the garage was the chauffeur's quarters; at least three men lived here.

By the time she returned to her room to prepare for dinner, Klara felt she had a good feeling for the layout of the villa. She'd resisted the urge to go back and check out the radio room when she found herself growing bored with her inspection. Still, there was more to the basement than her cursory examination had exposed, especially since the equipment had shown signs of recent use—not what one would expect from an abandoned hospital.

That thought reminded her of the notebook she'd stuffed into her handbag, but glancing at the clock, she knew there was no time to examine it before dinner. Annabelle was a stickler for protocol, and her meals were served precisely at the same times every day. Unless one enjoyed sitting in the hall until the meal was done, it was best to be in your seat ahead of the dinner bell.

At five minutes until six, Klara slipped into her seat at the long dining table and waited quietly until Annabelle and two other people entered from a different part of the house. Klara didn't recognize the middle-aged men, but from their dress and manners, she knew they had never been in the military.

"Ah, *Herr* Wagner, *Herr* Tichka, may I introduce you to my friend Klara Zelle. *Fraulein* Zelle is visiting us from America." She then spoke directly to Klara, nodding her head at the two gentlemen. "*Herr* Wagner is a director at Mercedes-Benz and *Herr* Tichka is with the Swiss Bank Corporation. We are in discussions about establishing a foundation to deal with the issue of war orphans across Europe."

Klara kept her face neutral. "A worthy cause. While adults

make war, it is often the children who suffer the most."

Pausing for a moment to let the servants place the first course on the table, *Herr* Wagner lifted his monocle to his left eye and nodded sagely. "Very well put, *Fraulein* Zelle. Our lovely hostess has made her appeal in much the same manner. While our lawyers need to look over the papers, I have no doubt my board of directors will certainly be on board, especially if the Swiss Bank Corporation agrees."

Herr Tichka sat back in his chair and sipped from his coffee before responding. "You flatter me, *Herr* Wagner. I have no doubts my directors will feel the same, pending, of course, the lawyers don't spot something I have not."

Annabelle's eyes sparkled as she lifted her hands toward both of the men. "Gentlemen, hearing these words fills my heart with joy. Let us toast to a swift recovery for all of Europe and better days ahead."

Klara joined the two men in lifting her wineglass and then let the dinner conversation flow over and around her while she concentrated on what was—and wasn't—being said regarding the foundation. While Klara was certain a foundation would be established and some children aided by these and other contributions, she also knew beyond a shadow of a doubt that the real account books would show this was funding Annabelle's spy organization, with possibly some funneled into Rheingold.

The conversation continued well after the meal, but eventually the two men were escorted to the front door by Annabelle. Once Johann had bundled the visitors into the town car and was heading down the driveway, Annabelle motioned for Klara to follow her and led her back to the sitting room.

"Your impressions?"

Klara sat for a few moments to collect her thoughts. "Both men are altruistic. *Herr* Wagner was not a soldier, but from the look in his eyes, he was at least close to some action. *Herr* Tichka is not native Swiss. I would guess he's originally from Bohemia or possibly Moravia. He probably fled in 1938 just before the occupation. Both completely believe your foundation is legitimate and both, most likely, will do everything in their power to sway their boards to support your efforts."

"That is good, because I have been cultivating their friendships for the past six months to get to this point. Any other impressions?"

"I also do not believe for a second this foundation is legitimate. Oh, it will look good on paper, and the odds are good that the best Swiss auditors would never piece the truth together, but a significant amount of funding will be diverted for other operations controlled by you."

Annabelle's eyes narrowed, but her voice remained amiable. "And why do you say that?"

"Because, in your position, that's exactly what I would do. I have not had the opportunity to interview your staff yet, but I suspect you have at least one expert forger on your staff, and if my eyes don't deceive me, one of the best accountants from the Reichsbank is working as your head butler." Klara leaned back in her chair, feigning a nonchalance she did not feel. "It's been a few years, but we were introduced when I was on assignment in Berlin. I have suspicions about the purpose of these funds, but since I have no evidence, I'll keep those thoughts to myself."

Annabelle favored her with another honest smile. "Very perceptive. Without direct support from a government, we had to acquire our operating funds through various means. Unfortunately, many still loyal to the cause are unable to contribute in a meaningful way. So, we do what we must. Unlike that group in Vienna, we have not lowered ourselves to black marketing, burglary, and pandering. This is merely a temporary bridge until we secure more lucrative funding."

The Triumverate . . . ?

"I see the puzzlement in your eyes, Klara. How much had those fools, Otto and von Kruger, filled you in?"

"Only what they felt was healthy for both them and me. I know about the council, but Baroness Blood and von Kruger are small fish. They cannot be the leaders of Rheingold, mainly because I don't see you working under them."

"You understand me very well, Klara. Once I finished

checking your bona fides, I will explain much to you." For a split second, Annabelle let her guard slip and Klara could see the weariness on her face and the slump of her shoulders. "I am not as young as I once was, Lorelei. Your return is an opportunity I will not let go to waste." With that said, Annabelle shifted as if someone had slammed a ramrod up her back and the inscrutable mask was back in place. "However, if you are *not* who or what you claim, this will be a short and painful 'reunion.'"

"You *know* there exists no identifying data on me. Von Bruno was very thorough about finding my medical records, any fingerprints in the files, even the one photograph of the interior of my eyes was secured from Gestapo headquarters and destroyed. So, while I know who I am, I admit a certain amount of curiosity to see how *you* intend to satisfy yourself to my identity."

"We will settle this tomorrow. I have had a long day. You are excused."

Klara's alarm went off a few minutes after one in the morning. She reached under the pillow and turned it off, hoping the thick, downy pillow had muffled the sound in case anyone was listening in the hall. The rooms in the basement interested her, but she preferred to inspect them without someone watching over her shoulder. Even though Annabelle had given her permission to go anywhere and examine anything, there was no sense in tipping her hand just yet.

She went through her wardrobe, getting ready for this evening's stroll. Putting on a black tunic and a black pair of slacks, she tied her hair back into a tight bun, and slipped a pair of gloves through her belt, hidden beneath her tunic. She picked up a pair of crepe-soled flats but held them in her hand before moving to the door.

Easing it open, she saw no sign anyone else in the household was awake, although she knew at least one person would be on guard outside, and one inside. That was standard operating procedure. Moving quietly, she made her way down the hall and entered the toilet. After a suitable time had passed, she flushed, ran some water, and then made her way back to her room. In the darkness, she quietly opened and then shut her door, while she remained in the hall. Staring into the darkness, she saw no sign of movement and hoped that if someone had noticed her door opening, her act would fool them into thinking she'd returned to her bed.

Cautiously, she made her way to the stairwell and crouched behind the balustrade, examining the room below. The faintly glowing hands on her watch seemed to crawl as she put her shoes on and waited. As expected, a large man made his way through the room and went down the hallway toward the front door. She noted the time he was gone and as he passed through again, headed toward Annabelle's suite, she eased down the stairs and found a good place to hide in the living room.

When he made his second trip, Klara knew exactly how much time she had to get to the basement. She had already noted where all the furniture was on her daylight walks and easily made it across the room, down the hall, and through the heavy wooden door before the guard returned. At the bottom of the stairs, she turned on her flashlight.

The examination rooms looked no better in the dim light of her flashlight than they had in the glare of the bright overhead lights earlier. The examination tools and medical equipment seemed normal, and everything was meticulously organized and ready to use at a moment's notice. The shelves beyond the examination tables contained rows of journals, which reminded Klara of the book still in her handbag upstairs.

Picking up one of the journals that dated back to before the war, she saw it described different techniques the doctors had employed in attempting to cure their patients. Bile rose in her throat as she read the descriptions of their methods—and their results. The mortality rate had been incredibly high, which angered and disgusted Klara, knowing these were children being experimented on. The more she read, the more she realized the doctors were less concerned about curing the patients than they were in proving or disproving various theories. In their own words, these doctors saw their patients as only slightly more valuable than the average lab rat. Still, she was not here to right the wrongs of twenty-odd years ago. Snapping the book shut, she returned it to its place before moving to the radio room.

Walking carefully, she searched the floor near the desk for pressure plates before turning her attention to the desk itself. Initially ignoring the radio resting on top, she noted there were no apparent wires attached to the desk, and none of the drawers showed any obvious signs of alarms or locks. Klara knew old desks were notorious for having hidden compartments, however, so she pulled out a couple of the drawers on the top right-hand side and was rewarded with a recess at the back of the middle drawer, in which she found a small iron key. She placed it into a pouch on her belt and returned to her examination.

Beneath the desk were two doors at the back, and a small mat on the floor. Curious, she moved the mat to the side to reveal a small metal plate in the floor—and a keyhole. A twist of the key she'd found resulted in a tumbler being released and the metal plate rising up and back, to reveal a hole, and a ladder descending into the darkness. The shaft was about eight feet deep with an opening at its base, so taking a deep breath, she lowered herself, feetfirst, into the pit.

A briefly claustrophobic descent brought her to a large room that showed signs of being newly constructed and was filled with modern furniture. There was a door in the far wall as well as a gun rack filled with both modern and vintage weapons. Three ammo cans were also tucked neatly away beneath the rack. Two metal doors with small grates toward their tops graced the left-hand wall. The right-hand wall was lined with maps and file cabinets while a large table with several chairs circling it dominated the center of the room.

Moving quickly, she examined the farthest door; from the faint breeze coming around the edges, she realized it opened to the outside. Finding no alarms, she carefully opened it to find a tunnel running upward at an angle. A glimpse of night sky through some brush revealed that the passageway came out in the small garden behind the garage.

Returning to the subbasement, Klara made her way to the iron doors. Through the open grate on the first one, she spotted a metal bed bolted to the wall and a bucket in one corner. It reminded her of the rooms above and she wondered what the connection could be. When she glanced into the other room, she had to force herself not to gasp. A man was manacled to the wall, his slumping body held upright by the chains holding his arms and feet. She couldn't tell how long he'd been there, but it was obvious he wasn't going to last much longer. She heard him mumbling in French in his delirium.

She fought against her instinct to try to rescue this man. He might be a prisoner. He also might be a plant set up by Annabelle as a test. The presence of the tunnel was explained. If she was bringing people back to her villa to interrogate them, moving them from the garage to the garden and then down through the tunnel to this room would ensure no one, even guests staying at the villa, would be the wiser. Klara forced herself to turn away.

She had just begun to examine the maps on the wall when the overhead lights snapped on and the door to the tunnel opened. Annabelle stepped through the door and moved triumphantly toward the table, flanked by two of her servants armed with MP-40 machine pistols.

"So, you have found our little nest, Lorelei. What do you think?"

"I think you've done quite well for yourself," Klara replied honestly. "Even with the relative isolation of this villa, it could not have been easy to dig this without drawing attention, especially without undermining the garage above. Your choice of engineers was exactly what I would expect from you."

Annabelle allowed a faint smile, and Klara was satisfied to realize her old mentor could still be flattered, if only briefly. "Yes, I found a young man assigned to an engineering unit during the war. He proved quite useful to me. Unfortunately, others in the organization also saw his value and requisitioned him away from me. Good help is so hard to get these days, but one does what one must."

"Must have been something—or *someone*—important, to requisition anything away from you."

Annabelle's eyes narrowed, but Klara could see the anger was directed elsewhere. "Quite. A dreadful inconvenience, but as you know, we all answer to someone. And since the cause was a good one, I couldn't kick up too much fuss."

"Oh?"

"Save your curiosity, Lorelei. You haven't earned that privilege quite yet. Bad things happen if one has *too* much curiosity about the wrong things."

Klara heard the implied threat in Annabelle's tone, nodded to show she got the message, and changed the subject. "And the gentleman?" she asked, indicating the second door.

"A French agent with the wrong kind of curiosity. He was snooping, so we decided to take him on a guided tour to ensure he saw what he was looking for. He was suitably impressed. Unfortunately, he's going to turn up beneath a boulder under some snow miles from here. I don't know if you've heard, but these mountains are treacherous. Why, fifteen to twenty hikers are killed every year in this area, and it sometimes takes *years* for their bodies to be found. I suspect the authorities will determine he starved to death or was crushed while trapped in a landslide. Poor unfortunate man."

"A most horrible way to die, I imagine."

"I can't think of many worse. Trapped, knowing you have no way to escape the inevitable. There are more merciful ways to die—a quick thrust with a knife or a well-aimed gunshot. But those deaths are reserved for those who cooperate. Obstinate people like our friend in there bring their own horrible deaths upon themselves."

Klara did her best to keep her face straight, but she couldn't help the cold shiver that ran up her spine. She'd been trained as a spy since she was a child and knew most spies met a gruesome fate at the end, her mother included. Still, this was a side of Annabelle she'd never seen before. Any humanity she thought her mentor had before was simply a façade. In this moment, she saw her mentor for who she truly was.

"You seem upset, Klara. Surely you're not feeling sympathy for the man in there?"

Klara straightened and looked her mentor directly in the eyes. "It's never pleasant to consider one's own mortality. If things had gone differently, that could have easily been me."

"Be sure you remember that. Just because the shooting stopped doesn't mean the war is over. For people like us, it is never over."

The next few days flew by as Annabelle put Klara through a battery of tests. Some as simple as being given a document for a minute and then being asked to reproduce it an hour later, navigating the house blindfolded against a stopwatch, and going outside and spotting staff members hidden around the grounds. All relatively straightforward tests, things she'd passed early in her training under Annabelle—things that von Bruno had waved away as stage theatrics.

In between the physical and mental tests, she knew her whole person was being evaluated by Annabelle. She watched every move Klara made, every decision she made, how she added sugar to her coffee . . . Klara knew everything was being cataloged and weighed against the image Annabelle had from nine years ago. While she had fooled some of the greatest spy agencies in the world with her disguises, how do you prove you really are you to someone who doesn't believe you? She felt her nerves fraying under the perpetual microscope, but she knew that also was part of Annabelle's strategy.

"Klara, do I have your undivided attention?"

She kicked herself mentally for letting her concentration drift. "Of course. The organization SMERSH, a counter-espionage unit, was created under the Main Directorate of State Security, which was itself under the NKVD. Officially, disbanded in 1946, it was subsumed back into the new Ministry of Military Forces. However, knowing Stalin and his paranoia, there is no reason to believe SMERSH is no longer operational. Even the possibility of its existence is currently the greatest threat to Rheingold."

Annabelle nodded before continuing. "The Americans and British believe they understand espionage, but they are still in elementary school when it comes to counterespionage. Their governments and agencies have been riddled with Soviet spies for years." She stopped and took a sip of tea, her mouth curling as if she was tasting something foul. "Honestly, if the *Abwehr* had been run by even slightly competent leadership, things would have been different. I swear, sometimes I believe Canaris was acting against the Reich instead of for it. No wonder he was executed right before the war ended."

Once she had recomposed herself, she stared at Klara and continued. "No, if we are to protect ourselves, we must become as ruthless as our enemies. Weed out the gullible, the fragile, the mentally and morally weak among our ranks. You cannot rely on loyalty or nationalism. Sometimes, you must remind them harshly who they should really fear. Rheingold is merely one facet of the plan. Even if the incompetents in charge fail completely, they are a small and easily survivable loss. Much as I hate to use old bromides, this organization is like a hydra. Cut one head off, two arise in its place. Unless you can reach the heart, you cannot stop this movement."

"I look forward to serving in whatever capacity I can. However, if Rheingold is underperforming, then perhaps it needs your personal touch?"

"No. I will cooperate with von Kruger and Blud, but I will not be subordinate to them. They do well enough, but their security is too light and Teufel is already compromised, though he'll never admit it."

"Teufel is involved also? What did the good baron do this time?"

"He believes no one knows about his encounter with an American mystery woman . . . an encounter that took place at a meeting I myself had been at earlier. And to make matters worse, the fool allowed her to escape. The only reason I have not acted is my sources tell me this costumed interloper has not been seen since. If this involved anyone other than the baron, I'd chalk this odd report to good schnapps, but the details are concerning."

Klara nodded sympathetically. "What is it about Americans and their garishly dressed heroes?"

"I blame it on decadent Hollywood. They need bigger and bolder visions for the lesser people to look up to. The costumes rally the people, make the wearers bigger-than-life. Ah, you must have missed when even the Fatherland tried creating super-soldiers like Captain Nazi and the Black Axeman. Propaganda at its finest."

"No, those reports did not filter down while I was on assignment. They sound like they're right out of those comic books so popular with American children."

"Still, it is concerning. Which is why I'm going to send you back to Vienna."

Klara straightened almost involuntarily. It was as if she was sixteen again and getting her first real assignment from *Fraulein Doktor.* "What do you need?"

"Return to Vienna. You are not to go to Istanbul, no matter what von Kruger may have in mind. You must eliminate this American mystery woman. She knows more than she should and if she has not acted, then she is planning something. We need to nip it in the bud before she can bring her plan to fruition. Tell no one of your mission and if asked, refer them to me."

"Do we have anything to go on besides one report about Baron Teufel?"

"No. Which is why this is a perfect mission for you, Lorelei. Use the skills I taught you, skills I see have not atrophied in the years we've been apart. Do not fail me. I'd hate for the authorities to find yet another tragic victim of the mountains."

As night fell in Vienna, Klara stepped out onto the fire escape of her new hotel in the American sector. She was curious to know what Lieutenant Colonel Phillip Smithson had discovered during her time in Innsbruck, but she suspected Annabelle would have people watching her old hotel. She'd already shaken four tails since she'd arrived back in Vienna. Whether they were from the Americans, the Germans, or Annabelle herself, she didn't know and really didn't care. All she knew was their presence was making an already difficult job even harder.

It's going to be difficult to produce evidence that I've completed this mission. After all, I don't feel particularly self-destructive. I guess I could check in the morgues for a woman who's roughly my shape and dress her in that ridiculous costume. I don't think Teufel got that good a look at me, so passing someone else off as me might work. Still, let's save that as a last resort.

Making her way down the fire escape, Klara crept though the alley and came out onto a street several blocks away from her hotel. She stopped at a different hotel and made a short phone call. A few minutes later, a car pulled up, and Otto Piske motioned to her. She got into the car, and they drove around in silence until Otto was satisfied no one had followed them and pulled over away from any streetlamps.

"I didn't expect you back in Vienna so soon."

Klara turned slightly to face him. "I didn't expect to be back here either, but the situation has changed. I need you to get me in contact with the council."

He shook his head in resignation. "We received a wire from Innsbruck instructing us to give you all the cooperation we could, but it's going to take time to make arrangements."

"Otto, I know you're a fixer, so *fix* this. I need to see the council no later than midnight two days from now. Otherwise, I'll go over their heads, whether that's contacting Istanbul or wherever to get the authority I need to get their lazy butts in gear."

Otto paled at her threat. "No, no, there's no reason to go to those lengths. Do you have a number where I can reach you?"

"I'm staying at the Grand Hotel Wien. Ask for Tatiana Simeonov."

"I'll see what I can do."

Klara put her hand on his shoulder, slowly tightening her grip until she was certain she had his full attention. "Otto, I'm going to tell you this because you've been straight with me. You're a marked man. If you don't prove yourself useful—and soon—it's likely the Russians will be buying nylons from your successor. Make this happen and I'll do what I can to protect you. Fail me, and as someone once told me, 'What's one more body being fished out of the Danube?'"

Otto's eyes widened in surprise, then narrowed. "Do I need to be there?"

"Do you think it wise?"

He didn't answer that question but asked another. "No later than midnight two days from now?"

"Yes."

"Expect it sooner."

Klara spent the next day familiarizing herself with the center of Vienna. Unlike the other sections of town, the Innere Stadt district was under joint control, so it felt like every time she turned a corner, she spotted a jeep driving down one of the city streets, each carrying a member of all four of the occupying forces. She was stopped every so often to show her papers and to answer questions about where she was from, why she was there, where she was going, and so on. She was half convinced she was getting stopped simply because she was an attractive woman without a male escort.

Returning to her hotel that evening, she stopped by the front desk to retrieve her key and was given two messages. She waited until she returned to her room to try and read them. The first message was long and rambling, but when she took the first letter of each word, the real message was revealed: Otto had accomplished his mission. The meeting was arranged for seven p.m. tomorrow evening. A driver would call about six thirty and she should be waiting outside the hotel. He also hinted some of the council members weren't happy with being summoned.

The second message was from someone she didn't know, but examining it closer, she smelled the faintest hint of lemon juice on the paper. Holding the paper near the light bulb turned the hidden writing brown and she was able to make out the real message. It was from Smithson. He was about to move on the Viennese portion of Rheingold and there would be a simultaneous raid in Istanbul.

He also had heard from an informant someone important was calling a meeting for tomorrow. He would wait until after the meeting broke up to move in to allow a certain someone to escape.

She didn't know if she was glad Phillip was wrapping things up in Vienna or if she was angry he'd discovered her presence so quickly. She carefully destroyed both messages and reinforced the lock on her window. She'd gotten enough unwanted visitors at the other hotel and wanted to have at least one night of uninterrupted sleep before the showdown.

She'd just laid her head on her pillow when she heard the by-now familiar sound of someone on the fire escape near her balcony. She grabbed her pistol from under her pillow and slipped out of bed, moving into the deepest shadows. Before she had reoriented herself, there was the sound of breaking glass, and she saw feathers fly up into the air as rounds from a silenced gun struck her pillow and comforter. She moved to confront the intruder, but she heard the clatter of running feet.

By the time she reached the window, all she could see was a dark figure climbing down into the alley and disappearing. She wasted no time dressing and then gathering her things once she was certain there wasn't a second team lying in wait. As quickly as she had finished packing, Klara descended the fire escape herself and disappeared into the darkness of the alley below.

Klara made her way down the Opernring, staying in the

shadows as much as possible until she reached the Hotel Bristol. It took a bit of negotiating with the night clerk, who was rightly suspicious of someone trying to check in at so late an hour, but eventually she managed to get a room. After securing it and making a small bed on the floor out of sight from any windows, she finally fell into a fitful sleep.

The next morning, Klara changed her appearance once again and made her way through the city until she found the alleyway leading to the building where she'd first encountered the council. It was unlikely there was anything of interest, as it was probably just a convenient place to meet. Still, with someone actively hunting her, there was no point in making assumptions anymore. She needed hard evidence—evidence Otto would be unlikely able to—or willing to—provide.

Once she was certain no one was looking, she approached the doorway and inspected it for any signs of alarms. Finding nothing, she quickly tumbled the lock and slipped inside. Remembering the alarm on the stairwell, she took her time descending and found the entryway she was looking for. She moved along the edge of the room until she found the main light switches, throwing the room into a harsh light.

It didn't look any more impressive than it had that night, just dingier. Examining the table in the middle, she noted the legs were bolted to the floor. A small smile settled on her lips as she found boards aligned perfectly with the width of the table, unlike the others in the room that were offset.

She investigated the area where Baron Teufel had disappeared through the wall and found two buttons hidden beneath a shelf on the wall. The first button revealed the false wall the baron had used to make his escape. The passage led up to a store front that was entirely too dust free to be as abandoned as it appeared at first glance. The broken furniture and glassware were strategically placed to make a casual passerby think no one was using the building, while not actually inhibiting the passage of people or items to the back room. The lock on the back room was designed to keep out the average thief, but it was childishly simple for her. Once through the door, she discovered an arsenal of weapons, not only German, but there were weapons and uniforms of all the Allied soldiers. No doubt there were jeeps of various styles hidden nearby too.

It wasn't a bad plan when you thought about it, imitating various military police patrols to smuggle goods or people through the city. With the mixed makeup of the patrols in the Innere Stadt, it was likely none of the allied soldiers knew all the members in their own unit, much less the other Allied forces. Besides, it had seemed the American and British MPs were busier watching their Soviet counterparts and vice versa than they were watching for actual criminal activity.

Finishing searching upstairs gave her no other clues to the council's plans, so she returned to the basement. As soon as she pushed the second button, she heard machinery starting and the table slowly rotated ninety degrees, revealing a stairway going down. She pulled her flashlight out of her handbag and made her way down the concrete steps. The subbasement showed signs of recent construction, and she found another button on the wall about halfway down the stairs. Pushing it caused the table to rotate back into place. A faint sense of claustrophobia settled in on her, but she pushed on to the landing below.

At the bottom of the stairs were two doors with frosted glass on the upper half. Standing still, she heard soft voices coming from one of the rooms. Moving closer, she realized it was a couple of men speaking over a radio set. She couldn't quite make out what was being said, but she decided there was probably more to be found in the other office.

Once again, her lockpicks flashed and the door quietly opened under her push. This was a utilitarian room, with a desk with a large leather chair dominating the space. A row of file cabinets rested against the left wall and a bookcase was in the rear right corner. She moved to the desk and found the drawers locked. Deciding to go for the low-hanging fruit, she opened one of the file cabinet drawers and discovered a series of files listing names, points of origins, dates of transfers, and ultimate destinations. Pulling out a small camera from her handbag, she began photographing as many of the files as she could.

This could blow the top off Operation Rheingold. Knowing who's missing and where they're at could help us unravel not only the people-smuggling part but lead us to what's really going on here. I think this is a lot bigger operation than Toby suspected. It's important we stop it before they put whatever they're planning into motion.

There's no way someone like von Kruger or even Teufel are the big fish. This feels like something put into motion before the Reich ever fell. A fail-safe, so to speak. The real question is, who are the Triumvirate and what is their ultimate goal?

Realizing there was a chance the radio operators had heard the table mechanism, she knew it was only a matter of time before someone got curious. She finished photographing the files from one set of the cabinets and reluctantly put them away in the same manner she'd found them. She turned her attention to the desk and picked the lock to the lower drawer.

The drawer contained information about the daily activities of the council—mundane records like expenses, salaries, and so on. All useful information, but nothing that brought her any clarity. As she went to push the drawer back in, she felt something catch on the bottom. Shaking her head at not considering such a simple trick, she felt underneath the drawer and found an envelope taped to the underside.

To her surprise, Klara found it was her old *Abwehr* records, listing missions she'd been on, efficiency reports, and so on. There were several photographs of her in the file, both from before and during the war as well as photographs of her in Vienna. Someone had been going to great lengths to keep her under observation, and that concerned her. The file listed her real name instead of her *Abwehr* code name, and she wondered how many people had access to this information. The last few pages were an account of her activities in Vienna up to the point she left for Innsbruck, and a copy of the message from Annabelle telling them that Lorelei was coming.

It was the last line of the message that caused her to take a quick breath:

Lorelei cannot be trusted. Eliminate with extreme prejudice.

Klara slipped the envelope into her handbag and made her way to the door. There was no sound in the hallway, so after securing her Walther, she eased her way out and headed toward the stairs. Just as she passed the door to the radio room, it suddenly flew open, and the operators rushed out. She had no time to fire, so she pistol-whipped the first man across the face, and he slumped against the wall. She leaped to the side, letting the other man barrel past her. She slammed her pistol's butt down on the back of his head, sending him crashing to the floor. The first operator's eyes were just starting to uncross when she slammed her knee into his groin and then hit him again in the side of the head with her pistol. His eyes rolled back in his head, and he dropped to the ground as if all of his bones had turned to jelly.

She hit the second man on the head again for good measure and then rushed to the stairs. She had to assume the radio operators had contacted someone while she was in the other office. She hit the button and waited impatiently while the table rotated. To her relief, she didn't see anyone in the room above, so she hurried over to the shelf and rotated the table back into place before shorting out the buttons. She knew the operators wouldn't die before the Allies had a chance to secure this building and collect the evidence in the files below. With the buttons destroyed, though, she couldn't use the passage to the storefront, so she hurried up the stairs and out to the alley.

She'd just reached the street when a bullet cracked a brick just a few inches above her head and she heard shouting coming from the other direction. She ducked around the corner and hurried down the street, slipping into the first store she spotted, then spent the next ten minutes ducking into and out of stores, restaurants, and hotels until she was certain she had lost her pursuers.

Klara wasn't certain whether the operators had identified her or if they were just reacting to an intruder. However, if the council managed to reach them before the Allies could, there would be no doubt who had been there. It was a race against time and Klara had to admit the odds were against her, since she only knew the council members and a few of their operatives. Anyone she encountered could be someone targeting her.

She slipped into a hotel and went to the washroom. A few minutes later, with a quick change of wig and turning her outfit inside out, she emerged as a middle-aged housewife, wearing a dusty-gray dress and flats. She stopped at the store next door, bought a couple of small items, and put her handbag into the sack. Armed with her props, she caught a local bus and took it for several stops before changing to a different line. She changed buses twice more before going into another hotel and emerging as a young blond woman in an elegant blue dress and heels. She had peeled the false sides off her white handbag, and it was now black. She caught a cab and had it drop her off a block away from the Hotel Sacher.

She walked past the hotel and turned a few streets down before working her way back through the alleys. She was about a half block away from the back of the hotel when she spotted two people hiding in a doorway with a clear view of the rear entrance, which meant the front of the hotel and all the fire escapes probably were under observation also. There was a chance operatives were already inside as well. Still, she knew dealing with these two was her best option.

She glanced down at her clothes and knew trying to fight or even flee in this outfit was going to be impossible. So, sighing heavily, she found a spot in the alley out of sight and unhooked the false bottom on her handbag. She slipped into her Miss Espionage costume and pulled out a special blue magazine for her Walther, loaded with anesthetic rounds. *I hope these work like the boys in the lab said they would. Now would be a really bad time to find out they're a flop.* She twisted the silencer onto the end of the barrel and, taking a deep breath, made her way down the alley, staying tight against the buildings, taking full advantage of the debris and trash cans to approach as close as she could.

Klara paused twenty feet away from the pair, and while she

hated to rely on untested ammunition, she had to take them out quickly, or the alarm would be raised. If that happened, any chance of reaching Lieutenant Colonel Smithson was doomed. She pulled the trigger in quick succession and the men crumpled without a sound. She dragged them into the shadows, where a quick frisk turned up no identification, but one was armed with a Mauser HSc, the other with a Sauer 38H—both standard issue for the German military back in the war.

She dashed across the alley and listened at the back door, then picked the lock and crept down the service corridor to the lobby. To her surprise, the usual British soldiers were not at their posts. She waited as long as she felt she could, but with time and her unseen opponents against her, she crouched low and hurried toward the door leading to Colonel Whitby-Smith's office.

She didn't know if it was experience, a faint noise, or just that little voice in the back of her head, but she shot forward and landed on the floor as a volley of bullets whistled through the air where she had just been. She rolled and snapped off two shots, just to try and make her opponent duck, and slipped behind an overstuffed couch in the lobby.

A familiar voice mockingly called to her. "So, Baron Teufel wasn't hallucinating. Come on out, you American peacock. Face me."

She shifted positions behind the couch before speaking. "Ah, Baroness Blood. I was wondering if that was your aroma I noticed." She moved again as another burst from a machine pistol ripped up the other end of the couch. "So much for your vaunted Teutonic bravery. Do you have the courage to face me woman to woman? After all, I'm not the Black Angel. Surely, I'd be no threat to you."

A volley of German profanities came in rapid fire before she heard the clatter of the MP-40 on the lobby floor. "I never feared the Black Angel and I certainly do not fear you, *schweinhundin*. Miss Espionage, I believe the baron said you called yourself? I know your kind, content to hide in the shadows while true warriors face each other and shed their blood for their cause, then you swoop in and claim the credit. Come, little peacock, and I'll show you why I was one of the greatest warriors, not just pilots, of the Reich."

Klara slid her pistol out to show she was unarmed and stood up, ready to move if the baroness had a second weapon, but she had stepped into the open. She was wearing her old red uniform from the war, and Klara noted the nasty black whip wrapped around her waist as a belt. She stepped forward and took a fighting stance as the baroness approached.

The two women circled each other, each sizing the other up. As one, they came together in a flurry of blows, parries, and counterblows. With a quick twist, Klara sent the baroness flying, but like she was doing a maneuver with her plane, the baroness twisted in midair and landed on her hands and feet, immediately moving into position before Klara could follow up.

"My commendations to your martial arts instructor. I guess I'll have to take you seriously now."

"*Mein Gott*, is that all you Americans do . . . talk?" With a wordless scream the baroness launched herself at Klara, knocking her off her feet, and the two women fell together in a heap. From there, the fight quickly devolved from a martial arts contest to anything-goes mode. Hair was pulled, body parts were struck with elbows and knees, and clenches were broken with both pressure points and teeth. This was not just a contest of strength and wills; it was a fight for survival.

The two women rolled apart for a moment. Klara felt like she'd gone a half against the Chicago Bears, but the baroness seemed to have come out worse, with blood trickling from her nose and the corner of her mouth. The two women came to their feet, but before Klara could press her advantage, the baroness yanked the whip off her waist and Klara had to dive to the side to avoid the coil of leather that snaked toward her face and body.

Watching the baroness's eyes intently, she saw the whip rise for another attack and Klara launched herself forward in a leaping somersault. The whip whizzed through the air just millimeters above her back, but she came out of the tumble and, putting all her remaining strength into one last punch, nailed the baroness right on the jaw.

Klara felt the shock all the way up her arm from the strike, but the baroness collapsed to the floor. Klara kicked the whip away and retrieved her pistol, then pressed the muzzle to the semiconscious baroness's head. "Why are you here? Not just the goons outside. Why are *you* here?"

"*Fraulein Doktor* told us the false Lorelei would try and make contact with the British once she returned to Vienna. Said you needed to be eliminated quickly, or failing that, ensure we placed enough evidence to point to you as being the head of Rheingold." The baroness's voice slurred as if she was about to lose consciousness, but there was no mistaking the next couple of sentences. "Just like she did to Mata Hari in the first war. *I* wanted to deal with you personally. Prove I was a greater warrior than you."

Klara felt like someone had just punched her in the gut, and she grabbed Blud by the shoulders to shake her awake. "What did you just say?"

The baroness shook her head to clear a few cobwebs. "You didn't know? It's been an open secret about the *doktor* for years. She betrayed Mata Hari to protect her own organization from discovery. Do not trust her, do not get close to her. She will use anyone and anything to accomplish her mission. We could have eliminated Lorelei several times, but the *doktor* insisted she had plans. Refused to tell us who she was. I swear that woman has no scruples at all."

Klara let the baroness slump back against the floor. With a struggle, Baroness Blood levered herself up with one elbow to stare at her. "Why do you look so surprised? Is not your name 'Miss Espionage'? You, above all people, should know that everyone is expendable. Only the mission is sacrosanct."

"You're right. I should remember that." Klara lifted her pistol and took aim at the prone woman on the floor. "Everyone is expendable."

She pulled the trigger.

She found the colonel, Sergeant MacDougall, and Philip tied up in the colonel's office. As soon as they were freed, she handed Philip her camera, told them about the subbasement and to hurry before the council had time to destroy the information, and that she'd be back to brief them later. Also, she mentioned the sleeping baroness and her two flunkies in the alley behind the building.

"Incredible. Absolutely incredible. But, dash it all, woman, who are you?"

"You've already met me, Colonel. I believe you remember being introduced to Miss Espionage. Now, if you gentlemen will excuse me, there's somewhere else I need to be. An appointment that's about thirty years overdue."

Phillip held up his hands, "Wait, you can't just go rushing off. Let us get some people to aid you."

"That'll take too long, and besides your people would merely get in my way. You take care of the gang still running around in Vienna—if you move fast, you'll be able to catch them before they scatter. And I do mean scatter. Just because you have their names now doesn't mean you'll have the names and identities they'll be using tomorrow."

Colonel Whitby-Smith stepped around his desk. "Miss, while I appreciate the rescue and your efforts to aid us, I can't just let you go."

She smiled a thin smile at him. "Oh?"

"Dash it all, miss, this is a secure area. You can't just come and go like you please. I have to at least know who you really are. There are protocols and such."

"Only if you report it, Colonel." She lifted her pistol, not pointing it at anyone, but ensuring they could see it. "And I'd really hate to have to undo all my good work by shooting you to ensure I can leave. As I said, I have a mission that cannot wait to ensure things are done according to Hoyle. So, not another word from either of you." She stepped back and put her hand on the doorknob, keeping everyone in the room in sight. "Now, again, if you'll excuse me . . ."

Phillip gave her a grim smile. "Good hunting."

And with that, she slipped out the door.

Unlike the last time she had arrived in Innsbruck, there was no posh town car to take her out to the manor. However, just like the last time, she was certain she had an escort, but this time they were trying very hard not to be spotted. Against a normal target, even against a normal espionage agent, they would have been successful. But between her training almost since birth, plus tricks she'd picked up from both her former Japanese allies and her current American ones, it was easy to spot shadows that weren't quite right or the faint steps of someone trying to match her rhythm.

Luckily for Klara's sake, her fury that had been a full blaze back in Vienna had cooled to a manageable ember during the train ride back. She knew Annabelle had probably learned of the Vienna cell's capture and her part in it but was counting on the fact it would be impossible for her to have learned of Baroness Blood's slip of the tongue. Klara was counting on being seen as a rival, not an avenger.

The moon was almost directly overhead by the time Ansitz Steyrer came into view, forcing her to move from shadow to shadow to avoid any additional watching eyes. Her tail had done a good job keeping up with her and was closer than Klara felt comfortable with but now was not the time to deal with him. She was still in her costume, having only taken the time to throw on a long coat over herself and store her mask and beret in her coat pocket. Again, she knew Annabelle would see through her disguise the second she laid eyes on her, but it might fool the staff, who'd only seen her in small doses.

Reaching into the coat, she checked the belt pouches and noted which contained the anesthetic bullets and which contained the 9x19mm Parabellum rounds. She hoped this could be handled with a light touch, but knowing Annabelle, that wasn't likely.

She found a tree that was bent slightly and carefully moved up to it before donning her mask and beret. The coat was hung on the tree to look like she was hunched over, observing the villa. It wouldn't fool her tail for long, but every second they were delayed was a second she could operate freely.

Using the shadows of a nearby tree to hide her approach, she dropped lightly over to the other side of a nearby wall, then made her way directly to the garage. She found the hidden entrance and made her way down the tunnel to the steel door, finessed the lock, and slipped inside.

She listened intently in the darkness until certain no one else was in the room and pulled out her flashlight. Nothing in the room had apparently changed, and a check of the cells revealed, to her relief, that the French agent was still in his room. He looked worse for the wear, but at least he was still breathing. She crossed the room, grabbed a couple of weapons off the wall, and stacked them near the outside door before approaching his cell. The lock resisted her attempt to pick it so she removed her bracelet. Working one of the beads free, she set the faux pearl in the keyhole and broke the seal. A few seconds later, there was a small pop, and the door swung open.

The Frenchman slowly opened one eye and with a strength in his voice that surprised Klara, he said, "A bit early for my morning beating. Is this something special?"

"Depends. Do you think getting out of here alive is special?"

"Oh, it would be *very* special, if true. But you've offered me this opportunity before only to snatch it away. One can endure many physical beatings, but the mental and psychic ones take their toll after a while."

Klara flashed her light up to her own face. "Well, luckily for you, I'm not with *Fraulein Doktor.* So, if you've given up, just say so and I'll get on with my mission. If you'd like to live, though, I have opened the doors and have weapons available for you."

The Frenchman looked her up and down and his lips parted in a grin. "If you're lying, what can it hurt? If you're not lying, I'd be a fool to turn down the offer of such a lovely angel."

"If you don't want to see angels for real, you'll need to get going as quickly as possible. This is a one-time offer, so make the best of it. However, if you *do* feel grateful, I would ask you to do one thing for me."

"What would you like, *ma chère*?"

She quickly picked the locks on his manacles. He vigorously rubbed his wrists and hands to return the circulation and leaned toward her to listen closely. "Once you get over the wall, count to thirty and then empty one of the weapons at the villa. I don't care if you hit anything, but I want all attention drawn to the walls while I'm in here. I know it's asking a lot, but it'll make it more likely both of us will survive tonight."

"I'm not ready for the Tour de France, but I'm not completely helpless." He paused, then regarded her with a warm smile. "If we survive and you find yourself in Paris, find a newspaper seller near the Eiffel Tower and ask if they have the latest copy of *L'aube Rouge*. He'll know how to contact me. I would like to show you Paris the way only a true Frenchman can."

"If we survive, it's a date. Now, please move."

Without another word, he followed her from the cell, still flexing his arms and shoulders to work out the kinks. She watched him inspect the weapons, ensuring they were actually loaded. He then listened carefully as she explained where the tunnel emerged, where the closest wall was, and how he could reach it without being observed. He repeated everything back to her, nodded once, and then slipped the door and disappeared into the darkness. Once he was gone, she made her way across the room to the other exit,

Taking her time and ensuring the alarm she'd missed her first time was disabled, Klara let herself into the basement, moved quickly through the radio room, and into the examination room beyond. Once certain no one was waiting for her, she made her way to the top of the stairs and waited. She hadn't been there long when she heard the first series of shots. Annabelle's former prisoner was apparently working off a lot of aggression, as he cycled through several magazines before the firing tapered off.

As she hoped, the area on the other side of the door was filled with the sounds of shouting and running feet. Screams of pain accentuated the tumult but Klara wasn't sure if they were from the Frenchman's fusillade or people simply stumbling over things in their mad rush through the darkness. Doors slamming indicated most of the household staff had to be outside now. Pulling her pistol out of its holster, Klara eased the door open and made her way down the hall toward Annabelle's quarters.

As she arrived at the door to Annabelle's sitting room, a soft voice called out, "Come in, Lorelei. It's unlocked."

Klara crouched down and opened the door just enough to slip in and shut it behind her. There was a soft light coming from a lamp and a fire going in the fireplace. Annabelle sat in her chair in front of the fire, like an empress preparing for court. Even though there were no visible weapons in her hands, Klara knew better than to underestimate her old mentor. She glanced around the room and found no sign anyone else was nearby, but again, that didn't mean anything.

Annabelle gave her an amused look. "I see you wasted no time putting our French guest to work."

"A useful distraction, nothing more. He seemed keen to put a few holes in this building."

"It did get you to this room, but what is your plan to escape?"

"Hadn't thought that far ahead," Klara admitted with a shrug. "My goal was to reach you, and I succeeded."

Annabelle slowly reached out and picked up a cigarette holder. She motioned to a box on her table and Klara nodded. She carefully extracted a cigarette from the fancy mahogany box and lit it with a silver lighter. The flash from the lighter illuminated Annabelle's face, and even though she appeared relaxed, she was staring at Klara with a snakelike glare. Klara forced herself to meet Annabelle's gaze and a smile slowly settled on her mentor's face.

"So, my stare no longer reduces you to quivering."

"I'm no longer the little scared girl you remember. The one who was eager to please to avoid punishments. Do you know why I am here?"

"Know? I have many suppositions, but no facts to base my

assumptions on. I know you managed to throw the entire operation in Vienna into turmoil, but I only heard of your antics a few hours before your arrival in Innsbruck. I knew you would return, though. Johann was all for meeting you at the train station with a machine gun; still, there was no reason to alert the local authorities to our presence."

"How do you know I haven't?" Klara challenged, chafing a bit at Annabelle's cool disdain.

"You haven't. When Sonje lost track of you about a mile from the villa, your intentions couldn't have been clearer. Your single-mindedness is probably the only reason Sonje is still alive. You could have eliminated her; you simply didn't want to waste the time or energy."

"Let's just say I'm here to collect a thirty-year-old debt."

Annabelle raised a hand to her chin in contemplation, "A thirty-year-old . . . Oh, my poor, sweet child, did you only just now learn the truth?" She gave Klara a look of pity. "I thought you'd learned that long ago."

"She trusted you. Why?"

"Why? It was simply business, my dear. You don't *have* friends when you are a spy. You have useful companions, useful sources, and useful superiors. If *any* of them prove to be a hindrance, you remove them. If you need to protect yourself, you find someone else to pin the blame on. The only person you ever trust is yourself. Everyone else is expendable."

Annabelle took a deep drag on her cigarette and blew a couple of smoke rings before continuing. "It was 1917. France and Germany were locked in mortal combat and nothing and nobody was out-of-bounds when it came to breaking the deadlock. When British and French counterintelligence came sniffing around my work at the hospital in Brussels, I needed someone, anyone to plausibly divert their attention to, and Mata Hari was the perfect foil."

"Even though we knew each other well, I had no clue whose side Mata Hari was on. She might have been a German agent, a French double agent, or even a German triple agent. She was sleeping with a German officer and a French officer and using their pillow talk to make her reports to higher headquarters. She was planning to sink her claws into an American once they arrived, but French counterintelligence agents found documents implicating her as a spy. It took quite a bit of doing to get her handwriting down—she had an atrocious scrawl—but it was worth it in the end. I was sad to hear she was executed, but all the attention directed at me was gone. A few months later, I managed to exfiltrate through the Allied lines into Germany before anyone realized my spy ring was still in operation."

"You *betrayed* my mother."

Annabelle's eyes lit up, and she almost rose from the chair as she straightened to look Klara in the eye. "Yes. Yes, I did. She died so *I* could survive. That was the most important thing. Not the mission, not the cause, survival. You can't complete a mission if you're dead. You can't complete a mission if everyone is watching you. Evade, deflect, misdirect, whatever it takes, *whomever it takes*, whatever sacrifice you must make, you survive and *then* you complete the mission."

There was a muffled shot and a sudden look of surprise and pride on Annabelle's face as the small pistol she had in her hand dropped from her nerveless fingers. With a sigh, she slowly toppled forward and collapsed on the sitting room floor. Klara stared at her old mentor's body before holstering her still smoking pistol. She took some of the more flammable items from around the room and placed them around Annabelle's body, then made a trail of items from the small pyre to the fireplace. As the first piece caught fire, she approached the window, glanced through the curtain and then opened the window, preparing to slip into the darkness beyond.

Glancing over her shoulder at the still form lying there and the fire creeping across the floor, she said, "Consider your mission complete, *Fraulein Doktor.* Give the *Kaiser* and the *Führer* my compliments in hell."

Klara looked up from the drink she held in her hand and let the noise of the Washington, D.C. bar wash over her. She'd finished her last debrief earlier that day, turned in her third copy of her report, and had talked to the psychologist for the sixth time since her return from Europe. She'd slipped out of Austria by way of Italy and caught a commercial flight home after her confrontation with Annabelle. There was no reason to return to Vienna—either Phillip had handled the situation, or he hadn't.

Toby wasn't pleased Rheingold hadn't been completely dismantled, but as Klara pointed out, while they didn't know the terminus of the pipeline, at least they'd ensured it would take a long time for the ex-Nazis to put the system back together. Toby agreed to give her some time to recover from this mission, but she was going to be heading to Istanbul by the end of the month to pick up the trail.

She motioned to the waiter to bring her a fresh martini and listened to the jazz trio playing at the other end of the room. While jazz wasn't really her thing, there was something about it that suited her current mood.

"The lady's drink?" a familiar voice said.

Glancing up, she spotted Phillip, who'd commandeered the waiter's tray and towel. She smiled and motioned for him to sit down. He handed the waiter a couple of bills and returned the equipment before joining Klara.

"I heard about what happened in Innsbruck."

"A shame that old villa burned down."

"Not quite. Several rooms were destroyed, but the fire department saved most of it. We found a lot of interesting information there. To include this . . ." He shoved a thick file across the table toward her. Another copy of her dossier. Apparently, Annabelle had been keeping tabs on her up until her disappearance in 1945.

"Interesting reading?"

"I wouldn't know. As soon as I saw it was yours, I secured it. It never appeared in the final report of Rheingold. As you said earlier, I had no need to know."

She smiled. "Thank you. I'm afraid I wouldn't have been

much further use to the Agency if my identity were known. But how is it, once again, you're right behind me? I did everything I could to ensure no one knew I was going to Innsbruck."

"Who do you think was following you all the way from the train station?"

Klara's eyes widened. "*You.*"

"I spotted your tail and incapacitated her before she could interfere. I guess you thought I was her on the way to the villa. Took me a bit to realize you'd fooled me with the old jacket-in-a-tree stunt. Luckily, your assistant pointed me in the right direction."

"The Frenchman?"

"Pierre Guillou. A rather resourceful fellow. I met him in the war years ago."

Klara wasn't surprised at that announcement. "Who are you really?"

A new voice spoke up from the booth next to hers. "They didn't call him the greatest spy America had ever seen for no reason, Klara."

Before either could react, a tall blond woman slid into their booth. She carefully placed her handbag and drink on the table and sat where she could watch them. In a soft but deep voice, she continued, "After all, Miss Espionage, who else could have possibly captured Germany's greatest spy than ZX-5?"

Klara felt her mouth fall open as she turned and stared at Phillip. "ZX-5?"

Phillip had the decency to blush and look sheepish. "Guilty as charged. Let me tell you, it's been tough not telling you the past few weeks." He turned to the interloper with a more serious look. "You seem to be incredibly well informed, ma'am. Since you're making the introductions, perhaps you could introduce yourself?"

"I am Cairo Jones. I specifically came to meet with Miss Espionage, but when fortune brought you to the table too, I couldn't resist the opportunity to get to know the both of you."

Phillip's body tightened at their visitor's name. "Cairo Jones? There was quite the manhunt for you not that long ago."

"Indeed. My late husband was one of the leading financiers for the old Reich. I didn't discover the truth until well after the war. If you're curious, the authorities have cleared me of any wrongdoing." She turned to Klara. "I'm using the money he had stored for the restoration of the Reich to create a group dedicated to ensuring it never rises again. Miss Victory and I are recruiting people who have the requisite skills and talents that would be of great use."

"Tempting, but I'm afraid I have a prior commitment."

Cairo leaned forward and handed her a piece of paper. "If you accept my offer, that will not be a problem. However, the highest authorities have made it clear this cannot be a sanctioned government organization. You will have to 'officially' quit your job, but it will be held for your eventual return, should you choose. Technically, we'll be working without official authority and if we get into trouble inside or outside the country, the government can't do anything overtly to help us."

"Working without a safety net? Wouldn't be the first time."

Phillip leaned in. "Would there be a place for an old spy hunter like myself?"

Cairo turned to him with a disarming smile. "Yes . . . and no. We have some specific individuals in mind for the field team. However, Miss Victory is putting together an operations cell to handle intelligence and logistics for the group. I believe the country's greatest counterespionage agent would be a great complement to their efforts. There might be some fieldwork, but ensuring these ladies aren't compromised is of utmost importance."

"'These ladies'?" Phillip asked.

"These ladies. Who exactly must remain confidential, at least until you accept our offer, ZX-5."

Klara lifted her martini glass to Cairo in a toast. "You've given me much to think about, Miss Jones."

"Please call me Cairo. If either of you decide to come on board, come to the address on this card or call the number. However, understand: if you call, we'll consider you in the organization and proceed accordingly. If you don't call, this conversation never happened." She glanced between the two and then motioned to the waiter. "Please, a bottle of your Tattingers, say the 1907?"

The waiter's eyebrows did their best to join his receding hairline, but he kept his voice steady. "Very good choice, madam. We'll have it out here in a moment."

Once the waiter had stepped out of earshot, Klara whispered, "Cairo. That's much too expensive."

Cairo sat back so she could take in the two of them in one glance. "Nonsense. If I can recruit two people of your skills in one shot, it's an event worth celebrating." Her face sobered a bit. "It may be quite a while before we can celebrate again, so let's enjoy the moment while we can."

"Now you're thinking like one of us, Cairo," Klara said, lifting the almost empty martini glass in her direction. "Live life to the fullest while we have the chance. How does that phrase go . . . 'eat, drink, and be merry' . . ."

Phillip lifted his glass in reply. ". . . 'for tomorrow we shall die.' But that's much too depressing with champagne on the way. How about we quote someone a tad more upbeat, like Mae West. 'You only live once, but if you do it right, once is enough.'"

Klara and Cairo raised their glasses in unison. "Here's to a well-lived life."

ABOUT THE AUTHOR

Richard C. White is multi-genre author. His latest release, *On Wings of Steel*, a steampunk novel, was released in April 2025. Other works include *Chasing Danger: The Case Files of Theron Chase*, *Harbinger of Darkness*, *For a Few Gold Pieces More*, and *Terra Incognito*, a non-fiction book on world building. He's appeared in Origins Game Fair anthologies (*Monsters*, *Robots*, and *Space*), as well as in pulp anthologies such as *Thrilling Adventure Yarns 2021*, *Liberty Girl: Fight for Freedom*, *All for One: Tales of the Musketeers*, *The New Adventures of Rocky Jordan*, and *Charles Boeckman Presents: Johnny Nickle*.

As a media tie-in writer, he's written for *Star Trek*, *Doctor Who*, *Battletech*, and *The Incredible Hulk* franchises. His novel, *Gauntlet Dark Legacy: Paths of Evil*, was a best-selling tie-in for his publisher. His latest tie-in works are *One Night in Freeport* and *Storm Wreck* for Nisaba Press (Green Ronin Gaming).

Richard is a member of the Science Fiction and Fantasy Writers Association and the International Association of Media Tie-in Writers. Additionally, Richard serves on the SFWA Writer Beware committee.

www.ingramcontent.com/pod-product-compliance
Lightning Source LLC
LaVergne TN
LVHW050616100826
845148LV00011B/1608

* 9 7 9 8 9 8 6 4 4 3 2 3 2 *